LEGACY OF A HUNTER

LEGACY
OF A
HUNTER

A NOVEL

EMERY BARRUS

FITHIAN PRESS • SANTA BARBARA • 1995

Published by Fithian Press
A division of Daniel and Daniel, Publishers, Inc.
Post Office Box 1525
Santa Barbara, CA 93102

LIBRARY OF CONGRESS CATALOGING-IN-PUBLICATION DATA:
Barrus, Emery
    Legacy of a hunter : a novel / by Emery Barrus.
        p.   cm.
    ISBN 1-56474-88-8
    1. Man, Prehistoric—Fiction.   I. Title
PS3552.A7413L44   1995
813'.54—dc20   95-9696
                                                        CIP

I dedicate this book to my dear wife, Mary,
who has always encouraged me
in my writing endeavors

Introduction

When the earth was still very young the ocean teemed with life and for millions of years the sea floor accumulated the calcium-rich deposits of the shells and coral. The flora and fauna of that ocean, in pursuit of survival, continually tested new environments. From the myriad mutated variations of that sea life, a few found a toehold, first in tidal mud flats and later on the moist terra firma.

The earth's ever-shifting plates lifted many areas of the densely compressed sea floor into mountains that later supported rivers and streams groping their way back to the ocean. The lifting process that created those mountain ranges also left cracks and fissures in the limestone strata below the swift descending waterways. The rain-fed streams and rivers, with their minute contents of atmospheric-supplied carbonic acid, permeated those cracks and fissures in their gravity-directed search for a more direct route to the valleys below. The water slowly dissolved and widened the fissures, creating long tunnels and caverns deep in the bowels of the mountains. Streams and large rivers often travelled many miles underground before resurfacing to continue cascading down the mountain slopes. Occasionally the earth's crust would yield to gravity and collapse the cavern roof, depriving the stream of its easy route. The millions of ensuing years modified those caverns with a kaleidoscope of various patterns. The eons of time allowed fantastic designs of stalactites to form, dripping their calcium-rich droplets onto the ever growing stalagmites below.

During the long process of erosion and lifting of the earth's crust, animal and plant life spewed out variations of their progeny in a continuous life or death struggle for a niche on the ever-changing earth. For millions of years size became a factor in that struggle, a period when the reptilian vertebrates dominated a world in which the first warmblooded mammals scavenged for the necessary scraps for survival.

After the cataclysmic event that ended the dinosaur era, mammals, exploiting the void, developed size as their own weapon of survival. When man's ancestors still dwelled in the canopy of the rain forest, each succeeding generation of many carnivore species grew larger, facilitating their acquisition of an adequate food supply. Of the herbivores that survived, many used size as their own armor of defense. Others found speed and wariness their tools. The browsers and grazers of those warmer climates, forced by competition, advanced to the limits of where the flora was tolerated by the cold and ice of the polar regions. Mammoth, wooly rhinoceros, reindeer, bison, and other species competed and adapted to the harsher environment.

Climatic changes forced our anthropoid ancestors, as refugees from a diminishing equatorial rain forest, to seek survival on the scrub plains and later on the grass savannah of Africa. For millions of years that survival was marginal and the extinction of the species would have gone unnoticed in the fierce drama that was unfolding on the earth. Man's descent from the trees carried with it a remarkable adaptation for survival. The hands that had earlier grasped limbs to escape the fangs of the leopard could now hold a club or spear in defense against the predators. Man inherited an additional adaptation for survival. His gregarious instinct from his earlier days in the rain forest served him well on the plains. With the dietary efficiency of omnivorous adaptation, our club and spear-wielding ancestors, closely grouped, became formidable competitors as scavengers and hunters. Intellect, and vocal communication, in the severe environment, also became increasingly important tools. As man's survival grew more dependent on his cunning, his cunning also rapidly changed. In the era of that change, when his logic accepted fire as a valuable tool of defense and warmth, the balance of power shifted rapidly in his favor. With the use of fire, the mold was cast. The outcome was inevitable. Man's survival was assured. A more relaxed life-style allowed that unique intellect to ponder its own origin. Man's ego demanded his own exaltation above all the other creatures of his environment. His desire to escape his mortality influenced his reasoning and directed the course of his future social development.

Very late in the chronology of earth's history, at a time when fire and tools eased the burden of man's survival, our Cro-Magnon ancestors found time to explore the earlier mentioned caves and, in rituals as yet only imagined, depicted images of animals of their hunting environment. Dozens of caves are adorned with thousands of paintings and carvings of bison, cattle, horses, mammoth, ibex etc. These paintings and carvings, along with symbols and groups of dots, captivate the imagination of all who study or observe these artifacts of our ancestors. Many paintings, dating from fifteen to thirty thousand years ago, remain as vivid today as when our Cro-Magnon ancestors assembled in whatever rituals motivated such an effort. What those rituals or motivations were now occupy the studies and imagination of all who visit those hallowed chambers. One can allow his imagination to relive the trials and joys of those courageous people who ushered in our own existence. Our civilization today is structured on the building blocks laid down by those who came before us. It is to those people that I extend my utmost respect and to them I dedicate this book.

-- Preamble --

As Jacques Marsal, the lifetime guide of La Grotte De Lascaux in southwestern France, turned on the lights deep inside the limestone cavern, my associates and I gasped in awe. An emotional surge sent spine-tingling ripples along my back. The vivid paintings of colorful animals surrounding us gave the observer a feeling of active participation.

Like the other four members of the University of California sponsored tour who were with me in the cave, we stood in silence, attempting to comprehend what we were seeing. Although we had been extensively briefed by David Abrams, our university professor, and by our guide, Jacques Marsal, we were still unprepared for what we were witnessing. The briefing made words unnecessary and Jacques wisely allowed us our own thoughts for several minutes.

I glanced down near my feet where carbon remnants of torches gave evidence that our ancestors, seventeen thousand years ago, in an apparent solemn ritual, had trod where I then stood while painting those life-size murals. In my imagination I became a participant in that ritual and easily envisioned the men of that time building crude scaffolding to perform their task. I witnessed larger than life pictures of cows, horses, deer, ibex and bison. There were paintings of mammoth and reindeer, animals nonexistent to that region, supporting evidence of man's periodic migrations farther north. As I allowed my imagination to run free, I saw those men, little different except in dress from my current neighbors. I envisioned those men building a shrine to their Gods with the same fervor that my neighbors today build their own shrines. Like the churches and temples of today, the scene I was witnessing revealed to me the search for security and eternal life that has motivated man since he first became aware of his own mortality.

In my imagination, I followed those men from that cave, returning with them to their families in the shallow limestone shelters left by thousands of years of river erosion. I saw the children at play and the women at work. I shared what I believed to be their hopes and fears on their long summer migration north in search of easy and abundant prey. In my mind I came to know many of those people and in these chapters are recorded what I believed to be their loves, hates and fears. As I thought about the paintings of the animals, I speculated as to when the first wolf was domesticated, and by whom the first cow was milked, and under what circumstances these things occurred.

One of the most prominent paintings in La Grotte De Lascaux is that of the leaping cow. Displayed just forward of the cow is what I could only construe as being a cage or perhaps a pole trap. In my imagination I could see the device used to trap the aurochs or wild cows that inhabited that part of the continent.

The seventeen-thousand-year time frame since that period is but a second in the evolution of life on this planet and but a day in the evolution of man. Had the ancestor who painted and worshipped in that cave been born thirty years ago, he could well have become the doctor or lawyer living next door, or perhaps the airline pilot who now travels in one hour the distance travelled annually in that era.

In the absence of knowledge as to the extent or character of the spoken language during the Upper Paleolithic Period, this author felt it would be doing a disservice to our ancestors to portray their vocabulary as any less expressive than the frontiersmen of the last century. In an effort to convey the emotions and frustrations of my characters, I felt the terminology and expressions of modern man would be most useful to that end.

The story is not intended as an anthropological study but rather as a fantasy journey into our past. In the following chapters, I offer you a peek into what my imagination suggests might have happened seventeen thousand years ago in what is now France and Western Europe.

- 1 -

Orin left the river, ambling slowly back toward the
shallow cave below the long, limestone cliff. The tall,
sandy-haired youth paused, lowering his flint-tipped spear to
the ground. After adjusting his deerskin garment he glanced
skyward, enjoying the warming rays of the midday sun. His
mind was preoccupied with the coming annual journey north
to the calving grounds of bison and reindeer.

Willows, bursting with new buds, swayed gently in the
spring breeze. Several days of steady rain had given way to
a blue sky, decorated by a few low, billowy clouds drifting
lazily across the valley.

The youth's heavy, fur, body garment had been replaced
with a lighter loin-skin for the joy of absorbing the warm
sunshine. He and his friends had yearned to escape the
confines of the cave during the cold rainy season. The
change in the weather offered reality to that yearning. As he
walked, he mentally reviewed the aspirations he had
nurtured throughout the long winter. His muscular maturity
gave an urgency to those ambitions.

I am now ten and seven years old, he reasoned. When
we reach the big meadows of the north country, I'll prove
I'm a good hunter and then Agar will surely honor me in the
Order of the Hunt. I'll prove I can kill as many reindeer as
any of the older hunters.

Being absorbed by thoughts of the coming clan journey, he was startled to see Nomi approaching from the shadows of the dense willow growth. They paused a short distance apart and after a few moments of silence, the girl lowered her eyes to the ground.

Orin broke the silence. "Are you going to the river?"

Nomi slowly raised her eyes. "I'm getting water for my mother and the new baby so they can stay by the fire." She extended her hand, displaying a skin water bag as a further explanation.

"I'll go with you to protect you," Orin volunteered, although they each knew there was little danger from animals at that time of day. The tall youth took the lead as they walked in silence along the winding path back to the water. Orin watched as Nomi descended the bank and lowered her slender body to her knees. She further lowered her head, touching her lips to the water to drink deeply of the liquid. Her long blond hair was tied neatly behind her neck.

As she raised her head, she waited for the reflection to stabilize in the disturbed water. Her eyes caught the reflection of Orin standing at her side. She lingered a moment in thought. *I wonder if he likes me? Mother told me that men have emotions similar to those of women even though they would never admit it.*

Nomi lowered the leather bag into the stream, allowing the current to fill the container. Raising herself to her feet, she turned to follow Orin back toward the cave shelter.

After walking a short distance, the young man stopped. "Does your mother need the water right away? Can we talk for a while?"

"Maybe for just a little while," she replied, glancing toward the cave.

"Let's go over there where we can sit," Orin suggested, pointing. "There's a good place by those old trees where we used to play."

Accepting her silence as consent, Orin led the way, cautiously stooping under the overhanging willow branches. Upon reaching the shaded clearing, Nomi glanced toward the cave and then lowered the water bag to the ground.

Orin eased himself to the grass before looking back up at the attractive girl. Her soft, tanned deerskin garment conformed snugly to her body, accentuating the mysterious metamorphosis that had recently transformed the young girl into womanhood.

Nomi was a happy child who generally inspired laughter and gaiety to those near her. Her mother's careful grooming and training had instilled a personal pride that enhanced the girl's natural beauty. Her fifteen years had not yet hardened her body into the muscular structure that was common to the older women of the clan.

"Everyone's talking about our trip to the north country," Orin said, ending the short silence. "I heard Dorik talking to the other hunters and they think we'll leave any day now. They all believe that Tomar will soon get a good sign from the Storm God. He's been whispering the chant to summon the omens and many believe the signs are favorable. I've noticed that many clan people have started preparing for the trail."

Nomi remained standing until Orin motioned her down to his side. Glancing again toward the cave, she lowered herself to a sitting position on the grass near him.

After a moment he continued. "When I was younger I always walked on the trail with the women and children, but now that I'm older, I'll be walking with the men. Dorik promised he'd ask Agar to let me hunt with the other hunters when they're out killing bison and reindeer."

Nomi glanced at Orin's developing shoulders and admired his heavy growth of sandy hair that was secured with a leather thong behind his head. The message in her eyes was one of fondness. "It's obvious you've become a man," she said. She was then embarrassed and felt the need to explain. "You're as tall as many of the hunters and taller than some. The hair on your face is getting thicker and you'll soon have a handsome beard." Nomi paused before continuing. "I've seen some of the clan women goggling at you and I don't like what they're thinking."

The remark stirred a feeling of embarrassment in Orin for he had never conversed that way with Nomi. His awareness of her rapidly developing body made conversation difficult.

As children, Orin had seldom joined in play with Nomi's age group. His two years age advantage kept him and his friends aloof and at separate play. It had been only a short time earlier that he had become conscious of the girl's developing breasts and hips.

He reached out to touch her shoulder and the warmth of the touch excited him. As his eyes continued to explore her body, he felt an excitement growing within him, and his imagination experimented with visions of himself and Nomi in the cave at night, sharing the bison-robe bed.

From her sitting position Nomi lowered herself fully to the grass and turned her eyes upward, looking at a white cloud high above. "Wouldn't it be fun if we could ride on that cloud and go wherever it took us?"

Ignoring her words, Orin raised up, supporting himself on one elbow. His attention was held captive by the sight of Nomi's breast, only partially hidden beneath her deerskin robe. It was not as though he had never observed her body, for in the warmer days of summer all the clan members often shed their robes for the welcome comfort and freedom of nudity. He had observed her that way on many occasions, and yet that moment was different. A daring excitement stirred within him as he reached under her robe to touch her breast. As Nomi turned her eyes to him, he pulled his hand back as though singed by a hot ember. He was then embarrassed, not by his aggressive action, but rather by his hasty retreat. He was grateful that none of the hunters had seen him. There was nothing in his youthful training to deter him from the advance he had just attempted. In fact, the hunters often laughed and talked of their exploits with clan women in almost the same way they would tell of their hunting experiences. Was that not proof of the rights and privileges of manhood?

The embarrassment of his hasty withdrawal subsided as his gaze returned to meet that of Nomi. He wondered if she was laughing at him as the hunters would, had they known. This thought again angered him for a man could never let a woman laugh at him. Encouraged by his new thoughts, he pushed the robe aside and cupped his hand firmly on her breast. His eyes, searching her face for a reaction, saw only a warm smile of affection. He relaxed his hand slightly.

Making no effort to resist, Nomi turned her head to rest it against Orin's arm. Like him, there was nothing in her training to generate guilt. Her emotion would be either a deep feeling of fright and resentment, or a warmth of willing submission that was then beginning to envelop her body.

"Do you like me?" she asked in a whispered voice.

"Of course I like you."

"Am I as pretty as that girl in the clan down the river?"

"I don't know what you're talking about," he replied defensively. "I hardly know the girl."

He suddenly realized she was teasing, that he had been tricked, but his new confidence encouraged him to play the game. "Of course she does have nice breasts," he added, "but I like you better."

She smiled but said nothing. Her silence relieved him of further conversation. He lowered his lips to Nomi's mouth and was excited and encouraged by the warmth of the response. He awkwardly fumbled with the thong that secured her body robe before moving the loosened garment aside. His eyes slowly surveyed her body and moved to meet the tender gaze that signaled her willing submission. After removing his own loin garment, he drew the girl closely to him. Feeling the warmth of her soft body, he experienced an increasing level of excitement. Their lips again touched in a long and passionate kiss.

Although the two young lovers had little experience to assist them, a deep mysterious instinct guided their intimate embrace to an exciting although awkward gratification.

For a long time Nomi lay snuggled in the arms of the young clansman. "I've dreamed of some day being here with you like this," she whispered. "I've watched you so many times and often thought about you. I hope you're pleased with me and we can meet again soon."

"I think about you all the time," he answered. "I hope someday, after I'm accepted in the Order of the Hunt, I'll be allowed to claim you as my mate." He paused and then added, "I love you, Nomi."

After such a bold revelation of his feelings, Orin regretted the declaration. He felt he had in some way reduced his masculinity by revealing his inner feelings. This uneasy thought, and the subsidence of his earlier passion, brought him to a sitting position. "Your mother might be worried," he said. "Maybe we better get back to the grotto."

Nomi leaned over and whispered, "I love you, Orin."

---

* * *

While walking on the trail toward the grotto, the two lovers saw Agar, the clan leader, approaching. Both Orin and Nomi stepped off the path, a symbol of respect and courtesy. When only a few feet away, Agar stopped. Orin waited for him to speak. An awkward silence followed as the clan leader looked, first at Orin, and then at the young, lightly robed girl. Agar's stern expression effectively cautioned the young man to remain silent until spoken to.

Orin's eyes, after searching the face of the older man in anticipation of his comment, were then slowly lowered.

The clan leader again surveyed the body of the young girl. He appeared about ready to speak but merely grunted and turned back to the path. Agar continued well beyond the two before stopping again to look back at Nomi. He studied the two for what seemed to Orin as a long time before continuing on down the trail.

- 2 -

The clan leader called his hunters together for a briefing. Agar, whose dark, wavy hair and heavy beard framed a face of olive skin with hazel eyes, had ruled the clan for several years. Muscular arms and a dense growth of hair on his broad chest emphasized his strength. His appearance, as well as his reputation for brutality, effectively discouraged any challenge to his authority. His height, a little short of six feet, was about average for the hunters of the clan.

"The time is getting near for our long trip north," Agar began. "We must get everything ready. Tomar tells me the moon is right for our ceremony to honor the Spirits of the Hunt. We will meet at dawn tomorrow to go to the Bison Cave to honor our ancestors and appease the animal spirits." He paused, waiting for questions before continuing. "The day after the ceremony, Vodim will take another man and some women down river to trade. We'll send all the flints and robes we can spare. Dorik and Gors will take some women to the Cave of Bears for a new supply of flint."

One of the hunters, attempting to clarify his own duties, interrupted. "Am I going with Vodim?"

Agar's short temper surfaced. "I haven't decided who's going with Vodim," he snapped. "Just wait and you'll learn soon enough."

The man timidly lowered his eyes and moved to the rear of the assembled hunters.

Tomar interceded to reduce the tension. "These past days I have seen many good omens for the coming journey. Tomorrow we will appease the animal spirits of our past hunts. Armid will draw new images in the cave where those spirits can dwell until they return to the bodies of newborn animals."

Tomar, the gray haired clan visionary, slightly stooped with rheumy eyes, enjoyed the respect of his fellow clansmen and the honor of serving as clan spiritual leader. His talent at interpreting omens had been learned partly from earlier clan seers and partly from his own experience. In early life he had learned that if he needed a sign regarding a coming event or death, and if his logic anticipated the imminence of that event, he could usually find a sign to prophesy it. The actual happening, of course, would verify the validity of the earlier omen. It had been several years since Tomar had participated in the actual hunting and killing of large game. His age and wisdom, along with his earlier status as clan leader, commanded respect from all the clan members.

Tomar's limited duties afforded him the time and opportunity to reminisce about his younger life. He often sat near the fire, recalling his youthful years and the annual early spring migrations from those same limestone grottos. The journey north was always an exciting experience for the younger children who were free of the heavy packs borne by the women. He remembered the excitement on previous journeys when the hunters, after capturing newborn reindeer calves, could easily slay the mothers of those calves as the animals attempted to defend their offspring. He enjoyed remembering his own acceptance as a hunter in the clan so many years earlier and the thrill of his first kill.

Tomar also frequently reminisced about the experience of his younger years when the clan leader of that time announced his intention to take Tomar's mate for his own. In desperation, and as a matter of honor, Tomar had challenged the leader. Upon witnessing the fury of the offended youth, the clan leader had relented, announcing his change of heart. Encouraged by the leader's indecision, Tomar had then challenged him for clan leadership. There was no fight. Intimidated by the other hunters' support for the young challenger, the older clan leader announced his desire to step down.

"I didn't want the responsibility anyway," the older man had confided to a few of the other clansmen. "Now I can devote my thoughts to hunting."

Tomar had become the unchallenged popular leader for several years. It was only when he was badly injured by the sharp tusks of a boar that he temporarily relinquished his authority to Dorik, his favored hunter and second in command. Later, after Tomar's injuries healed, he announced his decision to retire. He had learned to enjoy the leisure of inactivity in lieu of the arduous effort of hunting. He preferred the role of spiritual leader, a service that was vital to morale and to the survival of the clan.

As the hunters dispersed, Orin approached the old man.

"Tomar," he began, "I am now age ten plus seven and will be joining the hunts on our trip north. If I'm going to be hunting for the deer and bison, should I not also participate in the ceremony of the cave?"

Tomar reached up to place a hand on the shoulder of the tall youth. "Yes, Orin, you should. If you are to someday become a great hunter, it is important that you atone the spirits of the animals you slay. I'll speak to Agar, but I'm sure he'll consent."

Orin found sleep elusive that night. Since his earliest memories, a mystery had shrouded this most solemn of ceremonies. Although hunters often talked about the ritual, little was ever said of what the cave contained. He could not remember ever being forbidden to explore the cave, but such a restriction was unnecessary. All the children and many of the adults spoke in whispers whenever the cave was mentioned. His youthful conversation with other children evoked visions of frightening images and of wild animals whose bodies took the form of wisps of smoke.

His imagination finally yielded to a sleep that was interrupted in the early morning by his mother's hand gently shaking him. "Wake up, Orin," Amalee whispered. "The men are gathering for the trip to the cave. If you plan to attend, you better get up. I've prepared this small bag of dried meat and nuts for you to eat on the way."

The young man climbed from his bison robe bed and rubbed the sleep from his eyes. He glanced around to assure himself that no one was looking before kissing the woman on the cheek. "Thank you, mother," he whispered. "I thought we were out of food. You better save this for yourself and the girls."

"You need it more than we do," she explained. "We have all day to gather more. You'll be too busy to search for food. I also prepared you a lamp for the cave."

"But mother, you shouldn't spare the ibex grease for me. The other men will have lamps."

"I want you to have your own lamp, just in case."

Orin reluctantly accepted the seashell lamp which contained a woven fiber wick embedded deeply in congealed animal fat. "I won't use it unless we need it," he stated while carefully stowing it in his pack along with his food package.

Orin joined the hunters who were assembling near a fire at the edge of the overhanging limestone cliff. Poles, leaning against the stone wall, supported robes that served as wind breaks. Two of the men carried the turtle-shell fire box suspended from a pole. A fire smoldered in the shell and was occasionally stoked by a third hunter who carried a supply of oak charcoal.

When Tomar was assured that all the men were present, he nodded at Agar who moved off down the river trail, followed by all the adult male clansmen. Each man carried a wooden spear tipped with a long, slender, leather-bound flint point. Those who had received their rites of membership in the Order of the Hunt also carried a hand axe of broad flint, secured by leather straps on a wooden handle the length of a man's arm.

Orin fell in behind Tomar whose old age and aching bones made travel difficult. The old man carried a spear which functioned as a walking stick and a badge of honor from his earlier days as clan leader.

"Do the spirits of all dead animals live in the cave?" Orin inquired.

Tomar looked back at the youth. "No, son, not all the spirits, for there are many ceremonial caves used by other clans. The spirits use the caves only until they enter the bodies of newborn animals. The paintings and carvings provide a shelter for those spirits. The paintings appease the spirits and assure better hunting for our clansmen."

Conversation diminished as the column continued along the bank of the river. The men followed the well worn path until reaching a small tributary stream. The group then turned, and following the smaller stream toward its source, entered heavier brush. Orin stepped forward to assist Tomar across a fallen log.

"I'll be all right," the old man protested. "The men walk faster these days than we did when I was young. I don't know why everyone is in such a hurry."

The sun was well into the sky when Agar halted the group to consult with several men at the head of the column. When they again began moving, Agar and his hunters turned away from the stream and began climbing the steep mountain slope. The unmarked route required an occasional pause while the leader verified his position. The grade became steeper, occasionally requiring the men to grasp brush stalks to assist their ascent. Orin knew the general location of the cave from childhood stories but was surprised to suddenly climb onto a ledge and look into the dark opening of the cavern. The mouth of the cave was twice the height of a man and several times as wide.

"We'll wait right here until everyone is rested," Agar announced. He was offering a concession to Tomar who found breathing difficult after the steep climb.

"I'll be fine in a moment," the older man insisted. "By the time you light your lamps, I'll be ready."

Several hunters probed in their pouches, producing seashell lamps. After adjusting the wicks in the animal fat, a flame was transferred from the turtle-shell fire box.

There are enough lamps without mine, Orin reasoned, making no effort to produce his own.

The group, headed by Agar, Armid and Tomar, moved cautiously into the darkness of the cave interior. The lamps at first appeared inadequate, but as eyes adjusted to the darkness, the outlines of the cavern wall guided their movement. After proceeding until the last glow of light from outside faded from view, the cavern floor began to ascend. It was occasionally necessary for each man to hand his lamp to another hunter while he cautiously climbed over a large boulder or crawled on his stomach through a shallow opening. After one such difficult and precarious passage, the men waited for Tomar and then assembled near him. Orin's interest became intense when the old man spoke.

"These red dots on the wall were here when my father and my father's father first came to this cave. They are magical numbers. The wise men of the old clans tell us they were put here by the spirits. These seven marks, repeated four times, represent the four phases of the moon, and together they tell us the number of days the moon takes to again show its full face. These twelve red dots are also magical. They can be divided evenly into two groups, three groups, four groups or six groups. It is truly a magical number."

Orin became excited at the thought. He had never heard the logic of the mystical number. He thought of his ten fingers and reasoned that ten could only be divided by two and by five. It is truly a magical number, he reasoned. The Gods were very wise to create such a number.

As Agar continued deeper into the cave, Orin walked near Tomar at the rear of the procession. He glanced ahead and saw the hunters at the forward end of the column holding their lamps high in the air. He heard several expressions of awe and pushed forward to attain a better look. What he saw on the wall produced shivers along his spine and a strange emotional feeling spread slowly through his body. He had seen animal paintings and carvings on the stone of the shelter walls before but had never seen so many large animals painted with such bright hues of red, yellow and black. On the wall were murals of several large male bison. The paintings were life-size and of vivid colors, utilizing natural rock contours to represent curves of the animals' bodies. The drawings gave the viewers a feeling that the animals were alive. There were many other assorted carvings and paintings, but the bison drawings dominated this part of the cave.

There was no conversation as Armid scanned the wall, searching for the site of his next painting. He selected an area already covered by several smaller paintings and carvings. After opening his leather pouch, he carefully removed his shell containers of pigments. The black manganese dioxide and the red iron oxide had earlier been extracted from veins in another cave. The yellow ocher, collected from a rock outcropping along the river bank, and charcoal, taken from the fire pits of the grotto, were also used for shading and color blending.

Using the charcoal, the artist outlined a life-size image of a bison. He used a dark vein of the limestone wall to represent the shaggy beard below the animal's head. When the outline was completed, he dipped a pig's tail brush into his pigments and began filling, utilizing color tones to create a three dimensional effect. Although the mural was placed over several previously painted animals, as the painting progressed, the hunters saw only the mighty bison. As a solemn mood settled over the group, conversation ceased. After Armid had replaced his pigments and brushes, Tomar began a barely audible chant. As the volume of his rhythmic incantation increased, the other men joined his mournful plea. Their voices sent strange and awesome sounds echoing along the cavern walls.

"Oh, great Spirit of the Hunt," the chant invoked, "accept this cave and these images as a haven for all the spirits of animals that you have so generously given us. We appeal to all the animal spirits. Be not angry with us for we are your brothers. We beseech you to return each year to the plains and forests to provide food for our children, for it is willed by the Great Master of all who walk the face of the earth."

When the chant was finished, the mood lingered until well after all the men had returned to the bright world outside the cave.

As they walked back along the trail, Orin inquired of Tomar. "I saw paintings of bison, deer, ibex, cattle, horses and even of the mammoth and reindeer from the far north country, but I didn't see any images of tigers, bears or wolves. Why?"

"Of course not," Tomar explained. "We wouldn't want to provide a haven for the spirits of our enemies. Those beasts kill the animals that the Gods created for us. We want the spirits of those flesh eating animals to wander far away and never find a home in the newborn of their own kind."

Orin continued. "Tomar, I know that we should never draw pictures of people, for it might draw the spirits from their bodies. Do the paintings entice the spirits from the animals we hunt?"

"Yes, Orin," the old man explained. "If the spirits know they have a shelter in the cave, then those spirits are happy to leave the bodies of the animals and it becomes easier for our hunters to kill them. Now do you understand why we paint and carve the images?"

"Yes, Tomar, I do, but I noticed some small carvings that were in very hard places to reach. Maybe just a small image hidden in a crevice or under a low rock shelf. What are they?"

Tomar paused on the trail to give emphasis to his words. "Orin," he commenced, "the painting that Armid made today was for the benefit of the entire clan. It is to entice and please the spirits on behalf of all the clan members. But many hunters want their own personal image that will bring special luck to them on the hunt. They try to hide it somewhere in the cave where no one will alter or destroy it. When I was a young hunter, I carved an ibex in a very secret chamber of this cave. That image must still be there for I have been very lucky all my life."

Orin remained silent for a short while before asking his next question. "If the spirits live in the bodies of animals and people, how do they get there?"

"Surely your father taught you all those mysteries of life when you were young," Tomar answered.

"When my father, Dorik, was defeated by Agar, I was still too young. When Agar took mother and me to his hearth, it was only a short while before he became displeased with mother and we were then reassigned to Vodim. I think Vodim assumed I had already been told so he never said anything and I didn't want to ask. I've heard people talking about the spirits in our bodies but I don't know how the spirits get there."

Tomar looked seriously at Orin as the two slowed their pace, dropping well behind the other hunters. "I'll try to explain," the old man commenced. "Spirits live in the bodies of all living creatures. It is the spirit that gives life to the flesh and bones. When the spirit becomes displeased and leaves a body, then the body is dead. Sometimes, when our bodies get old, the spirit becomes restless and is anxious to find a younger body. The spirit then becomes reluctant to heal our wounds, or to make us well when we get sick. When the spirit decides our body is no longer a good place to live, it simply moves out, leaving the person or animal dead. Then the spirit must look for another body. While waiting for new bodies, human spirits live in the sky as stars, but animal spirits must stay on earth until they find new bodies. That is why we paint the animals in the caves. It provides a shelter for the animal spirits until a new animal is started in the belly of a female animal."

"I think I understood that part of it," Orin reasoned, "but what I don't understand is how the spirit enters the body of the new baby inside the mother. How does it get there?"

Tomar continued walking but hesitated a moment before explaining. "When a man takes a woman to bed and penetrates her body, spirits wait nearby until he is just about finished. They then enter the man's body and move through him into the woman's body, searching for the body of a new baby to occupy. When you experience that strong excited feeling just as you finish, that is the spirit moving through you into the woman. She sometimes also feels the spirit entering her. Sometimes the spirit doesn't find a baby inside the woman, so every time a man penetrates a woman, the spirit tries again."

Orin was satisfied with the logic of Tomar's explanation. Both men fell silent as they moved on, well behind the other clan members. Orin resolved that, at the first opportunity, he would carve his own personal offering to the spirits so that luck would always be with him.

- 3 -

After returning to camp, Agar assigned the vital tasks to be performed before beginning the long trek North. "Vodim, you will take one other hunter and six strong women to travel the three days' journey down the river to where it broadens out and becomes salty."

The river at that point was slowed by tidewaters and many clans lived permanently along the shores. Each year, many of the clans living in the interior region of the valley would send trading teams down the river to bargain for seashells and dried fish that were rich in salt. The fishing clans welcomed the opportunity of getting the animal robes the hunting clans would otherwise abandon before their long seasonal migration north. Flint tools for cutting and scraping were also prized by the fishing clans. The quartz nodules, from which the flint tools were knapped, were common in the interior region but unavailable in the lower river valley.

Agar pointed at Dorik and Gors. "You two will take four women to the quartz cave to gather flint to make tools for our coming journey."

Although every hunter knew the rudiments of flint knapping, none was so skilled as Dorik who had been trained by his father when still a child.

Orin approached his father. "May I go with you and Gors to the quartz cave?"

Dorik looked proudly at his son who stood taller than himself. "Of course you can go with us," he answered, "unless Agar has other orders for you. But remember that it's a long distance and the men will be expected to carry heavy burdens of flint the same as the women."

"I don't mind," the youth agreed. "I've carried heavy loads of wood before."

Dorik, like many of the clan men, was broad-chested with heavy muscled arms and shoulders. His thick blond beard concealed a wide rectangular face and firm chin. His soft blue eyes portrayed a gentleness that marked his normal personality. Only when provoked would his strength and determination manifest itself. He was well liked by all his fellow clansmen and usually respected by Agar. Any bitterness from the fight that had resulted in Agar's leadership had long since been suppressed. Dorik, although occasionally doubting the wisdom of the clan leader's decisions, usually declined the temptation to join in the gossip that entertained so many of the men and women.

During his younger years, as the son of Dorik, Orin had occupied a favored position in the clan. He remembered all too vividly the bitter fight when Agar replaced his father as leader of the clan. Although he was quite young, the experience left a vivid impression on the young boy. Orin had also heard the story told many times and often allowed his mind to review the frightening experience.

Many years earlier, as a maturing youth, Agar often goaded a younger fellow clansmen into wrestling, a sport popular with the young men. With Agar, his aggressive enthusiasm often carried the game far beyond simple competition. His muscles developed early and he quickly found himself with no one on whom to test his strength. The hunters tried to avoid the young man, declining the invitation whenever Agar was in a combative mood. Upon maturity, Agar's passion for physical contact sports soon left him without challengers. His membership in the Order of the Hunt did little to moderate his aggressive disposition.

Orin vividly recalled the winter day when his father, as clan leader, was called from the grotto where he was recuperating from a bad chest cold. Dorik was asked to settle a dispute between Agar and one of the hunters. A stuffy head and a sleepless night left him in no mood to arbitrate the problems of his clansmen.

"All right, what's the problem?" Dorik inquired as he approached the two men.

Gors held an empty leather thong in his hand. "Agar took a rabbit from one of my snares," Gors complained. "I've suspected it before, but this time I saw him."

"What do you have to say?" Dorik asked, turning to Agar. "Did you take the rabbit?"

"No, I didn't take his rabbit," Agar loudly denied. "I can catch my own rabbits."

Gors shook his head in disgust. "He's lying. I saw him take it from my snare. If he wants it that badly, he can have it, but after this I want him to leave my snares alone."

Dorik stepped forward to face the accused man. "I know Gors wouldn't lie about a thing like this. I think you better return the rabbit with an apology."

A fiery expression appeared on Agar's face. Without warning he plunged forward, driving his shoulder hard into the chest and stomach of the clan leader. The impact sent Dorik reeling backward with Agar lunging upon him and grasping at his throat. Dorik, gasping for air from the unexpected attack, struggled to free himself from the aggressor's grip. Summoning his maximum strength, Dorik drew a knee up and dug his heel into the ground. He arched his back, and in a twisting effort, rolled the two of them onto their sides. Agar regained his footing and again lunged at the still gasping leader. He drove his knee hard into Dorik's rib section and locked the leader's head under his arm. Twisting his body, Agar forced the helpless man again to the ground. While holding Dorik's head locked under one arm, Agar repeatedly drove his fist hard into the face of his victim, cutting the flesh around Dorik's eyes. Blood spurted in repeated surges from a wound at his temple. Dorik struggled desperately to free himself but found his strength ebbing. With each effort of withdrawing his head from the arm hold, Agar would grip his arms tighter, increasing the pressure. Dorik felt a dizziness beginning to consume him.

"That's enough," Tomar angrily shouted, moving to try to break the grip of Agar. "You have your victory. Now let him go."

Agar retained his grip until he felt the body of Dorik fall limp. He then released his hold. Rising to his feet, he looked around at the assembled clansmen and bellowed, "Is there anyone here who wants to challenge me for leadership of the clan? How about you Gors?"

Tomar stepped between Agar and Gors. "No one is challenging you, Agar," the older man stated. "If it's the clan leadership you're after, you have what you want. There's been enough fighting. We should devote our energies toward building this into a strong and productive clan."

The fight remained deeply embedded in Orin's memory. He often awoke from bad dreams, reliving the scenes of his father's defeat. He recalled how his mother had then been taken from Dorik as the mate of the new leader, but her moody compliance to Agar's demands resulted in early reassignment to Vodim. Those memories remained vivid in Orin's mind during the ensuing years.

Orin caught the attention of the young girl who had occupied so many of his thoughts the past few days. He left the evening fire area of the grotto and walked along the trail that descended to the river. He waited in the shadows and soon Nomi left her family hearth to follow him into the darkness.

"Over here," Orin whispered. "I'm glad you came."

"I wish I could be with you always," she replied. "It seems you're away with the men so much of the time."

Orin took her hand as she snuggled close to him. "Tomorrow I'm going with my father and Gors to the quartz cave to gather flint. We'll be gone two long days and I'm going to miss you terribly, Nomi. When we're apart I can't think of anything but you. I wish you could go with us."

"When I heard you were going with Dorik and Gors, I asked if I could also go, but Gors said I wasn't big enough. He only wants the real strong women. Maybe someday I'll grow bigger and can carry heavier loads."

"I like you just the way you are," was Orin's consoling remark. "Some of those women have muscles larger than men. Anyway, I'll see you when we get back."

"Please be careful," she said as she kissed him on the cheek. "I better hurry back to the hearth. I'm supposed to be watching the baby." She giggled at an afterthought. "Father and Mother went to bed early tonight. Father leaves with Vodim tomorrow." She then departed, moving rapidly back to the fire.

The next morning Orin waited where Dorik, Gors, and the women were assembling to begin the all day journey to the cave to gather flint. His mother, Amalee, was not selected for either of the journeys. She had lost considerable weight and Agar felt that some of the stronger women would be better for the task. In addition to his spear, Orin carried a small ration of dried meat and a few shelled nuts. He also carried the seashell lamp that Amalee had prepared for him the previous day. Pairs of women took turns carrying the precious fire in the turtle-shell fire box.

"Why is the flint found only in some of the caves and along the river bottom?" Orin asked of his father as they walked briskly along a game trail.

Dorik glanced back admiringly at his son but sustained the steady pace. "Tomar says the Earth God created the flint a long time ago and placed it in secret hiding places just for our people. I think our ancestors have always gone to this same cave for their flint."

"How did you learn to knap flint tools so well?"

"My father taught me when I was about your age, and his father taught him, and I guess it was always that way. I think you're now old enough to learn the craft."

"I've tried many times," Orin explained to his father, "but I can never get the chips to come off the way you do. I'm anxious to learn."

The small group continued toward the cave, pausing occasionally to fuel the fire box or to gather and eat roots and tender shoots of watercress that flourished in the occasional small streams they crossed. They saw a small herd of deer that Orin wanted to pursue until his father objected.

"Save your strength, son," Dorik advised. "You'll never get close to them once they've seen us. This project is more important."

The sun was still well above the horizon when they arrived at the mouth of the cave. There were several well worn paths leading into the cavern which prompted Dorik to make a closer examination.

"Some of the tracks are of other clans," he stated, "but some are of cave bear. I can't tell how old the tracks are. I should think the bears would be out feeding by this time of year."

The women began gathering firewood while the men searched for dry pine boughs, heavily laden with pitch.

"We might have to go quite a distance inside," Dorik explained, "so we'll each carry several torches."

They banked the camp fire outside the cave with a generous supply of wood and cautiously entered the cave entrance. One woman carried an oil lamp as an emergency light source. The men carried pine torches. The cavern floor descended rather sharply for a short distance and then became more gradual.

Dorik paused a moment to point up at a series of vertical gouges on the cavern wall at almost twice the height of a man's head. "Those are claw marks the bears scratch on the wall to claim this area," he explained. "It's similar to the way lesser bears scratch the bark high on trees to warn other bears away from their territory. These smooth, worn areas on the cave floor are where the cave bears have hibernated."

The group continued its descent along the winding cavern. It contained none of the picturesque columns of stalactites and stalagmites that were often characteristic of other caves.

Dorik occasionally lowered his sputtering torch to examine the cave floor, searching for fresh signs of bear. After a while he became more relaxed. "I think we're already beyond the area where bears spend the winter."

A woman laughed nervously and commented, "Maybe the bears don't know it's spring outside."

Although the small group began seeing a few nodules embedded in the limestone of the cave wall, Dorik continued deeper into the darkness. "Other clans have gathered all the best flint that was here," he explained. "We'll have to go on to where the better stones are located."

As the torches burned shorter, the clansmen continued deeper into the cavern where once a cascading river had worn the soft limestone away, exposing the long protruding nodules of flint.

Dorik paused with his group to examine a wall that some unknown, earlier clansmen had decorated with curved grooves, depicting several wooly rhinoceros. Just beyond, the artist had depicted several mammoth, parading along the wall.

"I don't remember ever seeing creatures like those," Orin commented. "What are they?"

"Once when I was very young, I saw some of those strange animals," Dorik explained. "Our clan had travelled farther north and east than usual, up near the ice mountain range." He pointed to the mammoth, adding, "Those animals are much larger than anything you've ever seen. They're more than twice as tall as a man and have long tusks curving out of their mouths like a boar, except the tusks are much longer than a man is tall and they curve in a large loop like these on the wall."

"I hope I never see one of them," a woman remarked. "This picture is scary enough."

The men and women stood transfixed by all the figures until Dorik reminded them of the mission. "We can't waste time looking," he admonished. "We have lots of work to do."

Dorik relinquished his torch to Orin as he carefully selected large, smooth nodules from the limestone walls. With a hand stone, he chipped a piece from each nodule to examine it for quality. If satisfied, he stacked the nodules on the cavern floor before returning for more. With the walls exposing vast quantities, they soon had more than the entire group could carry. Each clansman filled his leather carrying pouch with a load that he judged to be his maximum. The women appeared nervous when Gors reminded Dorik that the torches would soon be consumed.

"I hope you don't expect me to carry this load all the way back to the grotto," a woman complained.

Dorik consoled her with an explanation. "No. I'll select only the best ones in the morning and I'll chip away much of the outer waste."

The men and women struggled under the heavy load as they slowly worked their way back to the cave entrance. By the time they dropped their heavy burdens near the campfire, the sun had already disappeared. The exhausted workers nibbled at their meager rations and soon curled up in their light bed robes for a welcome night's sleep.

Gors, whose own mates were back at the grotto, made a feeble sexual advance toward one of the younger women. He welcomed the nervous rejection and soon fell asleep dreaming of what might have been.

Since his conversation with Tomar the previous day, Orin had been tormented by a thought. If I am to become a successful hunter, is it not also important to create my own personal shrine to appease the animal spirits? If other hunters went to such effort, could I afford less? Could I depend on the clan paintings that were drawn by Armid?

His determination to someday become a great hunter compelled him to make the extra effort. It will be my own personal, secret shrine, he vowed.

His excitement about the plan precluded the sleep that soon conquered the other clan members. When he was confident they were all asleep, he lit the small shell lamp that his mother had prepared. After reassuring himself that his flint knife was in his pouch, he picked up his spear and entered the cave. Although the feeble light made recognition of the earlier witnessed landmarks difficult, he cautiously continued on.

As he reached the area where he had earlier examined the bear scratches, he allowed his imagination to envision a large omnivorous beast just beyond the range of light. Don't be silly, he reminded himself. If there were bears in this cave, we would have found them earlier. Or they would have found us, was an additional nervous thought.

He was tempted to create his animal image at that location but reasoned that other hunters would soon find it when searching for flint. I must locate a place that no one else will ever find, he reasoned. If I'm to become a great hunter, I must show my courage now.

He readjusted the fiber wick in his lamp to increase the light before continuing on along the descending corridor. After arriving at the place where they had earlier gathered the supply of flint, he paused for a moment to again view the images on the wall. Seeing the carved outlines of the animals reaffirmed his dedication. He probed deeper and deeper, continually searching for a cavity that would fit his needs. He passed several such openings in the wall but each seemed too conspicuous. He continued on until he came to a fork in the cavern. After selecting the path to the right, he soon came to a solid end wall. He examined it carefully.

This is a perfect place for my carving, he thought. The spirits will be pleased to reside here until they return as newborn animals. After lowering his spear, and holding the lamp in his left hand, he began carving the image of a long-horned cow on the smooth limestone wall. The point of his flint tool easily dug deep into the soft stone as the image of the animal began to take shape. Upon drawing the outline of the cow, he continued using his flint point to deepen the groove. He moved the lamp to different positions to examine the various visual effects. Feeling pleased, he placed the lamp on the ground to better study his work and to meditate on the spirits that he endeavored to please. As he stepped backward for a broader look, his foot caught the shaft of his spear that he had earlier placed on the ground. With his body off balance, and in an effort to avoid falling, he quickly moved his foot backward. The spear was flipped across the floor surface, hitting the lamp. Sudden darkness closed tightly around him and fear exploded in his brain. He fell to his knees, groping for the shell, knowing the futility of his effort.

Stupid me, he angrily condemned himself. How could I have been so dumb? He sat down on the ground and tried to regain his composure. I must not panic, he told himself. I must pause and think about the situation. It can't be as bad as it seems. In the morning the other clan members will bring lamps and find me. Or will they?

A deep panic gripped his stomach and caused him to again jump to his feet. I didn't tell anyone where I was going, he remembered. They'll think I went back to camp. No, they won't think that because my bed roll is still there. My spear will be missing, so if they don't miss me until morning, they'll think I went hunting very early. They'll look for me in the forest and then eventually assume I'm dead. Why didn't I tell someone where I was going? Why was I so determined to keep it as my own personal secret? Why isn't there just a trace of light? It's so awfully dark.

He again sat down to collect his thoughts. He groped around him until finally locating his spear. If I try to walk out, he questioned, how will I know which way to go? I'm in this corridor that was to the right of the main cavern when I came in. I must locate the wall where I drew the cow and start working my way out. If I move to my right along the wall and always follow this same wall, I should eventually get back to the entrance.

He placed the shell lamp back in his pouch and after locating the wall began carefully moving to his right. He found that if he probed with his spear it became easier to determine his position in relation to the cave wall. Step by step he moved, probing first the wall ahead of him. Again and again he came up against large rocks in his path, often striking and bruising his toes.

Could I have entered a branch of the cave that I didn't see when I came in? Even if I did, every cave has its limit, and if I just continue along the same wall in the same direction, I should eventually work my way out.

Progress was extremely slow. When working around large boulders in his path, he took extra care to make certain that he relocated the wall. Again and again he stubbed his toe on smaller rocks he had missed with his spear. His foot ached with pain. He was certain his foot was bleeding, but because his feet were wet from the water and dampness of the cave, there was no way to be sure.

I'm moving so slowly, he thought. I'll never get out of here by dawn. In fact, I think at this rate it might take days.

A deep fear again began to dominate his thinking. How long can I live in here? Maybe I could get water from the dampness of the walls. I must not get turned around. If I end up going the wrong direction, I may never get out. Stay calm. I must stay calm and think clearly. I remember. The cave was always descending a little when I came in. Am I going up hill? I can't tell. It seems almost flat. If I move a little faster perhaps I can tell.

As he began probing faster, a sharp blow on his head left him dizzy. He sank to his knees, grasping his scalp.

"Who's there?" he shouted. As the echoes faded, a terrifying thought gripped him. Maybe it's not a person. Maybe it's a cave bear. Stay calm. Don't panic.

His logic returned and he dismissed the idea of an animal. Maybe something fell on me, he reasoned. After searching the nearby floor he rose to his feet and again his head scraped against the abrasive stone. As he reached above his head, he understood. He had walked into the low overhanging ceiling along the edge of the cave. After retrieving his spear, in addition to probing the wall and ground forward of him, he began probing above his head.

38

With progress continuing slowly, fatigue began influencing his judgment. If I could just lie down and rest for a short while, he thought. Sleep would feel so good. But father and the others outside would be terribly worried. Even though I would love to lie down for a short sleep, I better keep moving.

He forced himself slowly on. It must be daylight by now, he reasoned. In fact it must be the middle of the day.

Utter fatigue finally conquered his body. He slumped to the floor and lowered his head to the ground. Sleep quickly carried his mind into wild nightmares of cave bears and endless caverns.

Uncertain of how long he had slept, he was aroused to consciousness by a pain in his ribs. He reached under his body to discover a stone that had disturbed his rest. He again lowered his head and was about to resume sleep when his mind caught something. He raised his head, listening intently. Is that a sound?

A barely perceptible whisper brought him to a sitting position. Earlier he had been awed by the absolute silence deep inside the cave. I can hear something, he thought. I can, I can.

The sound was like a very faint rustling of leaves by the wind. He forced himself to his feet and again advanced slowly along the wall. Occasionally he would pause and strain to listen for the sound. I know I'm hearing something, he reassured himself. I must be getting near the cave entrance. The sound seems to be getting louder.

He was about to surrender to fatigue when his eyes again desperately searched for light. My eyes must be playing tricks on me, he thought. It seems just a little bit lighter up ahead than behind me.

Continuing on, he soon became certain. Both light and sound had increased. An excitement buoyed his energy to spur him on. After a few steps farther, he rounded a slight curve in the cave. He became jubilant. "That's a star I'm looking at," he muttered aloud. "It has to be. Could it be the spirit of an ancestor who protected me and guided me back to safety?" A feeling of reverence and gratitude humbled him.

He abandoned the wall and moved cautiously toward the point of light. The path began to ascend sharply and he realized it was the steep portion near the entrance. Upon emerging from the cavern entrance, he looked around to reorient himself. A thin partial moon and the low glowing embers of the campfire guided him to his sleeping robe. After rolling into his comfortable bed robe, he quickly released his conscious mind into the welcome arms of deep sleep.

Orin was awakened by a sharp chipping sound. His eyes slowly focused on Dorik who was sitting near the fire, breaking flint nodules into workable blocks. Orin looked around for the others. He would have enjoyed resuming his sleep but his frightening experience during the night brought his mind into focus.

"Where are Gors and the women?" he asked.

"Well, so you're finally awake?" Dorik responded. "They're out looking for food, and that's what you should be doing. Are you feeling all right? We tried to awaken you this morning but you wouldn't budge."

Without answering, Orin arose slowly to his feet. His toe throbbed with pain, forcing him to again sit down.

"What's that blood on your head?" his father asked. "And your foot. It's all black and bloody."

The question verified he hadn't been missed during the night and he debated whether to tell Dorik the truth. Knowing that his father would consider him stupid for venturing back into the cave alone, he searched for an excuse that would protect his secrecy and conceal his poor judgment. "It's nothing. I got up during the night to relieve myself and I tripped and fell. I'll be all right."

Dorik appeared satisfied with the explanation. "You should watch how I do this," he suggested. "I'm getting rid of the outer waste from these flint blocks to reduce the weight. When we get back to the grotto, I'll knap off the tools we'll need for the trip. As soon as the others return, we'll start back.

Orin pretended interest but his still sleepy mind drifted away. I won't let anyone know how badly my toe hurts, he thought. That will also be my secret.

Often pausing to rest, the men and women each carried a heavy load of flint nodules back to the home grotto. Orin tried to limp as little as possible. With no need to carry fire back, the empty turtle shell was strapped to the back of a woman.

It was late in the day when the weary clansmen dropped their heavy burdens to the ground near the grotto and searched for the comfort of their bedrolls.

- 4 -

Throughout the following days, while the clan waited for the return of Vodim and his group from the region of the sea clans, preparations continued for the long trek north. Dorik occupied his time from dawn to dark, knapping spear points, hand axe blades, and the various scraping and cutting tools that the hunters and women would need until their return in the late fall. Food gathering by the women was partially curtailed because of a cold rain that persisted for several days.

It was still raining when Vodim and his group trudged back into camp. Agar summoned him to his hearth. "How did you make out with those stingy river rats?"

"We had a few tense moments," Vodim replied, "but they wanted our robes and flints. When we convinced them we were going farther down the river to trade with another sea clan, they became a little more reasonable. The women carried back a full load of dried salted fish. Although we tried to keep the food dry, the rain made the task very difficult. I suggest that the wet fish be given to our clansmen to eat right away. The rest we can carry on the trek."

Agar looked critically at Vodim. "I'll take a look at it and then I'll decide when it's to be eaten."

Vodim shrugged his shoulders and returned to his own hearth where his mates, Olvi and Amalee, had prepared him a broth of roots and greens.

The following morning arrived with a clear sky. Agar, feeling an urgency to begin the journey, was noticeably restless, but he also knew that to begin such a venture without the favorable signs would be to invite disaster. He vented his irritation on Homan who meekly shared the hearth of the clan leader. "You can't even maintain a good fire anymore," Agar grumbled. "You share my food and hearth. You could at least maintain a good fire."

Homan remained silent although his mind passed harsh judgment on the clan leader. Homan, who had no mate, was assigned the responsibility of gathering fire wood and maintaining Agar's fire. He was also responsible for the fire box when the clan was on the trail.

The body of Homan showed little resemblance to what he had been as a younger man. At that time, as one of the mightiest hunters of the clan, he had been mauled by a cave bear. His mangled shoulder and arm had never healed properly and always remained a useless, scarred reminder of his helplessness. In earlier years, Homan's status as deputy leader under Dorik had given him an esteemed position in the clan. After the accident, Dorik decreed that Homan should retain his hearth which included one mate and five children. For three years much of his food was willingly provided by the other hunters. It was after Dorik was defeated by Agar that the new leader ordered a change.

"If the man can't provide his own meat," he argued, "he should relinquish his mate and children to an able-bodied hunter." It was out of respect for Homan that no other hunter chose to accept the woman and her children into his hearth. The woman was of strong body and a good worker which would have been an asset, but as one of the hunters commented to another, "I would always feel as though I was betraying my good friend Homan."

Agar at last assigned the woman to the hearth of Gors and the matter was soon forgotten.

Tomar, the elder clan visionary, also shared the hearth of Agar, although more often than not, he ate and slept at the hearth of other hunters. He also had no mate. He had outlived both of his previous mates and had no desire for the responsibility of another one.

Agar suddenly turned to Homan. "Go bring Tomar. He's never around when I want him. He loves to talk and flirt with all the old women of the clan. He should be out looking for signs."

When Tomar was seated at the fire of the leader, Agar spoke. "What do you have to say, Tomar? Have the Gods given you a sign?"

The old man scratched his long gray beard and his eyes became dreamy. He remained silent for a long time until, as if in a trance, he began to speak. "I have talked to the Gods and I have told them of our needs. We have had many days of rain. It is now the time of the flowers and new grass, and soon the leaves will return to the trees. The people of our clan are weak from hunger. There are few rabbits for the snares of our hunters. The deer have left the valley to feed in the forests of the mountains. Our women and children can no longer find the nuts that were hidden by the squirrels. Our dried meat is almost gone. The snow of the north should soon be melted and the reindeer will return to the meadows below the ice mountain to give of their calves. These things I have said to the Gods and we have waited for a sign."

Agar tried to hide his impatience. He was fully aware of the plight of his people and considered Tomar's long summary annoying. He was anxious for confirmation from a higher power that would support his decision to begin the trip. He was never certain how the spirits would react if he was critical of what he considered to be the ravings of an old man. He waited while Tomar continued.

"The Wind God has been silent for many days but this night he has spoken. He has told us that the time has come for Agar to take our people to the meadows near the ice mountain, that we may eat the flesh of the new calves and restore our strength. The Wind God has blown away the clouds, allowing the Sun God to warm our bodies during the long journey. This morning I saw many geese on their way to the lakes of the north. That is a very strong sign. While I slept last night the spirits entered my dreams, and in that vision I saw and remembered their message. I saw all our people on the trail. That is a very strong omen."

Agar wanted Tomar to say the critical words that would relieve him of the risk of a premature decision that might be flaunting the will of the great powers. He continued waiting impatiently.

Tomar closed his eyes and stroked his beard before continuing. "When the Sun God again rises above the hills, it will be time for our people to leave."

Agar turned to Homan. "Pass the word. We leave at dawn tomorrow."

- 5 -

The first light of dawn was penetrating the mouth of the grotto when Agar signaled the women to waken the children in preparation for the pending journey. Children were sent running to the other grottos to alert the clan members of the impending departure. Fires were fed to supply the needed light for the preparations. Babies cried as they were awakened and removed from their warm beds, allowing the robes to be rolled tightly and tied. Each woman bundled her meager food supply of dried meats, fish and nuts into pouches and secured the drawstrings. These special pouches would be treated as emergency rations to be used only if sufficient food could not be found along the trail. The gnawing hunger in their stomachs stirred memories of previous migrations north where reindeer calves were easy prey, and where the meat was so plentiful that only the choice portions would be saved.

"Come on," Agar shouted. "We can't wait all day!"

The clansmen, filled with enthusiasm, filed out to form a column near the mouth of the grotto. Behind the hunters, Homan moved into position, followed by five boys ages ten through seventeen. Two of the boys would shoulder the pole from which hung the precious turtle-shell fire box with its glowing coals. Orin led this latter group followed by a loose, mixed column of seventeen women and twenty-one additional children. Of the women and older girls, there were four who took positions at the very rear of the column, isolating themselves some distance back. Tomar had petitioned the spirits for the allowed exception which released these females from isolation normally required when they were under the curse of the Moon Spirit.

Agar consulted with Tomar. "You make the count," he ordered. "Make sure that everyone who is going is here."

An old woman, the mother of Armid's mate, Lana, was failing. Her vision had diminished until she could no longer forage for nuts and roots. Clan members had generously supplied her with the minimum food for survival, but everyone understood that when the clan began the migration, anyone unable to keep up with the clan would be left behind. The old woman had already announced that she wanted to be left behind. There was an extremely poor chance that she could find enough food and firewood to last until the clan returned in the fall. No one expected the woman to survive. The old woman confided to the other women that she was anxious to die and free her spirit to seek a new body.

Tomar walked down the long column, extending a finger as he passed each person. Each time he extended his tenth finger he would pause, drop a small pebble in his pouch and repeat the sequence. Upon returning to Agar he announced, "We have ten, five times, plus nine. There are two who will probably fall behind before we reach the meadows. There are four women who will give birth before we return. There is no need to delay. We are ready."

Agar raised his spear high in the air and waited. This signal created a reaction along the column as the women and larger children hoisted their heavy loads of sleeping robes, food pouches and miscellaneous possessions to their backs.

Orin stepped off the trail to look back at Nomi and to reassure himself that his mother, Amalee, and his two half sisters were there. He, like most of the older children, carried his own sleeping robe. The hunters carried only their spears, hunting axes, a small pouch of flint knives, and a heavier, extra fur body garment. The women carried sleeping robes for themselves and their mates, a supply of shell cooking and eating utensils, woven-reed gathering baskets and pouches of dried food and nuts.

When the heavy loads were hoisted, Agar lowered his spear and the clan began the long trek north.

The column proceeded along an old familiar path, roughly following the river toward its source. The river had created the valley over a period of millions of years, but in its fickle way had continually changed its mind during the spring flood season. The river formed repeated patterns of random loops, winding its way along the valley floor. The many sloughs and shallow channels gave evidence of the path the river had once travelled. Periodically the river extended its channel to the very edge of the valley, cutting deeply into the vertical limestone wall.

In the area where the clan walked, the trail was well worn and clearly defined in a fairly straight line from one river loop to the next, curving only to avoid a stand of heavy brush or the marsh of a slough.

"Come on," Agar shouted. "It's too early for anyone to be tired." The words were lost to the heavily burdened travellers far back on the trail.

Occasionally the path left the valley floor, ascending the bank of the foothills to detour the river at its point of attack on the limestone cliff. The increased effort to make the short climb was usually rewarded with a pleasant panoramic view of the valley. The column proceeded slowly, with Agar often calling back to prod his followers to a little faster pace.

The sun had made approximately one-third of its daily journey from horizon to horizon when Agar raised his spear high in the air and waited for the column to stop. He then lowered his spear and again raised and lowered it to signal an extended rest stop. All the members of the clan immediately shed their packs with the women and children scurrying off the trail onto the meadow of the valley. With digging sticks, they began rooting the soft soils for the familiar bulbs and roots that would stay the hunger gnawing in their stomachs. The hunters, who normally charged their mates with the responsibility of providing that type of ration, succumbed to the same hunger and, while pretending to stand guard, used their spears to probe the soil locally for any morsels that might be found. The women faithfully placed every alternate morsel in a leather pouch which they would soon give to their mates or any of their children who had been less fortunate in the search.

Agar walked leisurely back along the meadow. "In a few days you'll become hardened to the trail," he commented to a few women who were on their knees searching the ground. "Some of you have had it too easy all winter."

One of the older women smiled at the leader, but her later remark to another woman conveyed a different message. "If his advice was food, we'd all be fat."

Orin, after a few bites of tender roots that partially dulled his hunger pangs, walked back to the area where his mother and sisters foraged. He periodically glanced around to assure himself that no hunter was watching. His feelings were mixed. He was torn between his emotional family bond and his desire for identity as a hunter.

As he approached, Amalee struggled to her feet. "Have you found anything to eat?" She reached into her pouch, withdrawing several bulbs and roots. "Here, eat these. If you are soon going to join the hunt, you need food to grow big and strong."

"No, mother. You should save those for your mate, Vodim." He then glanced at his two siblings. "Are the girls getting enough to eat?"

Amalee's years of hard toil and sacrifice clearly showed on her stooped frame. Though never as heavy as many of the other women, her recent self-deprivation had reduced her body to a weight hardly more than half that of some of the larger women. Her hair had turned gray, and although her teeth were still sound, her sunken cheeks and dark eyes had become the gossip of more than a few of the clan women. Amalee was aware of her appearance and failing strength, but her concern was directed toward the welfare of her children. She constantly worried about what would happen to Carma and Retta after her spirit departed.

When thinking about her daughters, she often reminisced about her own youth. She remembered when, as a young girl, her body began to change. As her breasts grew and her hips developed, she enjoyed the attention that the young men and some of the older hunters displayed. Her long reddish hair and deep blue eyes attracted a young man, Dorik, who had only a short time earlier gained admittance to the Order of the Hunt. As a prerogative of that status, Dorik had selected Amalee as his mate. His broad shoulders and powerful arms discouraged other hunters from competition. It was soon after his son, Orin, was born that Dorik gained leadership of the clan. There had been no fight. The previous leader, Tomar, was happy to relinquish his power to his friend and second in command. They were fond memories.

Retta, the five-year-old, younger daughter of Amalee, moved to Orin's side and slipped her hand into his. "Why don't you walk with us, Orin? We miss you and I want you to be with us."

Amalee placed a hand on her daughter's shoulder. "Orin is a man now and is expected to walk with the other men."

"Then can I come and walk with you, Orin?" she pleaded.

Amalee interceded, relieving Orin of the need of rejecting the child. "Orin will walk with the men. You and Carma will walk with me."

Retta rejoined Carma in her search for food, and Orin, lifting his hand in a good-bye wave, turned and started back up the line. He paused when he saw Nomi watching him from a short distance. He started toward her but again stopped. He wanted to run to her and embrace her, but his status as a future hunter prohibited such an emotional display. After glancing around to see who might be watching, he waved a brief greeting before turning toward the forward column.

Agar called the hunters to his side. "We're getting far enough from the grotto that we might start seeing some larger game." He paused to study his men before continuing. "Dorik, you take your men and scout ahead of us along the river. I'll stay with the clan. We'll camp tonight at the meadow where Beaver Creek joins the river. Gors, you take your men along those foothills to our left and Vodim will take the right. We'll see you all in camp tonight. Stay alert."

As the discussion ended, Orin approached his father. "May I go with you? I want to help scout."

Dorik loved and admired his son but he had no desire to antagonize Agar. "You can help more by staying with the clan. When you make camp, you can help Tomar and Homan."

He rested his hand on Orin's shoulder before continuing. "Agar might need your help with the clan. Remember, you'll be the strongest man remaining with Agar."

Orin realized that Dorik was trying to make him feel needed and was grateful for the gesture although it failed to bolster his ego. Sure, he thought. Other than Agar, that leaves only Tomar, Homan and myself. When are they going to let me join in the hunt? How can I prove myself a hunter unless I walk with the hunters? He turned to take his place in the main column that was preparing to continue.

The scouting parties separated after which the remaining clansmen continued their steady advance along the valley floor. The column moved slowly enough to allow individuals time to leave the trail to satisfy their body needs. Agar, though frequently calling for greater effort, was careful to set a pace that would keep everyone within a safe distance of each other.

The sun had traveled only two-thirds of its daily journey when the column moved onto the meadow near Beaver Creek. Agar paused, waiting for the entire column to come to a stop. Holding his spear horizontally, he raised and lowered it three times, signaling the clansmen that the day's march was over.

Packs were rapidly lowered to the ground, allowing the women and children the opportunity of scouring the meadow for edible roots and bulbs. With the warming weather there were many succulent shoots pushing through the still dormant grass.

After Orin and his helper lowered the turtle-shell fire carrier to the ground, Homan relieved them of their duties and proceeded to blow the smoldering coals into a flame that could be transferred to a fire pit.

Orin grasped his spear and began running toward the river's edge. Slowing his pace as he approached the dense brush, he advanced cautiously below the overhanging willows to explore the shoreline. He was startled as a pair of frightened ducks, squawking loudly, took to the air. He began searching the bank looking for the nest he suspected was near and was alerted by the noise of a twig breaking behind him. Quickly turning, he saw Nomi watching him from the shadow of a nearby tree.

"What are you doing here?" he scolded. "You shouldn't be away from the camp alone."

"I'm not alone. You're here with me, or perhaps I should say I'm here with you."

"You might have scared away the game."

"You mean the duck's eggs," she said grinning.

Orin also smiled and moved over to the shaded area where the girl stood. He seated himself on a nearby fallen log and held out his hand to her.

Nomi sat beside him and placed her hand in his. "I like to be close to you. I wish we could always be together."

"And I want you to always be with me." Orin looked around to assure himself they were alone. "When I'm accepted into the Order of the Hunt and receive my hunting axe, I'll have the right to choose a mate. I hope no other hunter will have claimed you by then." The thought produced a worried look on his face.

Nomi shrugged her shoulders. "Why would you say that? I think that's silly. All the hunters have mates. Some have two or three, so why would anyone claim me?"

"I've been watching Agar. He looks at you every chance he gets and I'm afraid he might decide to take you as a mate."

"Agar has three mates already. I don't think he wants any more."

"He could give one of his women to another hunter and take a younger one. That's what he did with my mother. When he defeated my father, he claimed Amalee as his mate. I was quite small then, but he later claimed Anna and gave my mother to Vodim. He might decide to give away one of his other mates and claim you." Orin paused in deep thought before continuing. "Someday I'll challenge Agar. Some day I'll be the clan leader."

Orin lapsed into silence as Nomi snuggled near him, envisioning him as her mate and master of the clan.

Orin quickly rose to his feet. "We'd better keep looking or we won't find any food."

They had been searching the tall rushes along the bank for only a short time when Nomi called excitedly. "Oh look, here's the nest. It's loaded with eggs."

Orin knelt to examine the discovery, and after counting, looked up at Nomi. "There are twelve of them." It was a subtle reminder to Nomi that he could count.

Girls were taught to count to ten on their fingers but boys were taught by Tomar to count all the way to ten, ten times. Counting could be very important when reporting animals. They loaded the eggs carefully in Nomi's leather pouch, cautiously placing dry grass around them.

"I'll continue to search while you take them back to camp," Orin ordered, retrieving his spear.

Nomi had walked only a short distance when she called to Orin. Upon arriving at her side, she pointed up into a tree several paces away.

"It's a porcupine," he said with enthusiasm. "Put your pouch of eggs down and let's kill him."

After she gently lowered the eggs to the ground, they both ran to the tree where the animal was feeding on the bark of a limb about three times a man's height above the ground.

"When I get up on that limb, hand me my spear," Orin ordered. He jumped to grasp a lower limb and pulled himself up to a standing position. "Now hand me my spear," he again ordered. As he began maneuvering his way from limb to limb, he added, "Find a stick to use as a club in case he falls out of the tree."

When within reach, Orin made a sharp thrust with his spear, attempting to drive it into the porcupine's neck. His thrust merely wounded the animal which fell from the tree. While Orin was excitedly descending to the ground, Nomi tried to slow the animal's departure. She managed to turn it back after which the porcupine again began climbing the tree. Grabbing his spear, Orin succeeded in driving the weapon deep into the neck of the animal.

After clubbing the porcupine to death, he pushed the spear completely through the animal's neck, allowing it to be carried without the hazard of injury by the quills.

As they approached the campfires with their prizes, they were met by a cluster of curious children.

"What is that?" a child inquired. "Is that a porcupine?"

"Of course it's a porcupine," Retta stated. "Can't you see the sharp quills on its back? She then proudly walked beside her brother as she called to other friends, "Come see what Orin killed."

The porcupine was taken to the main fire pit where Homan congratulated them both.

* * *

The clan policy required that any game that size or larger be shared by the entire clan. Roots, bulbs, nuts, grains etc., as well as smaller animals such as squirrels or rabbits could be retained at the hearth of the individual hunter and shared with his mates and children. There were special circumstances in which the clan leader could confiscate food from one hearth to be given to another. Bad feelings could arise at such times but no one ever challenged the leader's authority. They realized, without question, that survival depended upon the cooperation of each individual under one authority. Weak leadership could allow divergent goals, fostering disputes and ill feelings among the clansmen. The individual hunters had authority over their families, but the clan leader had complete authority over all the clan members. A leader should normally try to avoid interfering with the affairs of the individual families, but if a hunter could not control his own mates or children, the clan leader would not hesitate to exercise his power. At times, the leader would order a woman and her children transferred from the hearth of one hunter to that of another. If a hunter was killed, it was the duty of the leader to assign his mate and children to another man. If a young, maturing women was not claimed by a hunter within a year of the time of her first moon curse, she could be assigned to one.

Orin and Nomi left the fire where Homan was heating the cooking rocks in the hot embers.

"You take the eggs to your hearth and let's go look for more," Nomi suggested.

"No, you found them, they're yours."

"We found them together," she countered. "Why don't we share them?"

Orin's concern for his mother and sisters prompted him to accept. "All right," he conceded, "but maybe later we can find some more."

By then several fires were burning at various locations on the meadow. Often, when on the trail, the families of two or three hunters would share a fire for companionship and for the convenience of sustaining the flame during the night.

There were jealousies and grudges among some of the women and the proximity of one campfire to another usually reflected those feelings.

Orin and Nomi, after dividing the eggs, parted to locate their respective family hearths.

As was custom, Orin remained a member of the hearth of his mother and siblings until he was accepted as a hunter and had claimed a mate. Amalee shared Vodim's hearth with his other mate, Olvi, and her one child. Olvi was Vodim's first mate and remained his favorite. Vodim treated Amalee and her children kindly and the two women maintained a cooperative, if not completely amiable, relationship.

Orin located his mother, who was storing a supply of edible bulbs and roots at the edge of the fire. Olvi's six-year-old son, Uval, and the two daughters of Amalee were busy foraging for firewood.

"Nomi and I found a nest of duck eggs," Orin explained. "It's too bad that the ducks heard us and flew away."

"You're a good provider," Amalee said proudly. "I hope you're careful when you hunt."

Ignoring her words of caution, his eyes searched the meadow. "I don't see Olvi."

"We remembered the watercress beds up the canyon of Beaver Creek. She and one of the other women went to gather some."

"You look awfully thin, mother. You've been giving your food portion to the girls, haven't you?" He noticed the bones of her face and shoulders protruded more than usual.

Amalee looked up from her chores, her sunken eyes clearly revealing her fatigue. "You won't understand until you have children of your own."

The sun was casting long shadows when four of the hunters returned to camp supporting furry bundles over their shoulders and broad smiles on their faces. Several of the curious children raced to meet the hunters and followed closely behind as they delivered their quarry near the main fire. Agar hurried over and stood at the side of Homan to hear of the hunter's exploits.

Vodim told of discovering a small beaver dam when crossing Beaver creek on their hunting foray. "Two of us circled carefully around the dam to locate the entrance tunnel to the beaver lodge. We swam to the lodge and positioned ourselves to intercept the returning animals. Armid and Umik chased the beavers while shouting to create confusion so the animals wouldn't notice we were waiting at the lodge. The diversion worked and we were able to spear them as they tried to enter the tunnel. We tried to get to the beaver pups inside the lodge but couldn't."

By the time the story was told, some of the women, using their sharp flint knives, had skinned and cleaned the animals and were cutting the meat into portions to be divided among the hearths. The four hunters would be allowed to keep the pelts which would be dried, cured and made into hunting pouches. The meat was particularly prized, for it contained more fat than most other game found at that time of year.

"Very good," Agar commented. "Now the women can save more of their dried rations for the hard days ahead."

The porcupine was not skinned but was gutted and lowered onto the bank of red coals where the burning quills and hair dispensed an acrid odor that kept the women cooks on the upwind side of the fire. After the coals had charred the skin into a dark greasy crust, the carcass was pulled onto the rocks at the edge of the fire to continue to roast.

The sun was low when Dorik and the other hunters returned empty handed and without news of even seeing any game.

"We saw some fresh spoor of deer," Gors related, "but apparently they heard us first. We tracked them for a while but they were too wary."

Though the apportioned ration was in no way a feast, it did help relieve the nagging hunger in many of the clan members.

With partially satisfied stomachs, the younger children congregated to initiate a game of hide and seek. One child stood at the base tree, slowly counting to ten while the other children attempted to hide behind trees or shrubs. The player at the tree then recited the verse that would warn the others that he or she was ready to search.

"Here I come, ready or not."

There was repeated loud squealing and shouting as an exposed player raced the seeker back to the base tree. The excited play lasted until darkness approached at which time mothers called their reluctant but tired children back to their bed robes. With the children secured, the mothers lost no time in collapsing into their own bedrolls.

- 6 -

The next few days found the clan moving into higher and cooler terrain. The valley had narrowed, forcing the migrants to edge along the narrow trail that looked sharply down at the swollen river. Storm clouds could be seen to the north, unloading their burden of water over the mountains ahead. Hunting had been sparse, necessitating the consumption of much of the hoarded emergency rations.

The sun was high overhead but hidden above a dark overcast when Dorik, of the center scouting party, excitedly returned to meet the caravan. He approached Agar. "We may be in luck," he announced. "We spotted a herd of deer in the willows up ahead. They're feeding on a neck of land where the river forms a long loop across the valley."

"Did they see you?" Agar asked. "Are they still there?"

"I believe so," Dorik answered. "They didn't see us and the wind was blowing from them to us. There are at least six or eight of them. The situation is ideal for a drive and ambush."

"Where are your men?"

"I left them to watch the deer," Dorik explained. "They'll report to us if the animals leave before we're ready."

"I want you to locate Gors and his men across the canyon," Agar ordered. "Bring them back as fast as possible."

He then ordered Orin, who had overheard the conversation, to climb the canyon slope and proceed upstream. "Locate Vodim and his men and bring them back here. Be quiet so you won't alert the animals, but hurry."

Instructions were passed along the trail for the women to maintain silence and they all unloaded their packs to enjoy a much needed rest. Orin and Dorik each departed in haste while Agar, Tomar and Homan discussed the possible strategy.

Orin climbed well up on the canyon wall before proceeding parallel to the river. Often he would pause to cup his hands around his mouth and give the call of the hoot owl. Waiting only long enough to listen for a reply, he would then cautiously continue. Trampled grass and fresh footprints offered clues that the scouting party had traveled that route and his call was soon answered by a similar call. Conforming to techniques that all hunters learned as children, he repeated the call three times. When the calls were returned, he waited for the hunters to join him. The group quickly returned to the clan, arriving almost jointly with the team from the other bank.

When the hunters had gathered near Agar, he issued the orders. "Dorik, you're familiar with the terrain. Is the riverbank suitable for the clan to drive the deer into the water at the end of the neck as we did two years ago at the big meadow?"

Dorik scratched his beard in thought. "Yes, but the stream is swollen and we might lose some wounded animals to the river. The cliff beyond the end of the neck is too sheer. If we station six hunters upstream from the cliff and six downstream, we should have a good chance to kill some of the animals."

Fortunately the caravan of women and children was on the correct side of the river. Instructions were given for the hunters to move back downstream to a suitable crossing. With their spears tied to their backs, the hunters waded into the rushing water and began swimming for the opposite bank. Though the current carried the men some distance downstream, they had no trouble crossing. The hunters congregated on the opposite bank, shivering from the cold.

Every man, woman and child of the clan could swim. They were usually taught before they were old enough to walk, for on the annual migration there were many times that the entire clan would have to cross streams that were too deep to wade. Swimming was not only a means of survival, it was a sport and usually a pleasure.

After crossing the river, the hunters separated, with six men climbing up and around the cliff to quietly establish their concealed ambush along the upper stream bank. The other six moved into position below the cliff.

Agar turned his attention to the women and younger clan members. "When the hunters are ready, we'll quietly form a line across the strip of land. I want all of you to find clubs or heavy sticks to carry with you. The deer may try to break through our line rather than enter the swift water. Even if that happens, we might be able to kill one or two of them."

When Agar was satisfied that all was ready, he quietly signaled the women and children to form the line across the neck of the peninsula. Upon the signal from Agar, the line advanced slowly along the peninsula toward the tip. They all understood that it was important to not panic the deer but to drive them slowly enough so the fleet-footed animals would not take to the water until reaching the bend of the river. As the drivers cautiously and quietly advanced, they occasionally saw an animal raise its head and move deeper into the security of the willows and brush.

After the deer had retreated to the shrubs near the tip of the peninsula, Agar felt that the time was right. He raised his spear and gave a loud shout. "All right, let's go," he yelled. "Let's see the mountains shake with the noise. Keep them moving fast."

All the drivers then ran forward, shouting to the fullest extent of their lungs. The panicked deer rushed to the river's edge and turned, following the gravel bank. As the animals rounded the curved end of the peninsula and reentered the brush, they were met by the shoulder-to-shoulder line of shouting marchers. The deer herd consisted of a buck whose emerging antlers were covered with velvet. There were five does and four yearlings. The animals turned, and taking their clue from the buck, plunged into the water, swimming for the opposite bank upstream from the cliffs. As the lead animals struggled to gain a footing on the opposite steep bank, the concealed hunters rushed forward to drive their spears into their helpless victims. The slower deer turned back to the river and were carried downstream by the current, swimming for the steep bank below the cliff. At the most vulnerable moment, the deer were met by the other waiting hunters. The animals, seeing no alternative, struggled against the spears that awaited them as they climbed from the water. One of the does, followed by her yearling, abandoned the steep bank and turned back to the gentle slope of the peninsula. Orin, who had been advancing close to Tomar and Homan, raced into the water to meet the doe just as she began to gain a foothold in the gravel bank. As she struggled to get out of the water, he plunged his spear deep into her neck. Homan rushed in to assist, and with his one good hand, held the doe as the youth tried to extract the spear. From the corner of his eye, Orin saw the yearling struggling against the current in shallow water. Seeing that Homan was holding the lifeless doe, Orin plunged into the water to grasp the neck of the younger animal. The yearling turned back into the current to swim downstream with the excited youth gripping handfuls of hair on its back.

Nomi called her support and caution from the bank. "Orin, be careful. Don't get hurt."

Orin and the yearling were swept around the bend of the river leaving Nomi and many of the women shouting encouragement. As they disappeared from view, Agar and Nomi raced through the brush, attempting to stay within sight of the endangered clan member. The trees and willows impeded their movements until, upon emerging at a lower clearing, Orin and the deer were nowhere in sight.

Panic stricken, Nomi attempted to follow the shore but was forced back into the brush by the overhanging willows. "Orin, Orin," she yelled. "Are you all right?"

The current was becoming swift and more turbulent. When she and Agar again emerged from the brush into another clearing, she was startled and surprised to see Orin, climbing up the gravel bank, dragging the struggling yearling by the rear legs. Agar rushed to his side and, with a flint knife, cut the deer's throat.

"How in the world did you get him to shore?" Agar asked.

"I didn't," Orin answered. "He pulled me to the shore. I held onto him by the hair of his back until he started up the bank. Then I grabbed him by the rear legs."

Agar let Orin shoulder the carcass and carry it into the camp that was being set up on the peninsula. Walking proudly at his side, Nomi extolled the bravery of Orin to the children who ran to meet them.

Upon arriving at the main clan, the women had begun skinning the earlier killed doe, and the hunters had extended a braided leather line across the river to aid in transferring the other dead animals to the peninsula.

Homan and one of the older boys had returned down the trail to retrieve and sustain the fire that still smoldered in the turtle-shell fire box.

By late afternoon, venison roasts were dispensing mouth-watering aromas from several camp fires. Women and children were singing joyous songs that hadn't been heard for several moons and an undeclared celebration was underway.

Tomar took the precaution of reminding all the adults that perhaps they should offer their prayers of thanks to the Spirit of the Hunt. "We should remember that the great spirit granted us this success. We must honor that great power."

Orin had eaten his fill from the strips of venison sizzling on heated rocks near the fire. His eyes searched the camp until locating Nomi. As their eyes met, smiles crept slowly across their faces. Orin rose to his feet and began walking out of camp, occasionally glancing back. Nomi soon followed, using a different route. Orin jogged ahead, moving to the path Nomi was following. He waited quietly behind a large tree until, as Nomi arrived near his hiding place, he jumped out to surprise her.

"Oh," she squealed, grabbing her hands to her chest. "Orin, don't you ever do that again. I almost jumped out of my skin."

He said nothing but took the girl in his arms and drew her frightened body to him. Their lips met in a tender kiss. When he did speak, it was in a soft and gentle tone.

"I didn't mean to frighten you. I wouldn't ever hurt you. I just want you all to myself. Back in camp there are too many people. Let's walk back down the trail where we can be alone together."

They walked hand in hand far back along the trail until Orin was sure they wouldn't be disturbed. He led her off the trail to a small clearing in the heavy willow underbrush, where, after lowering himself to the grass, he motioned for Nomi to sit at his side. No words were spoken as he drew her to him in a prolonged and passionate kiss.

The embrace lasted for a long time until the silence was broken by Orin's whispered voice. "Nomi, I love you more than I know how to say. I want you with me always."

She kissed him lightly on the lips. "And I love you, Orin. There is nothing on earth I want more than to someday be your mate."

The two lay together, speaking of their hopes and plans after Orin's acceptance into the Order of the Hunt. For a time they remained in each other's arms without speaking, each of them mentally experimenting with scenarios of their life together.

Nomi sat up, looking nervously at the deepening shadows. "It's getting dark and we better get back to camp before they start looking for us."

After walking hand in hand back to the edge of camp, they embraced and kissed once more before slipping unnoticed into the festive celebration.

The fires burned brightly, well into the night. The carcasses of the uneaten deer hung from limbs of nearby trees with a fire maintained nearby to discourage scavengers. The children went to sleep with gorged stomachs and the spirits filled their minds with visions of good times ahead.

As the first light of dawn penetrated the heavy overcast, a drizzle began to fall. There was a scurry of activity as fires were stoked and robes were spread over the piles of wood that had been gathered the previous evening. Homan loaded hot coals into the turtle-shell and moved it to the limb of a nearby tree where a robe was hung over it to divert the rain. As though it had waited for the precautions to be completed, the rain then intensified and soon became a deluge. Word was passed to conserve and keep the firewood dry. Sticks and small chunks of wood were wrapped and carried to the turtle shell.

No one was hungry and the children passed the time huddled under robes, retelling stories of past travels, hunts and spirits, and sometimes quarreling because one child had pulled the robe too hard, exposing another to the rain.

One of the favorite stories was the legend of Sandow, the boy who grew up and hunted with the wolves. It told of how he learned to speak the wolves' language and taught them how to hunt as a pack, rather than individually. The story explained that before Sandow, wolves could kill nothing larger than a rabbit, but with Sandow to teach them, they learned to hunt as a pack and to kill the bison and the long-horned cattle. After Sandow taught the wolves his secret, he went to walk with the spirits, and it was said that "Even today, when one hears the eerie wail of the wolf, you know they are calling to Sandow."

The rain continued throughout the day and the women portioned out the remains of the food that had been cooked the previous evening.

The plan decreed by Agar the night before was to remain in camp for two or three days, smoking and drying the meat which would sustain them for many days' travel. The clan leader sat gloomily under his robe, sharing the fears of all the clan adults.

Agar looked up as the bundled figure of Dorik approached. He signaled an invitation for the hunter to sit at his side. "If the rain continues for another day or so," he said, "the meat will spoil. We can't dry it in this weather."

Dorik raised the overhead flap of his robe to study the sky. "It doesn't seem to be easing up. Here in the mountains, at this time of year, the rain could last for days. I do have a suggestion, though, if you would care to hear it?"

Agar nodded consent. "What do you have in mind?"

Dorik continued. "It would be difficult, and not without risk on the muddy trail, but this is what I've been thinking. Do you remember the cave about a day's walk from here, the one where Homan was wounded?"

"Yes, go ahead."

"Well, if we left the children here with a couple of women and one or two hunters, the rest of us could carry part of the deer meat to the cave. With the large overhang of the cave entrance, we could build our fires to smoke and dry the meat. Do you think it worth trying?"

Agar didn't answer for a while, periodically grunting as his mind explored Dorik's suggestion. "It would be risky, but we can't afford to lose the meat. It's a good suggestion. We'll make arrangements to start at dawn tomorrow."

Agar called a meeting of his hunters. The rain-soaked men waited as the leader issued orders. "I've given a lot of thought to the problem and have made a decision. At first dawn tomorrow, all the hunters, and our strongest women, will carry the haunches and front legs of the deer up the trail to the cave where Homan was crippled. I think we can do it in one day. It looks like this rain will last for a few days and I don't want the meat to spoil. We'll leave the nursing mothers and the women heavy with child here to look after all the children. Tomar will stay here and be in charge. Any questions?"

Orin stepped forward to inquire, "Am I to go with the group tomorrow?"

Agar looked at the slender youth who stood half a hand taller than himself. Orin's success at killing the doe and capturing the yearling deer had impressed Agar and kindled a begrudging respect for the lad.

I'll soon have to make plans for his acceptance and initiation into the Order of the Hunt, he thought as he nodded assent to Orin. "You can help Homan with the fire."

Three women, with their own smallest children and two other expectant mothers, would be left behind to feed and care for the remaining children. Nomi was included with the women who would be carrying meat to the cave. Homan and the fire box would also accompany the travellers.

Agar consulted with Tomar. "The remaining meat will probably attract scavengers, so you must keep the fires burning brightly and keep everyone in camp. We'll leave enough meat to last you for several days, so there's no need to forage outside the area. I know I can depend on you."

During the night, Agar found sleep difficult and he worried about the success of the mission. He felt he should take extra precautions. Before dawn he alerted Homan and ordered him to stoke and enlarge the fire that smoldered under the leather awning. He put a couple of women to work cooking venison, and by the time it was prepared, he had roused all the travellers from their damp bed robes.

"It will be easier to carry some of the food in your stomachs than on your backs," he explained to the sleepy clansmen who were preparing for the difficult march. They all agreed.

Working in the continuing rain, the remaining deer meat was cut into manageable loads. The rear and front legs were removed, leaving the balance for those who would remain behind.

Homan and Orin shouldered the pole that supported the all important fire box. Dry wood, heavy in pitch, was tied to the pole with a robe hung over it to divert the rain.

Agar took the lead as the column moved out along the trail. With the heavy load being carried by each member of the party, walking became difficult on the slippery surface. The encouraging thought that pushed them to greater effort was the prospect of reaching the comfort of the cave.

The column proceeded slowly, with an occasional traveller slipping and spilling his load to the wet ground.

"You're a clumsy old woman," Agar shouted back along the column after a heavily burdened woman fell. The column paused only long enough for her to retrieve her burden and hoist it back to her shoulder. She mumbled a mild protest but resumed her chore.

"Don't you think they should rest for a few moments?" Vodim asked of the leader.

"I intend to get to that cave by dark," Agar answered, accelerating the pace.

Homan and Orin maintained the rear position of the column, occasionally stopping to locate a tree limb where they could temporarily suspend the fire box. On each occasion, while Orin held the cover aside, Homan stoked the smoldering fire back to life. They also watched for pine cones which, though wet, contained sufficient pitch to sustain the fire.

"Are we half way yet?" Agar inquired of Vodim and Dorik. The two agreed that more than half the distance had been travelled but noted that everyone was slowing down from exhaustion.

Agar called back along the column, "If we push a little harder, we should reach the cave by dark."

Word was passed and a renewed effort was made to sustain the pace.

The rain continued throughout the day with no indication of relief and the sky began to darken with the onset of twilight. As the trail detoured a rocky outcropping, Dorik suggested to Agar that he thought the cave was in the next ravine. It was welcome news to the trail-weary men and women as they turned away from the main trail, advancing up the narrow side canyon.

Darkness was setting when Agar and Dorik located the cave entrance. The travellers lowered their packs and waited as the men examined the dark opening. The entrance towered three times a man's height and was equally wide.

After examining the ground near the mouth of the cave, the two men inspected a well worn path to a nearby creek.

"What do you think?" Dorik asked. "It looks like the cave is occupied, but I can't tell what kind of animal it is."

"The cave has been used lately," Agar agreed, "but the signs aren't clear. The rain has destroyed the footprints so we can't be sure."

Dorik glanced back at the cave entrance. "After we killed the cave bear here at the hunt with Homan, I doubted that another bear would move in. There aren't many cave bears left any more."

"We can't take any chances," was Agar's advice. "It might be one of the smaller black bears, or it could be any of the big cats. I think we should move back down to the river and wait until morning."

The weary travellers again shouldered their loads and retraced their steps down the ravine to the bank of the river. Homan and Orin worked feverishly to nurse the fire into a large enough flame to enable them to transfer the fire to the ground. Pine cones and dead limbs of high pitch content were gathered by the travellers. By the time heavy darkness had set, there was a good fire burning in a pit. Poles had been located and a robe was suspended high over the fire to divert the rain. Dead limbs were broken from nearby trees and stockpiled near the fire.

"I don't want anyone to leave the area of the fire," Agar ordered. "It's too dark to gather any more fire wood and I don't know what animal is in the cave."

The meat was placed between the fire and the river bank where two guards were posted to maintain a vigil. Agar was concerned that the smell of the deer meat would attract, if not the occupant of the cave, any other foraging scavenger in the area. He felt the fire was inadequate to deter the big, night-hunting cats. "But I don't think the wolves will be a threat in this area," he commented to a few of his hunters.

During the night, the rain eased to a light drizzle. Agar questioned his own judgment of the previous afternoon. We should have established camp early enough to gather a better wood supply, he thought. The fire may not last the night and now darkness makes wood gathering dangerous, if not impossible.

The night passed with only one frightening moment. The guards were alerted by the snorting of some unknown night creature. As they began shouting, the yell was quickly taken up by the awakened clan members. The combined chorus of voices frightened the unidentified beast into making a cautious retreat. The next shift of guards spent a quiet time waiting for dawn.

As the sky began to lighten, a few men ventured away from camp to search for suitable firewood. Coals were stoked into a blaze that not only improved the security of the group but brought a welcome warmth to their numbed bodies. The rain ceased but the threatening sky offered little encouragement for the coming day. The morale of the group was buoyed by the anticipation of occupying the cave. Venison strips were soon sizzling on heated rocks, adding a new enthusiasm for the approaching day.

Conversation included speculation as to the identity of the cave dweller and what technique would be pursued to drive the beast away. Agar remained silent, but was watched carefully by his curious clansmen.

- 7 -

The hunters congregated near Agar to hear his plan and to receive instructions. Homan, with his vivid and ghastly memory of a previous visit to the same cave, stoked his fire box and helped carry it up the trail. Agar was grateful that the rain had temporarily ceased. He considered this a good omen. He assumed the Spirit of the Hunt was watching over them.

"I want a large supply of reasonably dry wood and also a large pile of green pine boughs," Agar ordered. "Stack them on the hill just above the cave opening."

No one was allowed near the cave entrance. Hunting tales and past experience told Agar that if the occupant was one of the great cats, it would evacuate the cave in a fury at the first provocation. The risk outweighed the glory and he didn't want to be one of the casualties. If the cave contained a cave bear, it would take considerable prodding to bring it out and it was understood by the clansmen that an attempt would be made to take it as a trophy. The Spirit of the Hunt would be proud and generous if the clan could overcome such a great beast.

The small flame from the turtle shell was propagated into a sizable fire on the steep ground above the cave entrance. With the women at a safe distance, the burning logs were pushed over the edge of the cliff to collect and continue burning near the mouth of the cave. The hunters remained above the cliff with instructions to not challenge even the cave bear if it came out at that time. The fire was fed from above until it was a sizable mound of burning logs. His memory from earlier visits reminded Agar that the depth of the cave, though reasonably shallow, gave ample room for a beast to instinctively retreat from the fire.

When the time seemed appropriate, the piles of green pine boughs were thrown over the cliff onto the burning conflagration below. Heavy dark smoke billowed out from the burning green needles, mushrooming around and into the cave entrance. The signal was given and the hunters raced to take up positions on either side of the fire. Adrenaline poured into the bloodstreams of the excited men as they faced the unknown with ready spears.

The men joked to relieve the fear and tension that each harbored. "If he doesn't come out soon, I'll send my woman in after him," one of the men joked. "He'll wish he'd found a different grotto."

Orin was allowed to participate only by assisting Homan above the cave. The two men coughed and choked with teary eyes as they continued to feed green boughs onto the fire below.

As the smoke penetrated the depth of the cave, the hunters became confident that the moment was near. Above the crackling and hissing of the fire, a series of protesting growls brought the men to a tense alert.

Gors was the first to see the huge cave bear bolt toward the entrance. "Here he comes," he yelled and the hunters braced themselves with spears raised.

As the bear approached the fire in a state of agitated confusion, he made two or three aborted lunges before retreating. Again he reared up, and with a series of whining utterances, vigorously rubbed his paws across his smarting eyes. As a thermal gust of air lifted the billowing smoke momentarily, the bear lunged toward the clearing, oblivious to the armed men in his path. Three of the hunters, with feet braced to absorb the force, drove their spears deep into his body. Two spears penetrated the shoulder near the neck and a third entered the body behind the rib cage. Vodim, whose spear was broken by the flailing paw of the beast, fell backward, directly under the path of the animal. The bear, in his frantic escape attempt, unknowingly trampled the hunter, and upon seeing the other men, lunged toward them in a ferocious attack. The hunters from the far side of the fire raced to protect their disarmed comrades. They arrived just as the beast reared to attack Agar whose spear had been deflected. Dorik saw the exposed belly, and putting the full weight of his body into the force of his spear, drove the flint deeply into the animal's chest. Agar scrambled frantically to escape the enraged beast, for although the mighty cave bear was mortally wounded, it was still capable of mauling or inflicting lethal damage to an adversary. The half blinded bear, suffering severe pain and confusion, decided to escape. It turned and began climbing the steep slope adjacent to the cave. Orin, who had been excitedly watching the action below, grabbed his spear and started across the slope to intercept the bear.

Homan watched in horror with a vivid memory of his own experience. He shouted a warning. "Come back, Orin.

Come back. He'll kill you."

Orin never heard the warning. As he moved along the steep slope to intercept the beast, his feet slipped on the damp grass. After quickly regaining his footing, he ran to a position directly above the climbing beast, exploiting the advantage of the steep grade. As the enraged bear approached, it reared up, snarling with open jaws. Orin, in an automatic reflex, lifted his spear and drove it with all the force he could summon, deep into the throat of the mighty cave bear. The beast, suffering a new source of pain, lost his balance and tumbled out of control down the steep slope.

When the hunters, with spears raised, ran to continue the attack, Agar ordered them to stand back. "No more," he shouted. "Don't damage any more of the skin."

The great cave bear was in his final death throes and could not get up.

The women came running in from their place of safety, and with exclamations of awe and admiration, congregated around the dead beast. Vodim was sitting up, regaining his breath and checking himself for injuries. He was not seriously hurt.

The hunters called Orin into their midst, slapping his back with congratulations. Agar raised his hand to subdue the ovation. "That was a brave thing you did, Orin. It was also a foolish risk. The bear could not have traveled far with his wounds and the hunters could have finished him off later."

Orin's exhilaration deflated somewhat but was again buoyed when Agar continued. "There is no doubt about your courage. You will be a great hunter someday. From now on, you may join us on the hunt." Orin waited for Agar's comment about his Order of the Hunt membership, but the leader added nothing more.

Orin knew that the normal procedure for a young man was to join the hunting forays as an apprentice until the leader felt him fully qualified. Orin's elation was dampened by his impatience, and his desire for Order of the Hunt status was far greater than the hunters would have suspected. He knew he could not claim Nomi until after his acceptance ceremony.

A spontaneous chant was started by Armid and was soon joined by all present. The hunters formed a column that circled the dead cave bear and soon their feet picked up the rhythm of the chant. The voices grew louder as the tempo quickened and soon the spears were being waved in mock thrusts toward the dead bear. The words that echoed up and down the canyon sang praise to the great Spirit of the Hunt and to the spirits of all those brave men who had died in glory. The song affirmed the special place in the spirit world for the hunters who died on the hunt, and petitioned the spirits of those men to protect all their comrades who still walked the forests of the earth.

- 8 -

Agar issued orders to the women. "Bring all the meat up from the river and then get busy cutting and drying it." The clan leader then cautiously led the hunters in an exploration of the shallow cave. He was aware that cave bears lived and travelled alone except when mating, but he felt it prudent to verify there were no more bears inside. The precaution was unnecessary.

While the women were bringing the venison from the river's edge below, the hunters began the ceremonial skinning of the giant bear. The task of skinning an animal, which would normally be the chore of the women, was in this case reserved for the men. The hide would be removed with the utmost care to avoid damage. The head of the bear would be cooked and the brains removed to be blended with certain ceremonial herbs. This would then be stuffed into the heart and roasted over a special fire tended by Agar, who by tradition, was the bravest of the brave. At the ceremonial feast to be held that evening, the entire clan would roast and eat of the bear flesh, but the hunters, in a separate and secret ritual, would also eat portions of the heart. To the hunters there was no question about the value of the ritual which would imbue great courage and strength into the bodies of any who ate of it.

The skull, which would be cleaned and preserved, would be buried in the cave floor where it would be retrieved on the return trip. It would then be taken to the winter cave where it would be displayed as a symbol of homage and gratitude to the spirits that controlled their lives.

The clan members were taught in early life that there were forces more powerful than the spirits. There was the God of fire, embodied by the Sun, and also the Goddess of the Moon, a lazy female who could not travel as fast as her master, the Sun God, on his journey across the sky. The children were taught that the Sun God was so powerful they should never look directly at the heavenly being or they might be blinded for such an audacity. The inferior Moon Goddess always displayed respect to the Sun God by never revealing her full face when traveling near her master. That was obvious proof of her inferiority. There were also the other Gods of Wind and Storm. The power of these Gods was incomprehensible. Man could talk to the spirits who accompanied the hunters, dispensing either good or bad luck, but he was rather helpless to influence the greater Gods. All he could do was pay homage to those great deities and pray that they not become angry and dispense their wrath on the face of the earth.

Nomi found time to slip away from her work to join Orin at the creek where he was cleaning his spear. The flint point had become loosened and he was tightening the leather binding.

She moved to his side and waited for his eyes to acknowledge her. "I'm so proud of you, Orin," she said. "I couldn't see what happened but I heard the men talking about it. You were very brave. I'm grateful to the spirits for protecting you. I would die if anything happened to you. I love you so very much."

Orin glanced around to confirm their privacy before drawing her to him. He kissed her lightly on the lips. "It was no more than any other hunter would have done," he said. He hoped she would catch the meaning without considering it bragging. "Agar told me I could now join the hunts. I can't wait until I receive my hunting axe at the lodge ceremony."

* * *

The sky was becoming darker and threatening but failed to dampen the mood of the enthusiastic workers. The venison was moved to the cave and was being cut into long strips to be suspended over the fires that burned at the entrance. The bear had been skinned and the carcass stripped of its flesh. The bear hide was suspended with the raw side facing the fire in hopes that it would dry before spoiling. The sun, which would be high overhead at that time of day, would normally have aided in drying the hide, but on this day the power of the Storm God prevailed over that of the Sun God. The clan conversation centered on the plans and anticipated joy of the evening feast.

Agar signaled Orin to his side. "The sky is looking darker. We may be getting more rain soon. I want you to run back to the camp of Tomar with a message. Tell them of our victory and that the cave is secure. Tell Tomar that as soon as weather permits, he is to move the rest of the clan to the cave here. We'll plan to stay at this site for eight or nine days. The men will hunt these hills while the women dry the meat."

Orin was disappointed that he would miss the feast and wanted to stay near Nomi, but he also recognized his duty to obey Agar's orders without question.

Before leaving camp he located his mother who was on her knees cutting meat into strips. The dark circles of her sunken eyes contrasted vividly with the paleness of her cheeks. He explained his mission and added a request that she try to eat more and to get more rest.

"Please watch over your sisters," Amalee implored, reaching for his hand. "I'm sure the other women have been caring for them but I want you to look after them as much as you can, particularly on the trail." She squeezed his hand and released it as he turned to go.

Carrying his spear in one hand, Orin set off at a jog. The trail had dried considerably during the few hours' respite from rain, and the trip, which had taken a full day's travel one direction, was now covered in one-fifth that time.

Upon Orin's arrival at the camp of Tomar, he was greeted by an excited and curious throng. He was deluged with questions but waited until the entire camp surrounded him before telling the details to an excited and wide-eyed audience. The episode, describing the victory over the cave bear, brought gasps and a buzz of whispers from his audience. Orin modestly accounted for his part of the action by merely saying that he participated in finishing the kill.

Carma and Retta pushed through the gathered congregation to grip Orin's hand. Retta took the opportunity to remind one of her friends that Orin was very brave. "I'll bet Orin killed the bear all by himself," she bragged. Her friend was so impressed that she never questioned the statement.

Orin relayed Agar's message to Tomar who responded, "We'll make that decision in the morning. We have enough food for another day or two, but of course, we are all anxious to rejoin the clan."

At dawn, Tomar studied the sky. A very light drizzle was falling but the low level of the clouds nestling against the hills suggested that the Sun God would soon defeat the Rain God when it climbed to a more advantageous height. Nearer the coast, the sun usually emerged victorious over the morning mist, he reasoned. It should here, also.

Tomar questioned Orin about conditions. "Just as soon as the trail is dry enough to be safe, I'd like to take these children to their mothers. What do you think?"

Orin was flattered to have Tomar ask his opinion. "I think it should be all right," he answered, and then after considering the responsibility of his statement, he added, "Unless it starts to rain heavier."

With the decision made, the children and few remaining men and women were soon laboring along the same path their clan mates had travelled two days earlier. The drizzle didn't cease nor did it intensify. Though he had misjudged the weather, Tomar was still glad of his decision. The pace was good and with Orin's knowledge of the trail, Tomar optimistically anticipated arriving at the cave well before dark. The old man set the pace, and with the women encouraging the children, the group made steady progress.

Tomar's optimism was vindicated. As they approached the cave, the children ran the last short distance to rejoin their mothers. There was hugging and kissing with a buzz of conversation as the children inquired about the bear. Bed robes and carrying pouches were lowered as they hurried to participate in the feast that was underway. The renewed celebration was less elaborate but no less enthusiastic than the feast of the previous evening.

Tomar reported to Agar on the events of the past two days. "We had no problems," he explained, "but I did want to bring them all here before Gors' mate, Wilma, has her baby. She's very heavy with child and the women think it could come soon."

Orin joined his tired siblings in ripping fat strips of steaming bear meat from the roast that hung skewered over the glowing coals. By the time the adults had eaten their fill, the children were resting sleepy heads on their mother's comfortable laps.

Assignments were made for the duties of feeding the fires and turning the strips of drying meat that hung on lines near the embers.

The following morning, Agar and his men paired off to make short scouting forays into the surrounding hills. Though the drizzle restricted their range of vision, one team brought back reports of seeing fresh tracks of a small herd of ibex near the cliffs that faced the river.

"I couldn't tell for sure but there appeared to be several animals," Gors reported.

Agar received this news with interest but knew that weather conditions and terrain would have to be ideal to successfully hunt the wary, long-horned mountain goats. One team had twice seen porcupines and had made a mental note of the location, knowing that the animals wouldn't travel very far. With an abundance of food at camp, they continued their search for larger, more desirable game.

The next morning they awoke to large patches of blue sky showing. A few dark clouds clung tenaciously to the higher mountain ridges but the gusty breeze offered encouragement to the hunters. Teams of men continued to scout the forest slopes while Agar took Orin to investigate the reported ibex. They followed along the river and then climbed a sharp slope that faced the cliffs across a deep ravine. They seated themselves on a log that offered a clear view of the terrain near the cliffs. A rock slide area below a jagged cliff terminated on a gentle slope that supported a heavy growth of scrub brush. Beneath the brush area was a second long, sheer cliff that had been eroded and cut, ages earlier, by the river that now wound its way in the valley floor far below.

"I see an ibex now," Orin whispered. "It's just below the upper slide on the far end of the brushy slope."

Agar stared for a long while before responding. "I see it now. There are three or four of them. They're hard to see until they move. Chances are there may be several more."

The two remained silent while Agar studied the layout. Orin surmised what the leader was thinking, and would have liked to present his own ideas, but tradition dictated that he could do so only if invited.

"I don't know," Agar finally said. "There would be a lot of area to guard if we tried to crowd them off the cliff below. We'd have to cover both flanks of the slide and brush areas, all the way from the lower cliffs to the upper cliffs. We'd need the entire clan. We have an advantage though. The face of the mountain is rounded enough to allow us to get fairly close before the ibex could see us." After an additional short silence, he continued. "We'd need to kill three or four to justify the effort."

Using his hand to shade his eyes, Orin continued to scan the ridge across the ravine. "I've spotted two more," he said. "They're hard to see until they move to a different feeding spot."

After an extensive study of the area, Agar concluded there were at least ten animals. The ibex finally moved across the base of the slide area, offering a better contrast for an easier count.

"If the weather holds good tomorrow, we'll give it a try," was Agar's final comment while walking back to camp.

Morning arrived clear with a misty haze lying low over the river valley. The plan had been discussed earlier and the clan was alerted to prepare for the drive.

Tomar approached Agar to report a problem. "That woman, the one I told you about, has started her birth pains. I don't think she can go on the drive."

"She can help dry the meat while we're gone," the leader said. "The other two women, who will be tending the meat and smaller children, will be here if she needs them."

Vodim was dispatched to the far mountain slope with about half the men, women and children. Two hunters were stationed below the lower cliffs and Agar commanded the remaining participants in the drive. Vodim's group proceeded to the river and along the trail to the canyon beyond the cliffs while Agar led the others to the canyon wall on the near side. The critical aspect of the hunt was the coordination of the teams while approaching the ibex, otherwise the wary animals might be alerted and escape. The two hunters assigned to slaughter any wounded animals which were forced off the cliffs were given the additional duty as signal men. With the turtle-shell fire box, the two men built a fire near the river below the cliffs. The fire was maintained with dry wood that produced a minimum of smoke. One hunter positioned himself higher on the hillside across the valley where he could watch the movements of both groups of drivers. He could also see the herd of ibex grazing at their accustomed place. Waiting until he felt that each group was in position, he then signaled the fire keeper who piled stacks of green pine boughs on the existing fire. Dark smoke belched upward, rising in a tall, thin column.

Tensions increased as the waiting clansmen saw the heavy smoke rising over the cliffs below. Agar shouted to signal the beginning of the drive.

"Here we go," he yelled. "Everyone stay in a tight line and keep moving."

The men, women and children surged forward, shouting and screaming loudly. Excitement increased as the two rows of clan members advanced toward each other with the upper ends closing first. There was added shouting and pointing as several clansmen saw the retreating rumps of the ibex bounding down the mountain slope. After the upper ends of the driving lines closed ranks, the chance of escape diminished.

Agar and Vodim were among the first to arrive at the irregular ledge that comprised the upper edge of the lower cliffs. Agar moved out to a point with a favorable view of the terrain below. He saw his two hunters waiting at the base of the cliffs, anxious to complete the kill of any ibex forced off the cliff.

Agar shouted to his men below. "Haven't you seen any of the ibex? We saw them coming down the slope toward this ledge. They must have gone over this cliff."

"We saw a couple of does running along that ledge to your right," one man shouted in reply, "but none came down here.

With Vodim following, Agar began exploring the cause of their loss. Hidden behind an area of brush growth on the face of the cliff, a narrow ledge, descending laterally, became too narrow for the men to go any farther. The unmistakable hoof prints told the complete and disappointing story. The ibex herd had escaped.

"The animals will be so wary now they'll move to another feeding ground." Agar grumbled. "There's no point in even considering pursuit. How could the spirits have failed us? Some evil force must have helped the ibex escape." To transfer any blame, Agar then turned angrily to Vodim. "You should have examined this ledge more closely before the drive. It was a terrible waste of our time and effort."

Before departing, Agar paused a moment before remarking to Vodim, "I want to make a clear mental picture of this ledge. Perhaps another year, if we find the animals on this slope, we'll try again. Next time I'll have a man stationed right here, and the ibex will be very surprised when they come running around this corner."

The two men returned to the disappointed clansmen to explain the failure. There was no singing as the people returned to the cave.

After leaving the brushy slope, one of the older women reminded the children to inspect each other for ticks. "They can be very bad this time of year," she explained.

Agar's anger and disappointment with the unsuccessful hunt became clear when he told Tomar, "Just as soon as the meat dries enough we'll be on our way. I don't know what we're doing here when we could be out on the plains hunting bison."

As the hunters approached the cave, Agar quickened his pace. "There's no one watching the meat," he shouted angrily. "Where are those useless women? A scavenger could have eaten it."

Vodim hurriedly entered the cave and quickly returned to where Agar waited. "Wilma is having her baby," he explained, "and the other women are helping her."

"Does it take both of them?" Agar grumbled. "We could have lost all of the meat."

"I think she's having a problem," Vodim explained. "The women said the baby isn't coming out right."

Several other women, returning from the ibex hunt, hurried to the hearth where the woman was moaning in agony.

"What's the problem?" Olvi inquired, pushing her way through the assembled crowd.

"I think the baby is turned wrong," a woman explained. "The head isn't coming out first. She's been in terrible pain for a long while. I could feel the baby's leg but the baby just can't come out. The baby was moving earlier but I think the spirit left it and now there's no life at all."

Olvi examined the suffering woman to confirm the other woman's observation. "The baby does seem to be crossed. When did the pains first start?"

"They started right after all of you left on the ibex drive. She's been straining awfully hard, but I think her strength is failing."

There were several comments of sorrow and sympathy until Olvi called for quiet. "The spirit hasn't left her body yet," she argued. "We better try to pull the baby out."

Though many of the women had experience as midwives, Olvi's training and experience gave her the extra status as a medicine woman. The other women usually looked to her for guidance in treating the sick or wounded. "Two of you hold her arms," Olvi ordered. "I'll see what I can do."

Her desperate efforts were futile. After several attempts to extract the baby, Olvi finally gave up. The failing woman had lost consciousness from loss of blood and her breathing became faint. Tomar was summoned.

"I think her spirit is about to depart," a woman explained to the old man. "I think it's time for you to talk to the Great Spirit."

Tomar examined the dying woman and then stood erect. He turned his face upward, and with closed eyes, began an incantation. "Oh, Great Spirit of all the clans," he began. "Please find a resting place for the spirit that is about to leave this woman's body. Allow the spirit of this woman to find a new home in an unborn child of our people, that she can grow to become a mate to proudly serve her mate and the hunters of this clan."

He paused, listening to the moaning of all the sympathetic women gathered nearby. Olvi continued to check the breathing of the failing woman. As darkness settled outside, additional lamps were lighted. A few of the women bedded the children at hearths deeper in the cave. The men silently remained at the fire near the cave entrance.

Tomar emerged from the cave to inform Agar and the other men who waited silently near the fire. "The spirit has departed the woman," he said unemotionally. "I have instructed the other women to move the body out of the cave. They'll place it in the ground tomorrow."

Gors consoled the three children of his dead mate. "Don't grieve for your mother," he said. "Her spirit is now free and will soon find a new body."

Agar reassured Gors that his children could remain in his hearth under the care of his other mate.

The body was buried with a minimum of sorrow. Wilma would be missed by her children and friends but the clansmen all knew that her spirit had been freed to find a new body. There was no reason to grieve.

Each day found Agar testing the drying meat and complaining that it had not been cut into thin enough strips. "I sometimes think you women do things like this on purpose so you can sit around camp a few more days."

He ignored the fact that the women, who were not watching and turning the drying meat, were scraping and curing the bear hide and deer skins.

The following days found the hunting poor. The hunters had, on two occasions, located a small herd of deer but were never able to successfully stalk the wary animals or drive them into ambush.

On the ninth day following the cave bear kill, Agar conferred with Tomar. "Isn't that meat dry enough yet so it won't spoil? The uncured pieces can be strung and carried on the women's backs where they'll continue to dry."

Tomar was aware of Agar's impatience and nodded approval. "I'm sure you're right and I know your hunters are also anxious to move on. I've watched for signs and perhaps the spirits are also anxious for us to reach the plains where there are more animals than a man can count. I believe the spirits have been warning the deer and the ibex for that very reason. Perhaps we shouldn't ignore these omens."

Agar called a gathering of the clan. When all the adults were near, he announced his decision. "We will take to the trail tomorrow at dawn. We should reach the hot springs above the fork of Salmon Creek in a few days, and if the spirits favor us, the fish will be starting their run."

Though not generally inclined to commit himself, or to disclose his plans, Agar continued as if thinking out loud. "And after that, it'll take us about two days to the North Pass and another four days to the great plains of the bison."

Agar was a hunter, and though he loved eating the juicy tender salmon that was easily speared, his heart was in the hunt and the challenge of the kill. He suddenly felt that he had said too much. "That's it, then," he added. "Go prepare for the trail."

Armid was instructed by Tomar to leave a symbol on the wall of the cave to honor and pay homage to the Spirit of the Hunt. Using a flint point, he scraped a crude outline of an aurochs, a long-horned cow, on the face of the limestone wall. He then added the symbol of a spear near the carving. A short chant by Tomar fulfilled the minimum traditional ritual necessary to placate the appropriate spirits.

* * *

The sky promised good weather as the long column moved onto the trail. Enthusiasm ran high among the children in anticipation of the hot springs.

"I can hardly wait," Carma said to her mother. "The last time we were there we had so much fun. Do you think we can stay there a long while?"

"Perhaps, if the fish run is good," Amalee answered. "It all depends on Agar." Then, with a strong hint of sarcasm, she added, "Unless he gets an oat barb up his rear end and decides to move on."

The two girls giggled, looking at each other to share their mother's remark.

While the column was stopped for a badly needed rest, Carma and Retta gathered bright red poppies from a small meadow near the trail. They each carried a handful of the colorful flowers to Amalee who sat at the trail side, her head resting in her hands.

"Here, Mother," Retta offered, "Carma and I brought you some flowers."

Amalee looked up to accept the gift. "Thank you my darlings," the exhausted woman said. "The only things more precious than these beautiful flowers are my children. I love you dearly." Large tears welled up in her dark eyes. "If it wasn't for my precious daughters," she continued, "I think the spirit in this tired old body would escape and go in search of a new one."

Carma placed her arms around her mother's shoulder to console her. "Mama, please don't talk like that. I think you should lie down and rest."

Retta, caught in the emotions of the moment, and with tears rolling down her cheeks, ran to also embrace her mother.

Amalee felt very tired. Although she had plenty to eat the previous few days, the self-deprivation during the moons of late winter had taken its toll. Her thirty-four years found her shoulders stooped and her weary head bent as she struggled under the heavy load of sleeping robes and rations.

* * *

The hunters scouted ahead and on either side of the trail. On the third day, Dorik, with three other hunters, succeeded in killing a doe and her new fawn. He and his men had been advancing in a flank pattern, keeping each other within sight. One of the hunters located a newborn fawn huddled motionless in the tall grass.

For the first few days after birth, the small spotted animals, obeying a strong survival instinct, remain motionless, low near the ground. The alert hunter noticed the grass in a small meadow was matted where an animal had bedded down. He paused to closely scan the area and search for fresh spoor to determine the freshness of the site. He was about to move on when his eyes fell on the motionless infant.

"Over here," he called to Dorik. "I think our luck has changed."

With a leather thong, the men tied the helpless fawn to the trunk of a nearby tree. Two hunters, waiting in the overhanging branches, exploited an inherent weakness in the otherwise alert and cautious doe. The men knew, from legend and experience, that deer never look up to avoid danger. It was a weakness that was often fatal. When the doe approached her fawn, crossing under one of the hunters, the man dropped from the limb above with his full body weight behind his spear.

The animal was cleaned and strung from a pole. The two men shouldered the load and attempted to catch up with their hunting partners.

"She wasn't very fat," Dorik commented to the other hunter, "but it's better than we've been doing. "I hope the others have some luck."

The other hunter's luck was minimal, managing only to catch a partridge. The "sitting hen snare technique" was again used successfully. The men easily located the nest after the startled bird took flight. A hunter then uncoiled a long, flexible line of cured, oiled, deer gut and suspended a noose over the nest. The line was strung out to a bush some distance away where the hunter hid, motionless. Within a short time, the bird returned to her eggs, confident of her safety. After the bird was seated on the nest, the hunter gave a sharp pull to tighten the noose around the neck of the startled fowl. He then killed the bird before she could escape. The hunter, with the bird and the eggs, then moved on to rejoin his fellow teammates.

Vodim's luck was even greater. Leading the center team, Vodim found fresh signs of several pigs. The wild animals had been rooting under the trees near the river and could easily be tracked. They were soon located wallowing in the mud of a slough. Vodim surveyed the situation to determine a plan of attack. After the older tusked boar was alerted to the hunters' presence, he, with a couple of the younger boars, took up a defensive position between the hunters and the sows.

Noting the well-worn pig trail along the bank of the slough and through a small grove of poplars, Vodim issued instructions to his companions. "I want you to circle around behind the boars and take up an ambush position in that far poplar grove along the pig trail. I'll try to distract them until you're ready and then I'll try to stampede them back along the trail."

With full appreciation of the possible danger from the sharp tusks of the boars, Vodim looked nearby for a tree that could easily be climbed. He edged toward a large oak whose limbs hung low beneath a canopy of foliage. The defensive boars moved laterally with him, grunting threats and snorting. When Vodim was confident his men were in position, he ran forward in a mock attack. As anticipated, the large dominant boar charged. Vodim turned sharply left, racing for the tree a few feet away. With a running leap, he caught the limb that hung an arm's length above his head. He unfortunately miscalculated both the distance and the boar's speed. As he jumped to pull himself into the tree, the boar's tusk ripped a finger-length gash along the calf of his leg. Vodim pulled himself onto the limb and examined the shallow wound. Suffering little pain, he turned his attention back to the boar. The animal was charging madly around below him, slashing his head and tusks back and forth in a futile attempt to reach the hunter. The sows and young pigs had failed to panic as Vodim had anticipated and were grouped behind the lesser boars, squealing in nervous excitement.

His spear, Vodim realized, had been dropped as he leaped for the limb. After withdrawing his hunting axe from his garment belt, and while hanging from the limb by one arm and entwined legs, he reached down to measure his swing. The boar, seeing the new threat, again charged at the suspended arm and axe. Vodim swung the hand axe, driving the sharp flint point into the eye socket of the enraged beast. The boar turned to continue his attack. Again Vodim was able to deliver the full force of his swing against the head of the bewildered boar, dropping the stunned animal to his knees. Vodim quickly judged the distance and mood of the lesser boars as they squealed and snorted encouragement to their leader. The hunter, knowing that the stunned boar would soon be back on its feet, dropped to the ground and quickly grasped his spear. Nervously watching the other boars, he quickly drove the flint tip deeply into the rib cage of the wounded beast and then continued his attack with the hand axe until the large boar rolled onto its side in its final death throes. The other pigs, witnessing the death of their leader, panicked. They turned, racing in wild retreat along the path into the waiting ambush of the other hunters.

After the last of the surviving animals disappeared into the brush, the hunters took inventory of their success. In addition to the boar, whose tusks would later adorn the necklace of Vodim, the hunters counted two sows and three half-grown pigs.

"We were getting worried," one of the men remarked. "I was about to leave my ambush to go check on you."

Vodim smiled as he told the full story of the boar's attack. "That old tusker was faster than I expected. A moment longer getting into that tree and the pigs would have been feasting on me."

"You should have seen Gors," one of the men remarked. "He couldn't pull his spear out of that sow fast enough. She turned on him and he went up that tree like a squirrel. I had no idea he was so fast."

Gors grinned. "I'm sure glad pigs can't climb trees."

Vodim, after washing his wound at the river bank, wound his garment belt around his leg to slow the bleeding. He limped back to where the other men were dressing and hanging the six dead animals.

"Well," Vodim remarked, "I'd say that we've had a very good day. The spirits certainly favored us."

"But I hated to see those others get away," Gors said. "There must be eight or ten more of them."

"Maybe they'll still be here when we come back this fall," Vodim said. "They should be good and fat by then."

The men, knowing that the main clan would soon catch up with them, stretched out on the grass to absorb the heating rays of the sun. Vodim cautioned them to remain alert. There was the possibility that the blood scent might attract any large carnivore that might be hunting in the area.

There was considerable excitement when the clan arrived to witness the bounty of the pig ambush. The hunters were pressed for details of the kill by the arriving clansmen who gathered near them. The prospect of fresh meat, and especially tasty roast pig, activated many saliva glands among the hungry travellers.

Agar glanced at the sun to judge the time. Although he had hoped for greater progress that day, the problems of moving the pig carcasses by the already overburdened women prompted his decision to establish camp.

Orin was dispatched to find and advise the other hunters of the new camp location.

When the less successful hunters returned to camp with their additional game, the fires were already burning brightly and the women and children were singing the old familiar folk songs of the clan. The lyrics that echoed throughout the valley gave praise and thanks to the spirits for the food and protection enjoyed by all. There were songs that paid homage to the Gods, petitioning them for mercy from the many catastrophes of legend and experience.

After a period of play with their friends, and with darkness increasing, Carma and Retta returned to Amalee's side at the fire. Retta rested her head on her mother's lap. "Mama," she said, "those boys teased me and wouldn't let me play games with them. They said I was only a girl. They said girls and women are supposed to just cook and carry loads and do whatever men want them to do. Why did they say that?"

Amalee stroked her daughter's head while offering an explanation. "I guess that's just the way it is, darling. Men are the hunters and the women do the work. It's always been that way and I guess it always will."

Carma pondered the thought. "When I grow up," she commented, "I'm going to find a mate who will be nice to me. I don't want one who's mean like some of the hunters."

"Carma, my dear," Amalee explained, "when you grow up, you'll be assigned to a hunter who will treat you any way he pleases. We just don't have any say in the matter. I don't want you to worry about such things. You're much too young."

Carma said nothing more, but her mind rejected what she felt was such unfair treatment of women.

Darkness settled that night on a group whose distended stomachs testified to the pleasures of feasting on succulent roast pig. The partially consumed carcasses of the three smaller pigs remained suspended on green skewer poles above the embers of the dying fires.

As children surrendered to sleep, the spirits controlled and guided their minds into wild fantasies that awed and sometimes terrified the suddenly awakened victims.

"Why do we have dreams?" Retta asked her mother.

"When you're tired and go to sleep," Amalee explained, "your spirit plays games in your head. Your spirit controls your thoughts with things that it wants to think of."

"I wish my spirit wouldn't scare me so much," Retta commented. "I sometimes dream of awful animals that want to eat me."

"I know, dear," Amalee explained. "Just remember that dreams aren't real. They can't really hurt you."

- 10 -

With the rising of the sun the next morning, Agar called a council of his hunters and told them to pass the word to cook all the remaining pork. The pig meat wasn't suitable for drying and in two days it could possibly become poisonous. Cooking would add at least one more day to its useful life.

By noon the meat had all been roasted and everyone again ate his fill. The camp was alerted. Soon the women had loaded their packs, and with the additional cargo of roast pig wrapped in deer skin, they moved off along the trail that would eventually take them to the land of bison and reindeer.

As the next few days passed, there was only a token effort at hunting. Excitement grew when Tomar announced their nearness to the tributary known as Salmon Creek. The column turned away from the river, proceeding up a narrow canyon where the hunters periodically stopped at the stream's edge to look for spawning salmon. After reaching a narrow stretch of cascading water where the stream splashed eagerly from one boulder to another, Agar called a halt to the column. The hunters raced to take positions on the rocks where, with spears raised, they watched for salmon struggling against the swift current. The women and children waited impatiently.

The sun was still high when Tomar approached Agar. "The children are excited and anxious to get to the hot springs, and the women would like to set up camp. Do you think Homan, Orin and I could move the clan on to the campsite? You could bring the hunters into camp when you've checked for the spawning run."

Agar was embarrassed to realize that, in his enthusiasm, he had left the column standing for a considerable time. He resented being reminded of an error in judgment, but couldn't think of a sound argument against the request.

"Yes, of course," he answered. "You go ahead and we'll join you shortly."

* * *

As Tomar, with the remaining clansmen, approached the familiar campsite, he was suddenly alerted by the smell of smoke. He raised his hand, bringing the column to a halt. After searching the treetops ahead, he saw wisps of smoke floating slowly upward. Holding a finger to his lips to signal for silence, he beckoned Orin to his side. "Go get Agar and the hunters," he whispered. "Hurry."

Within a short time the alert hunters were all at the side of Tomar who pointed at the lingering smoke. "There are several campfires," he whispered to Agar.

Without speaking, the clan leader signaled the women and children to return back on the trail. After they had retreated a reasonable distance, Agar signaled the men to take positions on either side of him. With spears and hunting axes ready, they cautiously advanced toward the camp.

Their forward progress had hardly commenced when a series of shouts from the campsite gave evidence to Agar that his group had been discovered. They moved a few feet farther into a clearing before the clan leader stopped and motioned his men to do the same. "We'll wait here," he said. "Their leader should show up soon." Agar reasoned that an advance into the camp could create a panic that might unnecessarily precipitate a fight from the unknown clansmen in defense of their women and children.

A silence was soon noted from the area where the shouting had originated. An unarmed, older, white-bearded man emerged from the pine grove ahead and advanced only a few feet before stopping. He raised his hands, motioning for Agar and his hunters to stay in position.

Nervous glances over his shoulder, by the old man, told Agar that the men of the clan were apparently away from camp, but he also knew that in a fishing environment, the hunters would be nearby. Agar wanted to avoid a conflict with an unknown enemy. He lowered his spear point to the ground as a signal of peace and awaited the arrival of their leader.

Growing impatient, Agar at last called to the stranger. "I am Agar. Where is your clan leader?"

The lone emissary from the camp made no effort to communicate but remained motionless except for an occasional glance over his shoulder. Agar ordered his men to guard against any surprise attack on their flanks or rear.

After what seemed an eternity to the tense hunters, a tall, dark-bearded man emerged from the grove, followed closely by eleven armed companions. The dark-haired man, whom Agar assumed to be their leader, halted his men and advanced alone a few feet toward Agar. Taking the clue, Agar motioned his men to remain in position as he also advanced half the distance that separated the two hunting groups. He placed his spear on the ground with the knowledge that he could quickly grasp the hunting axe tucked under his belt. The other leader also dropped his spear and moved slowly forward, his hand also resting on his hunting axe. When within arm's reach, the two men extended their right arms to grasp each other's hand.

Tradition, dating beyond the recollection of clan historians, demanded that, in any confrontation, the protagonists must grasp each other's combat hand, not only to prevent a sudden attack, but also to assure the other person of his own peaceful intent. The precaution had gradually taken on a symbolism of friendliness.

"I am Agar," the stocky clan leader began. "My people are of the Nordo tribes. We are on our way to join with our brother clans at the feeding grounds of the reindeer."

The bewildered look on the other leader's face slowly gave way to a friendly smile. He directed a short command over his shoulder before returning his attention to Agar. After placing his left palm across his chest, and with exaggerated pronunciation, he sounded his name.

"Izek," he slowly enunciated. Again he repeated the name and offered a few more words that held no meaning for Agar.

The two men finally relaxed their grips and withdrew their hands but made no move to rejoin their men. Agar ordered his hunters to slowly advance to a position a few feet behind him. As the men started forward, the armed men of Izek's clan moved forward to a similar position. Without turning his head, Agar called to his hunters. "Lower your spear points to the ground, but keep them ready."

The awkward confrontation was finally eased when a woman, carrying a small child, appeared and was pushed forward by the men of Izek's clan.

Izek gave the woman a crisp order which directed her attention toward Agar.

"I speak the tongue of Nordo," she said. "My name is Alma. I was born to the clan of Jenk, which is of the tribe of Nordo. Our leader wishes to know of your clan and your destination."

Agar was surprised to hear a familiar tongue. "First tell me what you're doing with this clan," he said.

"It is a long story," she explained, shifting her baby to her other arm. "It was about four years ago that I became separated from my clan. We were on a bison hunt and the large herd was on the move. I was left to skin a calf and was told to wait for the hunters so we could all rejoin the clan at the camp near a river. A pack of wolves drove me away from the dead calf. I became lost. Four days later when I finally located our camp site, the clan was gone. I think they probably returned to the bones of the calf and assumed I was dead. I wandered for three moons before this clan found me and nursed me back to health."

Izek, whose face had assumed an irritated look, interrupted the girl with a sharp command.

Alma said something to Izek and then turned back to Agar. "My leader is anxious to learn of your clan."

Agar glanced at Izek and then back to the woman. "We summer on the meadows near the ice mountain. We spend our winters in our grotto far to the south. We are on our way north and plan to camp here at the hot waters as we have done every year. We always come to this place at this time of year to fish for the spawning salmon." Agar paused a moment before adding, "Tell your leader what I have said and ask him to tell of his clan and where they are going."

The message was relayed to Izek whose lengthy reply was translated for Agar. "Our clan is on its way to the plains six days travel from here. The men hunt the bison and calves that return each year. The clan spends the winter three moons travel east of here, across the high mountains that extend all the way south to the sea. We trade with the people who live on the slopes of those mountains." Alma glanced at her leader and continued, but with an altered tone that gave Agar the impression that she was supplementing Izek's statement.

"The people in the land where we winter are very strange. They don't hunt as we do but kill and eat the sheep that come back to their wooden caves each night."

Agar interrupted her. "What do you mean? I can't believe that sheep would walk right to the cave to be killed."

Alma turned to Izek for permission to answer Agar's inquiries. After an approving nod, she continued. "The sheep are different from the sheep we hunt. The people of the wooden caves tie the lambs to trees near their caves and the sheep always return to nurse the lambs. At night the sheep are put in enclosures which are made by piling logs on top of other logs. The enclosures are near the fires by the wooden caves so the wolves do not attack the sheep. The sheep are not killed until the people need the food, and because of that, the people of those villages never go hungry. They don't even have to dry the meat."

Agar's eyes portrayed his amazement. "Why do you travel then? Why don't you stay there?"

"Because there are too many of those people. They claim all of that territory. They let us camp near their villages and trade us fresh meat for the furs that we make into body garments. We also spend our winter days making necklaces and trimming deerskin clothes with the animal teeth that we collect on our hunts. By spring we have nothing more to trade. Our leader is ready to leave by then."

Agar pondered the information for a few moments before dismissing the idea as being very impractical. His thoughts returned to the local situation. He turned to Tomar to ask if the spiritual leader felt the signs were favorable for the clan.

Tomar replied affirmatively. "The Spirit of the Hunt has favored and guided us these past few days. I'm sure he would not forsake us now."

As Agar began speaking, Alma's eyes opened wide. She was unable to hide her nervousness while listening to the words she would have to interpret for Izek.

"We have traveled a long way to occupy this campsite by the hot water," Agar stated. His words were slow and solemn. "We occupy it every year at this time. We intend to occupy it now. Ask your leader if he is now ready to move his clan out of this area."

As Izek listened to the woman's interpretation, his muscles tightened and a frown appeared on his face. After questioning her for clarification, his eyes surveyed the men of Agar's clan and then turned for a reappraisal of his own force. A long, tense period followed during which the hunters of each side summoned their courage and adrenaline for a possible conflict.

Finally Izek appeared to relax a little and spoke to the interpreter. One of his men shouted an angry protest but was quieted by a sharp order from his leader.

Alma turned to Agar. "Izek said to tell you that he was planning to leave here anyway. He is very anxious to reach the plains by the time the bison arrive."

Agar studied the interpreter for a short while. "You are of the tribe of Nordo," he said. "We are of the tribe of Nordo and we speak the same tongue. If you desire to join our clan, you may do so."

A frightened look appeared on the woman's face. "Oh, no," she answered. "I am now a woman of the clan of Izek and the mate of a hunter. I also speak their tongue and I have a child. I appreciate your offer to let me join your clan, but if you will allow me to decline, I will stay with this clan and my present mate."

Agar considered the problems and then dismissed the idea of taking the woman by force. "You may stay with your present clan," he said.

The members of Izek's clan hurriedly gathered their belongings and moved past Agar's hunters behind whom the women and children of Agar's clan had gathered. When the last departing migrants of Izek's clan disappeared down the trail, Agar instructed his hunters to follow them for a short distance to insure that they didn't circle back.

Tomar approached Agar on behalf of the children. "Do you think it would be all right if they run ahead to swim in the warm waters? They're getting excited and children are so very impatient."

When Agar waved his consent, there was a wild scramble of children, running toward the warm springs that were remembered from previous years.

A short distance beyond the camp site, steam rose and vanished from several springs as bubbling water overflowed the limestone encrusted banks. Small streams merged and descended a few hundred feet of crusty slope to join the main, fresh water stream below a gravel bar. The colder water eddied around the bar to mingle with the hot water in a pool whose depth increased gradually to more than a man's height. Robes were cast aside and left strewn on the bank as the children tested the water before splashing and wading into the warmer areas of the stream.

The women and older children moved into the grove where they hurriedly established their territories by spreading bed robes and food pouches onto the more desirable camp sites. The rapidly abandoned campfires made it unnecessary to transfer the precious flame from the turtle-shell fire box. The many fish heads and bones that lay near the fires' edge gave welcome testimony that the salmon were running and available to the hunters.

With confidence that the other clan was no longer a threat, Agar released his men to return to the boulder-strewn rapids where glistening salmon could be easily speared as they struggled against the swift current.

Orin joined the hunters and his excitement mounted as he positioned himself on a partially submerged boulder. In tense anticipation, he scanned the stream below him where the water cascaded from one boulder to another. Above the roar of the stream, he heard the shouts of success from other hunters upstream but refused to allow his eyes to abandon his search. Encouraged, he saw the outline of a large salmon moving toward him from the pool below. As the fish accelerated to enter the narrow channel of swift water, Orin drove his spear in a swift thrust into the salmon. Continuing his forward thrust, he raised the spear tip above his head, impaling the fish on the shaft. Balancing the spear and fish above his head, he stepped from boulder to boulder until he was able to drop the heavy prize on the bank. With a shout of excitement to advertise his success, he looked around in search of a witness.

Dorik, downstream of him, waded back to the shore and proceeded to where the salmon still struggled. He put a hand on the shoulder of his son to offer his praise. "What a beauty! I wouldn't be surprised if it isn't the largest salmon caught today. Your mother will be very proud."

Orin became choked with emotion for it had been a long time since his father had offered more than advice. He understood that a hunter could never publicly display his feelings and was grateful that the two were apparently unobserved. Trying to hide his feelings, Orin said, "I'll take the fish to camp and then come back. Maybe I can catch another one."

"I suspect that most of the hunters will be returning to camp soon," Dorik suggested. "It's getting late in the day and I'm sure that after our meal, everyone will go to the hot pool for a celebration."

As they prepared to return to camp, Orin's pride and enthusiasm were only slightly diminished when he saw the three salmon his father picked up from the grassy stream bank.

A tantalizing aroma activated the salivary glands of Orin and Dorik as they entered camp. The women had heated stones at the fire's edge and salmon strips were already cooking. Dorik paused at the hearth of Vodim to watch the reaction of Amalee upon seeing her son's catch.

Amalee raised up from her stooped position and viewed the salmon in the arms of Orin as well as the three being carried by Dorik. "You don't have to give us any of your fish," she said. "I'm sure Vodim will be bringing some in."

"Amalee, you're mistaken," Dorik protested. "I'm not giving you that fish. Orin caught it and deserves full credit."

Amalee's haggard eyes turned back to her son. "Oh, Orin, I'm sorry. I guess I wasn't thinking. I'm very proud of you. The girls will be thrilled when they get back from the pool." A short silence ensued as Amalee gazed admiringly at her son.

Dorik started to leave but turned back, pausing near Amalee to offer advice. "You're not getting enough rest or enough to eat. You've been giving too much of your food and labor to those girls. They're big enough to give you more help. Everyone is worried about your health."

"I'll be all right," she tried to assure him. "When we reach the summer hunting grounds I'll get my rest."

Dorik reached out and touched his hand to her shoulder. He opened his mouth to speak but changed his mind and moved on toward his own hearth.

Orin watched his father for a moment before returning his attention to his mother. "Dorik is right, Mother. You're getting awfully thin and your eyes don't look good."

A short time later Vodim returned to his hearth carrying two additional fish. Olvi and her son, Uval, rushed to meet him, showering praise and admiration for the catch.

Vodim complemented Orin on his success after which the two men discussed the days experience and their hopes for the following days.

After the meal, at which the clansmen gorged themselves on the salt-rich salmon, enthusiasm mounted for the pleasures of the warm springs.

"I want to remind everyone," Agar cautioned, "you should hang any fish that you don't eat high up on the tree limbs. There are many animals out there, including black bear, that would just love to get an easy meal."

- 11 -

The sun was still well above the mountain tops as the adults and older children started for the hot springs. Agar assigned Orin the task of moving a fire to the stream bank where the children had already collected and piled stacks of wood in anticipation of the celebration. Fur robes were shed and stacked on rocks or fallen logs to avoid the dampness of the ground. Many of the adults were soon enjoying the luxury of the warm water with expressive "ohs" and "ahs" of pleasure and an occasional squeal as someone moved into a current that was too hot or cold.

Orin's participation was delayed by his difficulty in finding a pitch-laden limb to sustain the fire while being carried from the camp to the pool. After the fire was at last burning adequately, Orin removed his fur body robe and waded into the water. There was already much laughing and teasing, with water being splashed into the faces of the celebrants. Orin located Nomi and was soon at her side. She made a playful attempt to jump on his back but became the victim of her own game when they both lost their footing and together took a dunking. They came up sputtering and laughing and quickly resumed their play. The mood had become contagious with many of the older children and adults participating.

The fire was burning brightly as the sun descended below the horizon, displaying a red silhouette of the western mountain ridge. The playful activity ceased as fatigue from the long day's effort took its toll. One of the women began a mournful song and was joined by many of the other bathers. The song told of the joys and sorrows of the trail and of the ultimate relief that would come from that final journey into the world of the spirits.

Nomi joined in the song as she moved to nestle her head against the chest of Orin. Though slightly embarrassed to display his feelings in public, he was encouraged by watching the affection displayed by two of the hunters with their own mates. Orin responded by resting his cheek against the head of Nomi and encircling her body with his arms. Agar watched from a few feet away where, in contrast to his earlier playful enthusiasm, he settled into a moody silence.

After a few other songs were sung, a quiet mood settled over the group. Women with younger children had departed, taking their offspring to their hearths to be placed in bed.

Orin's love of Nomi, and the excitement of the day, became an intoxication, stimulating his mounting passion. His encircling arm explored her breast, and feeling unobserved, turned her to him to kiss her in a long embrace.

Orin heard the voice of Agar but was slow to grasp the significance of the words.

"Well, what do we have here?" the clan leader asked. "It seems that one of our girls has suddenly become a woman. Where have I been? Why haven't I noticed your beauty before?"

As Nomi hung her head in embarrassment, Orin looked directly at Agar, hoping to verify that the clan leader was teasing. He couldn't be sure.

"Come over here and let me have a better look at you," Agar continued.

Nomi looked up at Orin but remained motionless when he failed to release her from his arms.

"Nomi, I told you to come over here," was Agar's repeated command. "I'm not going to hurt you." Agar's tone left little doubt that he was serious.

All conversation at the pool ceased with everyone's attention concentrated on Agar.

Orin's arms slowly released the golden-haired girl who, with head lowered, moved to the side of Agar.

"That's better. I'm not a monster, but I am your clan leader, and I'm in the habit of having my orders obeyed. Here, look up at me so I can see your face." He placed his hand beneath her chin, tipping her face up toward his. The absence of conversation only exaggerated the sound of the stream. The fire cast flickering light on the partially submerged bodies, enhancing the beauty of the frightened girl.

Agar took the girl by the hand, pulling her into shallow water nearer the fire. "Let's have a better look at you. That robe you've been wearing has been hiding your beauty. I didn't realize you had become a woman."

Orin clenched his teeth in anger as adrenaline surged into his bloodstream. He wanted to rescue Nomi and remove her from the threat, but a lifetime of training restrained him.

Agar again took the arm of Nomi, pulling her back into deeper water. He then placed his arm around her, drawing her to his chest as Orin had done earlier.

Nomi wanted to resist but was afraid to offer more than a token struggle. "Please, please let me go," she pleaded.

Orin failed to control himself any longer. With the fury of a charging cave bear, half swimming and half wading, he lunged toward Agar. "You son of a snake. You skunk. Let her go!" he shouted.

Agar released Nomi, bracing himself for the charging youth. As Orin struggled to gain a solid footing, and to raise himself from his semi-prone water position, he was met with a brutal, hard thrown fist that crashed into his face. Orin tumbled back, off balance, but was pulled upright again by Agar who, grasping a handful of hair, dragged the sputtering challenger toward the bank. Upon reaching solid footing, Agar lifted the head of Orin and sent it crashing down to meet his knee that was swung upward, delivering the full inertia of his powerful leg. Orin fell backward, unconscious, but the enraged leader continued to kick the motionless youth.

Dorik, who had witnessed the fast, unmatched action, raced from the water to block any further damage by the still irrational leader. "Stop it," Dorik shouted. "That's enough. He's out cold. Do you want to kill the boy?" Dorik placed himself over his son to prevent any further assault from Agar.

"You've got a bad memory, Dorik," was the angry clan leader's reply. "I'm still able and ready to tear you to pieces."

"I'm not challenging your leadership," Dorik responded, "and neither was the boy. He was only reacting to your teasing of the girl." Dorik then kneeled to assist Nomi in helping Orin, who was regaining consciousness, into a sitting position.

Agar looked down at the bleeding face of the young man and shook his fist to accentuate his raised voice. "So your old father thinks I was teasing. Well, now let me tell you something and hear me well. When we arrive at the summer hunting grounds, I intend to take this girl as my mate. That is my privilege. And until you are man enough to challenge me, you'll have to live with that fact." Agar turned, and after gathering his body garment and spear, disappeared into the darkness of the night.

Dorik turned back to his son. "That was very foolish. He could have killed you."

"Someday I'll kill him. He had no right to treat Nomi that way."

"He has every right. It seems you have to learn everything the hard way. Until you or someone else can defeat that man for clan leadership, he can do anything he wants."

Orin struggled to his feet, and with Nomi and Dorik to steady him, gathered his clothes and stumbled toward the campsite.

Amalee, who had not been at the water, became terribly

disturbed. "Orin, what happened?" she asked as he appeared in the fire light. "You're all bloody."

"He'll be all right," Dorik assured her. "It's nothing serious. Just a misunderstanding with Agar."

Amalee carried the leather water bag to where her son was seated. "Let me wash some of that blood off. Let's see how bad it is."

Olvi returned from another hearth where she had been visiting. The two women washed and examined Orin's bruised face. "He'll have a black eye for a few days," Olvi commented, "but I think he's going to be fine."

The days passed rapidly with the excitement of a bountiful catch. The salmon were at the peak of their spawning run and soon the supply exceeded the women's capability of stripping and drying the flesh. Fish were freely passed from one hearth to another to compensate for less luck, or to acknowledge a greater need. On the day that rain settled over the camp, poles supported bed robe shelters so as to continue the drying process. The flesh of the salmon had to be quickly smoked and dried or it would spoil. The effort was only partially successful.

After several days of a steady fish diet, many of the same mouths that had, upon arrival, salivated for the delicacy of salmon, now complained and yearned for a meal of hearty red meat.

On the evening of the eighth day at the campsite, word was passed that Agar had decided to break camp. There were many complaints, inspired by the need of discarding much of the fish that had been stripped and strung. The clan leader had not given them time to complete the drying process. A sullen mood settled over the camp. A few of the hunters were urged by the women to try to dissuade Agar from his decision but their efforts were met with a reminder that the decision had been made and he wanted no further talk of it.

The women urged the children to eat as much as they could, but the food didn't rest well. For the children, the eight days had been a happy time of feasting and frolic. They didn't want to leave. As for the adults, a sullen gloom permeated the clan.

"Do we have to leave this camp?" Carma asked her mother. "We've been having so much fun at the hot pool. All my friends want to stay here for a long time."

"I also wish we could stay here for a while longer," the woman agreed. "I think everyone could use the rest."

Amalee was deeply concerned about her daughters. She fully realized that she had only a few years in which she could sustain the rigors of the annual hunting migration. Her belief that her spirit would someday return in the body of another baby was unquestioned and she was consoled by that thought. If I can just survive until my girls are old enough to take care of themselves, she reasoned, then my spirit will be happy to escape from this tired old body. I must force myself a little harder.

Agar remained moody and aloof during the minimum time that he spent in camp. No one attempted to converse with him and he remained indifferent to the mood of his clansmen.

The morning departure was delayed, allowing the women time to cook and to encourage everyone to eat his fill. The fire box, under the watchful eye of Homan, was placed in the care of two of the older boys.

Dorik approached the hearth of Vodim and beckoned Orin to his side. "I think you'd be wise for the time being to walk with the women and children while on the trail. Agar is still in a nasty mood, and until he gets over it, I think you should try to stay out of his sight."

Orin lowered his eyes, and although he felt strongly disappointed, he nodded agreement. "All right," he mumbled. "I don't want to be around him anyway."

Orin felt totally frustrated. All his plans for membership in the Lodge of the Hunt, and his subsequent selection of Nomi as his mate, seemed to be slipping away. His mind posed questions that seemed to have no answers. If Agar takes Nomi as his mate, what can I do? If another hunter would challenge and defeat the man, then maybe I'd have a chance, but of course, there's no one who could or would want to challenge Agar. I don't know what I'm going to do."

As they moved out along the trail, Carma and Retta walked at his side. The sisters had not witnessed the fight but had heard many and varied accounts of it.

Retta was very defensive of her brother and after taking his hand, offered her consolation. "Someday you'll be the clan leader and that man will get what's coming to him."

Orin squeezed the child's hand but remained moody. "I don't want to talk about it and I don't want you to talk about it either."

Agar set a fast pace that resulted in a long column with some of the weaker migrants gradually dropping back. As the day wore on into afternoon, Orin noticed that his mother was falling farther behind. He lowered his pack to the edge of the trail, instructing his sisters to remain there until their mother caught up. He then walked toward the rear of the column until meeting Amalee. "You look awfully tired," he told her. "Let me carry your pack."

"I'm all right. This is a woman's chore. It wouldn't do to have the men see you carrying my pack."

Orin lifted the heavy load from her back with the firm statement, "I don't care what the others think. I'm going to carry your pack."

Amalee attempted to protest but Orin had already moved forward of her on the trail. Upon reaching the waiting girls, he let them carry part of his own pack.

It was later than usual when Agar finally raised his spear to signal the overnight stay. The hunters had scouted ahead but with no success. By the time the last stragglers of the long, loose column arrived in camp, several hearth sites had been established and fires were being relayed from one fire pit to the next.

Orin and the girls had dropped back to stay with Amalee. Upon their arrival, they located the site that had earlier been established by Vodim's other mate, Olvi. The girls dropped their bundles to accompany their half brother, Uval, in search of additional firewood. Amalee wrapped her robe tightly around her body and sat on the ground near the fire.

Orin touched her forehead. "You're shivering, Mother. Do you feel all right? Do you have a fever?"

"I'm just cold. I'll be all right when I warm up," she whispered before lapsing into silence.

Olvi walked around the fire and paused near Orin. "It might help if we get some warm food in her. I'm afraid it'll have to be fish. That's what we're all eating tonight. I think some of it is going to spoil."

By the time Vodim had returned from scouting and had located his hearth, Amalee was already asleep.

At dawn the following morning, the women began coaxing their sleepy children out of their beds. Agar had sent the word that he wanted an early start. The smell of cooking fish again permeated the camp as women attempted to use the marginal salmon that might otherwise spoil.

Olvi performed the few morning chores, insisting that Amalee rest. "You need all your strength for the trail," she insisted.

Orin stooped to his mother's side. "You've hardly touched your food," he protested.

Amalee raised her hand to object. "I couldn't eat a bit more. I'm still full from last night."

"But you didn't eat much last night," Orin said. "I'm very worried about you."

Amalee's failure to respond only deepened his concern.

As the clan returned to the trail, Orin again carried a greater portion of Amalee's trail pack. He walked beside her and encouraged her when she dropped farther back.

"I don't know why Agar can't set a slower pace," he grumbled, "or at least have an occasional rest stop."

The sun was high overhead, intermittently showing through fleecy clouds, when the long column crossed the mountain divide and began its descent. The trail avoided the steep ravine by turning to follow the crest of a ridge that gradually descended to the broad plains ahead.

"At least it's downhill for awhile," was a comment made by one of the weary women.

The hunters had rejoined the front of the column and all eyes were strained, searching for signs of the bison herds that historically migrated through the great grassy meadows ahead. Again Agar pushed the migrants late into the day, establishing camp at the upper edge of a pine-timbered ravine. A cold wind descended from the mountain range behind, chilling the exhausted travelers. Dry wood was frantically gathered and stockpiled to last the night. The women doled out meager portions of their emergency rations of nuts and dried fruit to supplement their diminishing supply of smoked fish.

Darkness settled slowly over the landscape. After the evening meal was finished the only activity was an occasional stoking or refueling of a hearth fire. The moon had not risen and the black sky displayed uncounted numbers of twinkling lights that the clansmen knew were the spirits of brave and heroic hunters.

The pine boughs of the trees near the sleeping camp moaned in protest as gusts of wind bent them to their will. During the night a long crying wail was heard from a distance and slowly faded, yielding to the sound of the wind. Several bedrolls stirred in acknowledgment of that wail and a small girl cried out to her mother, "Mama, what was that?"

"Go back to sleep, dear," the mother said, attempting to reassure her. "It's a wolf, but it's a long way off and it won't bother us here by the fire."

"I'm afraid. I want to get in bed with you."

"All right, bring your bedroll and come over here."

The fires were stoked a little brighter as the wailing call was repeated again and again, each time a little louder. Some of the bedrolls were moved closer to the circle of fires.

As dawn removed the curtain of blackness, many eyes searched in the direction of the wailing. Soon fingers were pointing and disagreement ensued as to the count.

"There aren't more than six or seven," was the judgment of Homan.

"We'll just have to keep the group a little closer together," Agar suggested. "We'll soon be at the bison hunting grounds and the wolves shouldn't bother us there."

Tomar, who had been silent for some time, offered his opinion. "This may be a bad sign. I should think that, if there were bison in this area, the wolves would be following the herds. We may be too early for bison."

"We'll know before the day is out," Agar added, and the statement seemed to terminate the speculation.

As the day's march began, with the column established on the trail, there was a noticeable change. Each clansman attempted to stay just a little bit closer to the one in front.

Amalee, Orin, and the two girls started out near the middle of the column but as the morning wore on they were overtaken and soon found themselves at the rear.

"Mama, I see two of those wolves on the trail behind us," Retta complained. "I'm afraid."

Orin moved to her side to reassure her. "Those are camp followers," he said. "They won't hurt us. Don't you remember, last year, how they followed us for many days? They're just old wolves that can't hunt with the regular pack. They tag along behind us to eat the scraps of meat we leave when we break camp. There's nothing to worry about. In fact, some people believe that camp follower wolves are a good omen. They stay just out of camp and never attack anyone, but if any other predators come around, they attack them or at least warn us."

"But they were there with that other pack of wolves."

"They aren't regular pack members," Orin explained. "They sometimes follow the regular packs the same way they follow people so they can get the scraps after the pack wolves finish their meal and move on."

The explanation seemed to console and satisfy the younger girl, for she continued along the trail in silence.

- 12 -

The sun had traveled only a quarter of its daily journey when the travelers crossed a rise that offered a view of a broad basin of meadow land. Agar waved his spear, calling the other hunters to his side. He needlessly pointed ahead. The hunters were also witnessing the action. A wolf pack was attacking one of the long-horned cows from a small herd of about a dozen animals. Defensively, the cattle had formed a tight group with the bulls and several of the cows repeatedly charging at the attacking wolves. The pack had concentrated their attack on a cow whose rear legs were bleeding badly. The wolves repeatedly raced in to slash at the cow's legs, while the defenders, with lowered, menacing horns, futilely charged at the agile attackers. The cow under attack repeatedly turned to face one of the wolves, only to have two others lunge at her hocks. While the hunters watched, the wolves succeeded in cutting the tendon of the cow's left leg. With the loss of support, her body quickly sagged to the ground. The remaining cattle continued their futile defense.

"I count only about eight wolves," Agar said. "I think we could drive them off."

Tomar looked back at the other waiting members of the clan who by then had grouped closely together. "You better get ready, then," he suggested. "The cattle will soon give up and leave."

Agar shouted orders. "I want Homan and Tomar to bring the women and children up here closer where we can defend them if necessary. The rest of you hunters leave your traveling bundles with your mates and come with me."

Tomar's prediction proved accurate. Moments later the remaining cattle abandoned the defense of the crippled cow and ran some distance away where, as a group, they stopped to watch the wolves continue attacking the wounded cow.

"Come on, get a move on," Agar called to the hunters. "Keep your spears ready and have your hand axes available. Now, let's stay close together."

Orin, looking for a clue as to whether he could participate, glanced at his father. Dorik smiled, giving a slight nod of his head to offer at least his own approval.

Thank you, the young man thought. I know I can handle myself as well as most of the others.

The hunters formed a tight group, advancing rapidly toward the downed cow. As the men approached the wounded animal, they slowed to a stalking pace.

The wolves ignored the approach of the hunters, concentrating their attack at the cow's head and throat. Walking shoulder to shoulder with spears ready, the hunters advanced to within twenty paces before the wolves displayed their first sign of concern.

"Stay very close together now," Agar shouted. "They're about to turn on us."

Two of the wolves turned their attention from the cow to face the hunters, baring their teeth and growling defiant threats. The men, taking their clue from Agar, stopped advancing when one of the wolves lunged toward them. Dorik stepped forward of his companions where, with a quick thrust of his spear, he struck one of the animals in the rump. The wolf emitted a series of yelps before quickly retreating to the far side of the downed cow. Two other wolves lunged at the men in a simultaneous attack. Agar drove his spear into the neck and shoulder of one attacker, pinning the animal to the ground. To assist Agar, Vodim stepped forward and swung his hand axe, delivering a fatal, bone-crushing blow to the head of the struggling animal. The other wolf suffered a nonlethal wound in his rib cage before retreating. The remaining wolves then abandoned the dying cow to join their pack leader as he circled the men, searching for a weak defense. The hunters, in close rank, waited for the attack. The men shouted encouragement to each other.

"Protect your legs," Vodim shouted to his clan mates as he saw one of the growling animals advancing low to the ground.

The wolf pack leader, with two other wolves at his side, lunged at the tightly grouped hunters. A half dozen spears were thrust, two of which entered the pack leader's neck and back. The mortally wounded animal emitted two short yelps before falling to the ground, motionless. The other two animals suffered painful, if not fatal, wounds before retreating to the company of their pack mates. The surviving wolves appeared disoriented, suffering from lack of guidance from their dead leader. To exploit the loss, Agar lunged toward one of the bewildered wolves that quickly retreated several paces before turning to face the hunters.

"I think we can rush them now," Agar shouted. "They won't attack. All together now, let's go."

The men followed Agar in a surge of brandished spears, racing toward the remnants of the pack. The animals hastily retreated a safe distance where they grouped to wait and watch the men.

The remaining cattle, that earlier had witnessed the loss of one of their herd, had departed and were nowhere in sight.

With a signal from Homan, the women and children ran forward to the downed cow. "We'll have fresh meat again," he called. "Let's get the animal skinned and cleaned."

The throat of the dying beast was opened and the women began the chore of removing the skin. While the carcass was being cut into pieces, the hunters stood guard between the wolf pack and the working clan women. The pelts of the two dead wolves were ignored. The shaggy winter hair was being shed and the fur had little appeal. "It would be just that much more to carry," one of the women remarked.

Orin felt a moment of disappointment that he hadn't been in a position to spear one of the wolves. At least I was with the hunters, he thought. I know I could have killed one if I'd been in position.

Agar scanned the horizon in a complete circle before conferring with Tomar. "We have at least two day's walk ahead to find timber for our campfires. I think we should cut the meat and retrace our path back to where we camped last night. Anyway, it appears that we're too early for the bison herds."

The cowhide was left behind. There was no time to cure and soften the skin, and it was far too heavy to be carried on the trail. With their sharp flint knives, the women cut the meat into manageable chunks, adding the loads to their already heavy packs. The head and larger bones were left behind, but the liver and heart were taken to be cooked separately and served to the hunters as a traditional ritual.

The last clan members had departed only a few paces from the carcass before the camp follower wolves raced to scavenge the remains. Tomar periodically turned to look back, speculating on how soon the remnants of the hunter pack would drive away the camp followers.

The sun was still high as fires were stoked and strips of meat sizzled on heated rocks or were skewered and cooked on green willow sticks.

"Mother, you're not eating," Orin protested. "The girls and I have eaten our fill and you haven't touched your meat." He held a juicy morsel before the stoop-shouldered woman.

"I'm sorry, I just can't eat a bite," she answered. "I guess I'm just too tired. Just make sure the girls get enough."

Although the wind had moderated and the temperature warmed, Amalee pulled her robe a little tighter around her body and sat staring through dark hollow eyes at the glowing embers.

Agar called a council of the hunters. "I don't want to delay any longer," he explained. "We'll probably find the bison herds farther out on the plains. We'll eat our fill of meat in the morning and carry enough for two days. It shouldn't spoil in that time. Have your women ready soon after sunup."

The news was soon passed, generating considerable grumbling. "Why can't we wait just a day or two longer?" Olvi complained to Vodim. "Amalee is in no shape to travel."

Vodim started to answer and then, after looking sympathetically at his ailing mate, merely lowered his head and turned away.

As darkness deepened, Orin slipped away from the hearth fire where only he and Vodim had remained seated. The other weary hearth members had already bedded down. Vodim glanced up, assuming only that Orin was leaving to care for his body needs. Orin moved silently through the pine grove to near the fire where Nomi quietly sat. After waiting in the shadows until catching her attention, he beckoned her to his side. Signalling for silence, he took her hand to lead her deeper into the woods. As he took her in his arms, he found her lips in a long and passionate kiss.

"You don't know how I've longed to hold you like this," he whispered. "It's on my mind all the time. I dream of you every night."

Nomi's arms encircled his waist as she whispered, "And I love you Orin, more than anything in the world, but I'm afraid."

"Afraid of what?" he asked.

"I'm fraid of Agar. I'm afraid of what he might do to you if he saw us together."

Nomi's remark prompted Orin to turn and peer nervously into the darkness. "He's an evil monster. Someday I'll get even with him. Someday I'll challenge him, and he'll regret that he ever saw me."

"Someday may be a long time off," she said. "Someday might be too late. It isn't fair. It seems to me that a woman should have some say as to who will take her for a mate."

Orin gave her another affectionate kiss before whispering, "You better get back to your fire. I'll see you on the trail tomorrow." After he reluctantly released her hand, she moved quietly away.

As dawn approached, fires burned brightly and the smell of roasted meat permeated the camp. Olvi stoked the fire where strips of meat sizzled on rocks embedded in the glowing embers.

Vodim knelt near the still huddled Amalee. "I know you don't feel well, but you're going to have to get up. We're going to move out on the trail soon and you haven't bundled your robes. Also, I don't think you've eaten anything."

"She hasn't," Orin said, adding his concern. "I'll bundle the robes, if she'll just eat a few bites."

"Is Mama sick? Is she going to be all right?" Retta asked, moving to Orin's side and searching his face for an answer.

"I hope she'll be all right," Orin responded. "I hope the spirits will give her strength."

Carma handed a strip of meat to Amalee and pleaded, "Mother, at least take a few bites."

Amalee attempted to chew on the food, but after a few swallows she stopped chewing.

Olvi touched her hand to the brow of the sitting woman. "She does have a fever. If we were back at the cave we would have dried willow bark and a clay pot to brew some tea. There's not much we can do here except let her rest."

Vodim stood up and looked away. "We all know the clan rules. The clan can never alter the schedule for one person." As he stepped away from the fire, he added, "I don't make the rules."

There was much whispering and staring at Amalee who remained indifferent to the activity around her. Orin wrapped and tied the woman's traveling bundle, placing it at the edge of camp with the packs of the other clan members.

"Come on, Mother," Orin begged. "Carma will walk with you and help you. I'll carry the bundles."

Amalee looked up at her son with tears sliding slowly down her cheeks. "I can't," she said. "I'm sorry, but I just can't." Her voice was barely a whisper. She held out her hand to Orin who knelt at her side. "Promise me you'll look after the girls. Carma will be all right, but Retta is so young. Help Olvi look after them."

Tears also dampened Orin's eyes. He attempted to speak but his voice failed.

"Don't feel bad," Amalee managed to whisper. "I think my spirit is anxious to find a new home."

Agar raised his spear to start the procession, but had moved only a few steps when Vodim trotted forward to his side. The two men conferred a short time before being joined by Tomar. After a few more words, the three men returned the length of the column to where Amalee sat. Orin and the girls still waited at her side.

Agar remained silent as Tomar knelt beside the woman. "I understand that you're sick and unable to continue. How do you feel now?"

Amalee slowly looked up at Tomar. "I'm tired," she whispered. "I'm sorry, but I just can't go on."

Tomar turned back to Agar. "Perhaps if we stay here for a couple of days, she'll be able to go on with us."

Agar glanced down at the seated woman and then back at Tomar before speaking. "And then after we've lost a couple of days waiting here, she still might not be able to travel. It isn't fair to the rest. We have always lived by that rule when on the trail, and we won't change now."

Tomar shrugged before reluctantly returning to the column. Agar looked at the two crying girls and then at Orin who stood back a few paces. "Get back in the column with the others," he ordered. "You are members of the hearth of Vodim, and you will immediately join Olvi on the trail."

Olvi hurried to the two girls and gently pushed them toward the waiting column. She then rushed to her traveling pouch and produced a large piece of partially cooked meat. She placed it on the stone near the feet of Amalee and started back toward the column. Olvi stopped, and for a short time looked back sympathetically at the woman she had known for so many years. Without speaking, she then turned and rapidly took her place near her son in the line.

Agar took several paces toward the column before turning to look back at Orin. "I told you to join the others," he shouted. "Take those girls and get in line."

Amalee looked at her son with a pleading look. "Please. Please, Orin, for my sake."

An emotionally torn Orin slowly placed his mother's bundled robes at her side. He then ran from one hearth to another gathering surplus firewood which he stacked near her side.

The clan leader accepted the delay, waiting until Orin had joined the column. After taking his position at the head of the clan, Agar raised his spear high in the air, and the long file began moving slowly along the trail.

Walking beside his two sisters, Orin strained to hide his emotions. "You've got to be a big girl now, Retta," he said. "Mother would want you to be brave. When Mother is in the spirit world, she'll look down at you and be proud. She loves us all, and I'm sure she knows that we love her." He then lapsed into silence.

When the column passed near the scene of the previous day's kill, the only evidence remaining was the skull. One of the hunters stepped out of the line and unsuccessfully attempted to break off the long curved horns.

Orin walked in a daze. His hatred of Agar mounted, and yet he knew that the rules were important for the survival of the clan. His thoughts shifted from grief for his mother to his fear of losing Nomi to the arrogant clan leader.

"If only I was older and stronger," he thought. "If only I could have Nomi with me all my life, we could then look after Carma and Retta as mother requested. If only I was a member of a different clan, but then I wouldn't have Nomi and I couldn't look after my sisters."

The thought hit him like a rock, starting his mind racing. Why not? Why not take Nomi and my sisters and run away from this clan until we can find another clan to live with? I remember the other years when our clan hunted bison and reindeer. We often encountered other clans of the Nordo tribe. Why couldn't we join another clan? Then I could claim my Nomi. I realize that, if I later encounter Agar, I'll have to fight, but by then I'll be older and can protect my rights.

The more he thought about it, the more his mind raced. How would he accomplish it? Would Agar follow him? What would Vodim say if he took the girls? Most important of all, would Nomi approve of the plan and go with him? It was a daring and desperate thought, but he could think of nothing else.

After testing plan after plan and weighing the possibilities, he decided he should act soon. If he waited until the clan was far out on the grass plains, it would be far more difficult to survive their escape. Desperation forced his decision.

If we leave early tonight, he reasoned, we could be back at the timber slopes by morning. I must act tonight.

Orin watched his sisters at the evening meal. The fires were fed with dried grass and small twigs from the low brush that dotted the meadows. He ate a larger portion of food than usual, stuffing himself with the reheated meat that Olvi prepared. When he encouraged his sisters to eat more, he wondered if Vodim or Olvi could guess his plan.

As darkness deepened, the weary travelers prepared their bed robes for a welcome night's sleep.

"The girls are still upset about their mother," Orin explained to Olvi. "If you don't mind, I'll have them place their beds near mine. It might make them feel better."

Olvi looked at him quizzically and then consented, feeling that Orin needed the company for his own sake.

Without the larger pieces of firewood, the flames soon diminished and darkness deepened. Orin walked through the camp to where he could observe the hearth of Nomi. The girl looked up from the bedroll she was adjusting. Orin nodded his head in the direction of the darkness beyond the fires and waited for an acknowledgment. From the look in her eyes he was certain she understood. Pretending to turn back toward his hearth, he then moved toward the planned meeting place. While watching from the darkness beyond the fires, Orin was reassured when he saw Nomi begin walking in his direction.

When she was near, he whispered, "Over here, Nomi."

"Oh, Orin, I'm very sorry about your mother." Her voice was choked.

"Thank you, Nomi, but we can't talk about that now. Let's move over where we won't be heard." Taking her hand, they carefully moved farther from the fire. He turned her toward him, his eyes straining to see her face. "I have a plan that could be very dangerous," he whispered, "but I've thought a lot about it. You may think I'm mad, but I'm so desperate to have you with me that I can think of nothing else."

As she began to speak, he placed a hand to her lips. "Now listen, carefully. Would you agree to run away from this clan with me and we'll find another clan where we can live together, far away from Agar?"

"Oh, yes, Orin," she answered without hesitation. "I've dreamed about something like that. But how could we leave and how could we survive?"

"I can't promise we'll survive, but I'd rather die than live any longer in this clan."

"And I'd rather die than be without you," she whispered, drawing herself close to him.

"Are you sure?" he questioned.

"Of course, I'm sure," she affirmed. "I've never been more certain of anything in my life."

"All right then, listen carefully. The moon will come up in a little while and that will be our signal to meet. Be very quiet and bring your sleeping robe. We'll meet just beyond the south edge of camp. I plan to take my sisters, so wait for me there. I promised my mother I'd care for them, and I can't break that promise." He kissed her tenderly before releasing her, allowing her to move quietly back to her hearth.

13

Orin waited for what seemed an eternity before a dim light on the horizon signaled the imminent appearance of the moon. He turned to where Carma lay sleeping beneath the folds of the reindeer robe. He placed one hand over the girl's mouth and gently shook her shoulder. As she stirred, he whispered very faintly, "Shhhh-- don't speak. Do you understand?"

A few moments passed as the girl shed the heavy veil of sleep. She then nodded affirmatively.

"Come with me," he whispered as he unfolded the robe and took the girl by the hand.

He quietly gathered her bed robe and his spear, and with his other hand led her into the darkness. When they were at a sufficient distance to safely speak, he explained his plan. "We're going to take Retta and go back to where we stayed last night."

"Will we find Mother and help her?" Carma begged.

"Yes, we'll go back to where we left her. I don't know how she'll be but we'll go back and find out."

"Oh yes, Orin, yes. I want to go." She had difficulty keeping her voice low.

"Then you wait right here and hold my spear. I'm going back to get Retta. Now don't move. Stay very quiet until I get back. Do you understand?"

"I understand," she replied.

Orin quietly moved back toward the hearth. Crawling on hands and knees to avoid alerting the camp, he located his own bed robe and draped it over his shoulder. He then located the bed robe that contained Retta. Carefully picking up the entire bundle, he carried the sleeping child slowly out of camp. He reached Carma just as the moon cast its first beam of light over the low horizon. Handing his robe to the older girl to carry, they moved quietly to the southern end of the camp.

The moonlight was dim, but by stooping low, he finally located the silhouette of Nomi. Without speaking, the four moved silently away from camp, proceeding back along the trail in the direction from which they had travelled the previous day.

After walking a safe distance, Orin stopped and lowered the awakened Retta to the ground.

"Where are we going, Orin?" the child asked.

"We're going on a long trip," he explained while wrapping the child's robe into a tight bundle. "Maybe we'll join another clan."

Carma started to whisper and then realized she could speak aloud. "Aren't we going back to Mother?" she asked. "That's what you told me."

"Yes, we're going back to Mother, but I don't want to build up your hopes. Mother may not be there when we get back."

"Where would she be?" Carma asked.

"Let's not talk about it. Let's get going. We've got a long way to go."

"Is Nomi going with us?" the smaller child inquired.

"Yes, darling Retta. Nomi is going with us."

The partial moon gave sufficient light for the small group to move steadily along the trail. Occasionally a cloud crossed the lunar face, slowing them down, but by proceeding cautiously they continued their progress. Several times Orin handed his bundle of robes to Nomi, freeing his arms to carry the smaller child.

Retta gripped her arms tightly around his neck, occasionally complaining. "Can't we stop and sleep for awhile?" she asked.

"No, we can't. We have to keep moving." Though Orin was deeply worried about his mother, he was also haunted by the thoughts of what would happen when the camp was alerted to their absence. He often stopped to peer back along the trail, listening intently for any sound.

While exploring the hazards of being overtaken by Agar, a nearby commotion summoned a surge of adrenaline.

"It's only a rabbit," Nomi explained. "It almost scared me to death."

* * *

The exertion drained their strength as they pushed themselves throughout the long night. The moon continued its journey across the night sky and the first glow of dawn appeared as the weary travellers passed the aurochs skull.

"Look," Orin said to his sisters, "we're almost there. We only have a little way to go."

The landmark, and the light of dawn, gave new energy to the exhausted group.

When within view of the pine grove at the earlier camp site, Orin halted his companions and handed his spear to Nomi. "I want all of you to wait right here," he ordered. He then turned to Nomi to explain. "Don't follow until I signal you. I don't know what I'm going to find."

The girls nodded assent before lowering their packs to the ground. Running toward his goal, Orin's worry suddenly increased. He saw two wolves standing motionless a short distance from camp. Orin shouted a curse, inducing a short retreat of the animals before they stopped to wait and watch. Approaching the camp, he scanned the area, hoping to see his mother sitting where he had left her. His doubt deepened to grief when, at a distance, he saw her empty bed robe laying open near the hearth site. He slowed to a walk and approached. Lifting the robe, he was somewhat relieved to see no blood or evidence of attack. As his eyes continued scanning the campsite for any clue to his mother's fate, his attention was caught by a wisp of smoke from the ashes near his feet. It took a moment to comprehend the significance of the smoke.

He excitedly raised his voice to a loud shout. "Mother, Mother. Do you hear me? Are you all right? Do you hear me? Amalee, where are you?"

Hearing no response, he again frantically examined the camp site and the surrounding area. He studied the two wolves that waited and watched from a distance.

I don't see any sign of a struggle, he reasoned. Could mother have left the camp and then been attacked by those beasts? Or could she have been carried away by a larger animal?

The uncertainty tormented his mind. He was about to return to Nomi and his sisters when the corner of his eye caught a movement in the wooded area. He looked again to verify what he could hardly believe. From a distance, his mother was moving slowly toward him.

He hurdled several fallen logs, racing toward her. "Mother," he shouted, "are you all right?"

The frail woman stopped, steadying herself against a tree. "I'm all right," she answered, her voice barely a whisper. "What are you doing here? You're supposed to be with the clan. You promised to look after the girls."

"We came back," he explained. "I couldn't stay with Agar or the clan any longer so I brought the girls back with me." He placed an arm around the shoulders of his mother to steady her before adding, "We'll find another clan."

Amalee shook her head, her hollow eyes staring into his face. "I wish you hadn't, Orin. The girls would be safer with Olvi. I'm not sure I can survive any more travel. I wish you'd take the girls back to Olvi."

Orin opened his mouth to speak but paused momentarily, weighing his words. "I also brought Nomi. We can never go back to the clan now. We don't care what happens. We had to get away from Agar."

Orin steadied his mother as they slowly walked back to the campsite. "What were you doing out in the woods?"

"I was trying to gather firewood. I knew it was futile, but it was better than just sitting and waiting for the end."

Orin seated the woman on a log before quickly gathering a few unburned, dry twigs from the edges of the adjacent dead fire pits. He then knelt to carefully blow the existing coals into a small flame. Running a short distance deeper into the woods, he retrieved some of the lower dry, dead limbs from the pine trees of the grove.

With the fire safely burning, Orin ran to signal Nomi and the girls.

"Mama, Mama, I'm so happy to see you," Retta cried as she knelt to throw her arms around her tearful mother.

"The spirits have truly been generous," Amalee said, stroking her daughter's hair. "I didn't think I would ever see my children again."

After the emotional exchange, Orin questioned his mother. "Do you feel any better than yesterday? Do you think you could walk?"

"I think my fever is gone. I don't know what was wrong with me, but I do feel a little better. I'm not sure how far I can travel, but I can walk a little ways."

Orin looked nervously to the north. "I'd like to get away from the trail and find a place where you could rest a few days. I'm afraid Agar might come back here looking for us."

"You and the girls must be exhausted," Amalee whispered. "You've been walking all night. Don't you need some rest?"

"The girls need sleep, badly, but we can't take the time now. I think we should at least get away from this camp. This would be the first place Agar would look." Orin again glanced nervously back along the trail.

Amalee loosened the draw cord of the pouch that hung from her waist. "I still have this meat that Olvi left. I want you to have it. You must all be starved."

"No, we're not starved," Orin protested. "We're still in good shape from last night. I'll have Nomi carry it for you, but that meat is for you. If you don't get your strength back, we won't be able to travel very far. You should eat some right now."

"I did eat some this morning. I'll be all right." Amalee looked down at the glowing coals. "How are you going to carry the fire?"

The young man's eyes surveyed the camp as though expecting an easy solution. "I don't know. I haven't had time to think of that." He stared at the fire as he pondered the problem. "We'll have to carry torches for now. It'll slow us down, but we better not lose the fire. Tomar told me about clans that made fire with a whirling stick but I don't know how they did it."

"You shouldn't count on that," his mother cautioned. "If it was that simple, Tomar would have done it."

Orin secured some dry, pitch-laden pine limbs and soon had one flaming with lively sparks. He then urged his sisters onto their feet, and with Nomi carrying her own and Amalee's bundles, he led the small band in a westerly direction away from the trail.

He guarded his fire carefully, stopping periodically to nurse it back to life with pine needles and dry twigs. His mother and the girls enjoyed the welcome moments of rest but when ready to continue, Retta often had to be scolded to get her back on her feet. "Come on, Retta," he urged. "I know you're tired but we can't stop now. We must get farther off the trail."

Their progress was tediously slow. Orin led them in a westerly direction along the timber covered slope, paralleling the mountain range to the south.

As the day wore on, he paused occasionally to nervously study the dark towering cumulus clouds building over the higher mountain range. The sun was nearing its midday journey when Orin halted the small group at the far edge of a broad meadow, allowing his mother and the girls a much needed rest. His fire was established in the clearing, fed with an armful of dried twigs and small limbs from the nearby pines. He urged his mother to eat some of the remaining meat and gave a small portion to the youngest sister.

Nomi, Carma, and Orin, using digging sticks, began probing the soft, damp soil, retrieving and eating a variety of the juicy, tender roots and bulbs of the new spring growth.

As the foragers worked their way onto the meadow, they were startled when a young fawn, that had been hiding motionless in the tall dry grass, panicked and ran for cover in the security of the woods.

Orin raced after the frightened young deer while shouting to Nomi. "Go get my spear and come with me. Maybe we can get him."

Nomi quickly retrieved the spear and, with Carma and Retta following, ran into the dense timber growth where the young hunter had disappeared.

"Over here, come over here," Orin shouted. "I think he's hiding behind those logs in the brush over there."

By the time the girls finally located their impatient brother, the sky had darkened, hampering the already impaired visibility in the dense growth.

"Find a stick and work around those fallen logs," he ordered. "I'll wait here and when you drive him this way, maybe I can get him. Nomi led the two sisters in a wide arc and, after what seemed ages to the impatient hunter, approached from the far side. Orin crouched and tensely waited behind a large shrub.

A lightning flash illuminated the dense grove, followed almost immediately by a crash of thunder that startled the small hunting party. Orin understood the threat but was torn in his desire to find the young deer. Looking nervously up at the rolling dark cloud overhead, he abandoned his ambush to advance toward the logs.

"Hurry up. We can't wait," he called. "Start shouting and rush into the area now to drive him out."

The girls began shouting and beating the underbrush while moving rapidly into the designated area. With spear poised, Orin ran from one shrub to another peering into the low growth. Another flash of lightning and a loud sustained roll of thunder commanded the attention of the frustrated hunter. As he looked up, the first few drops of water struck his face and rapidly became a downpour.

"Forget the deer. Let's save the fire," he shouted as he turned to run back to the meadow, but before he could reach the clearing, the rain had become a deluge. He frantically ran toward the fire site that was by then sending plumes of steam into the dark sky. He grabbed his bed robe and pulled the thong of the bow knot that held it tightly packed. The knot failed to slip free and the moments dragged as he struggled to free the pack. Managing to loosen the bedroll just as Nomi and Carma arrived, he shouted for them to hold the robe over the steaming black fire site to divert the rain.

"Try to keep the water off the fire," he pleaded. "Hold the robe up over the coals."

Dropping to his knees, he groped through the ashes, searching for any indication of fire. With the sharp reaction of sudden pain, he jerked his hand back. Grasping a charred stick, he carefully turned the ashes until, with a surge of relief, he saw a small, red glowing ember.

"Bring me some dry moss and twigs," he shouted to Nomi. "Retta, you help Carma hold the robe over the coals." He leaned very close and gently blew on the fading red ember, reviving the red glow. "Hurry with the moss and twigs," he again shouted without looking up.

Nomi called back from where she frantically searched for the vital tinder. "Everything's wet," she explained. "I can't find anything dry anywhere." The pounding rain and sudden strong, gusting wind drowned her frustrated reply.

A surging wind gust caught the edge of the robe, tearing it from the hands of the younger girl. She tried to recover her grip, but her numbed and slippery hands failed her. She gave up and began to cry.

Orin sat back, frustrated. "Don't cry Retta," he said, attempting to console the girl. "You did your best. It's my fault. The fire is out because I waited too long. I was stupid to try to catch that fawn anyway." Orin pounded the ground in a gesture of self condemnation.

Nomi moved to his side to place a consoling hand on his shoulder. "I'm sorry Orin, I just couldn't find any dry tinder."

Amalee struggled to her feet to approach the other shivering and disheartened travelers. Her words were barely discernible. "I should have been tending the fire instead of sleeping. It's all my fault. If you hadn't returned to get me this morning, it would never have happened."

"It is not your fault," he argued. "I'm the one to blame. I should never have left the meadow. Let's all get under our robes or we'll die of the cold." Orin repositioned the robe around his mother's shoulders and seated her against a nearby pine.

Within a short time the rain ceased and the clouds retreated, exposing the late afternoon sun. The five disheartened wanderers sat motionless, pondering the unknown future of survival without fire. Amalee condemned herself, accepting blame for the wrath of the Storm God. Nomi felt that the Spirits had deserted her as punishment for her feelings against Agar. Carma and Retta were confused and frightened, hopefully waiting for some word of encouragement from an adult.

Orin's guilt encompassed many of his actions since leaving the winter cave. If I had just not antagonized Agar, he thought. If I had just not neglected the fire. He had no regrets about his escape from the clan with his sisters and Nomi. He was grateful that his mother was still alive and with them, but he was beginning to have second thoughts about his leadership.

14

Orin sat, deep in thought, staring aimlessly across the meadow when a movement emerging from the far woods caught his eye. His heart began pounding as he identified it as the form of a man. His hopes and plans began disintegrating as he contemplated the confrontation with Agar. Suddenly he considered, and quickly dismissed, any thought of flight. Possibly, he and Nomi could escape, but he would never abandon his mother and sisters. He reached out for the reassuring feel of his spear. He knew he had little chance to defeat the experienced leader, but circumstances offered no acceptable alternative.

Only Nomi was alerted by the grave look on his face as he rose to his feet to shed his robe. Her eyes followed the direction of his stare and soon focused on the object of his concern. Saying nothing, she also got to her feet and went to his side.

"Do we have to move on?" Retta complained as she watched her brother draw his spear to his side.

"No, little sister," he answered. He then turned to Nomi. "I want you to keep the girls here with mother. I'm going out to meet him. I don't want any of you there."

Nomi grasped his arm. "No, Orin, no. Please don't go. Let's run away. Please don't fight him."

Orin looked down into the pleading eyes of the girl. "We have no choice," he said. "We can't run. Mother or Retta could never keep up with us, and I just can't leave them."

Nomi again looked out at the approaching figure. Tears dampened her eyes.

Orin searched the face of Nomi before continuing. "If anything happens to me, I want you to return to the clan. You and the girls could never survive alone, and you'll be much better off back with the others."

A look of panic spread across Nomi's face as tears accumulated in the corners of her eyes. "Oh, no," she protested, her voice breaking with emotion. "I could never go back with that awful man."

Orin drew Nomi to him and they embraced with a short but tender kiss that conveyed the emotions that tortured their frantic thoughts. He slowly released her from his arms but paused with his hands on her shoulders, looking longingly into her tear-filled eyes. "I love you, Nomi. I love you more than anything in the world. I'm sorry if I've failed, but I'm not sorry I tried. Please don't say anything. Just do what you can for my sisters and mother."

Orin turned abruptly away from her and started across the meadow toward the approaching, fur-robed, figure. His mind searched frantically for an alternative but quickly dismissed the thought. He mentally rehearsed the evasive movements necessary to escape the lunging spear of Agar and envisioned his own counter thrusts that might luckily exploit a moment of imbalance or carelessness.

A sickening feeling began penetrating his stomach and again he had an urge to run. Why couldn't we have gotten away? he thought. Why did he have to follow us? Why have the spirits abandoned me? His feet grew heavy as, in a partial daze, he advanced across the large meadow.

As he approached the distant figure, he was startled and then puzzled to see the robed man wave his hand, not in a threatening gesture, but as a signal of friendship. His mind searched for an explanation. Could this be a devious scheme of Agar's to confuse me or to cause me to lower my guard?

Again, the approaching figure waved a greeting.

Orin stopped and studied the man who was increasing his pace. Could Agar be doing this to maneuver the confrontation closer to where Nomi waited? His mind raced wildly. His eyes again strained and refocused. Suddenly his brain, that had earlier anticipated and feared the outcome of inevitable combat, exploded in joy upon recognition of the robed figure.

Orin ran toward the man, shouting and waving his arms. "Dorik, what are you doing here? How did you find us?"

As they approached within talking distance, the hunter called to his son. "Wait a moment, one question at a time. First tell me if your mother is all right and what about the girls?"

Dorik approached to place an arm around the shoulders of the excited youth. As the two men walked back toward camp, Orin began telling of the escape and their experiences since leaving camp. He was only a short way into the story when the girls also recognized the robed figure and ran to join the pair.

Dorik knelt by the woman who had once been his mate. "Are you all right, Amalee? Are you feeling any better?"

Amalee took his offered hand. "I'm feeling much better, but I'm very weak. My fever seems better, but I can't travel very fast. They should never have come back for me."

Dorik's gaze lingered on the face of the woman. "I should have been with them," he said. "There are many things that I should have done differently." Dorik then told of the excitement at camp following the escape. "Agar planned to follow Orin, threatening to kill him and take the girls back. He was ready to start back along the trail to catch up with all of you, but then changed his mind. I think he had some lingering doubts about his fellow hunters and suspected the clan might not be there when he returned. In any event, he suddenly ordered everyone to pack up and move on. I simply picked up my bedroll and walked out of camp. I looked back and saw the commotion as they watched my departure, but no one attempted to follow me."

"How did you locate us?" Orin asked.

"As easy as following a bison trail," Dorik explained. "I knew you'd return for Amalee and from there you left a well-marked trail of burned torches. What happened to your fire?"

"It was my fault," Orin quickly offered. "We were trying to catch a fawn that had bolted into the thicket but a thunderstorm caught us before I could get back to the fire. I don't know what we'll do now."

Dorik's eyes searched the sky. "This time of year we might be lucky and find a fire that was started by the Storm God. We'll figure something out."

"Are you going to stay with us?" Retta pleaded to the older hunter.

"If you want me to," he responded, lifting the child into his arms. He then looked at Orin. "I presume you plan to look for another clan."

"That was our plan. We just wanted to get away from Agar."

"We'll manage some way," Dorik reassured the small group. "Do you plan to camp here tonight?

"I don't know," Orin answered. "Now that you're here, I'd like you to act as leader. I've sort of bungled things so far."

Dorik laughed, attempting to console the young man. "You've been doing a fine job. If every leader stepped down with each mistake he made, the clans would soon be without leaders and the women would be giving the orders." They all laughed at such a humorous thought.

Dorik suggested the group remain overnight at the meadow and start early the next morning in search of another clan. "We need more hunters if we're going to be successful in killing big game out on the plains. Two men might catch an occasional deer, but we could never kill a bison or long-horned cow."

The remaining daylight time was spent probing the ground for edible roots and bulbs. As night approached, the temperature dropped rapidly. They shared their robes, forming a ground spread and a top cover, between which they all snuggled together to conserve body heat.

Orin held Nomi cuddled closely in his arms. His mind reviewed his decisions and actions of the past day and explored the possibilities of the future. I should never have lost the fire, he reasoned. If we can find a fire that was started by the Storm God, I wonder if that would be a bad omen. Would it be safe to use the fire that the powerful Storm God stole from the sun and sent crashing to the ground? Is the Storm God laughing and mocking the Sun God when he roars so loudly after sending the fire down to earth? Tomar believes that the Storm God sends the fire down for the benefit of man. There is no doubt that the Storm God is more powerful than the Sun God, for the clouds can hide the sun whenever the Storm God desires. But the Sun God is friendly to man. He gives us warmth when we're cold, so why would the Storm God treat us so badly most of the time and then relent to offer us fire? It's all very confusing, and I'm so tired. Regardless of what happens, I'll never regret leaving the clan. I now have my Nomi with me and my mother is still alive. If we can just find a place to rest for a few days, maybe she'll recover her strength. We'll need a place where we can hunt and gather roots. Oh, how grateful I am that Dorik joined us. What would I have done alone with four women? How can we hunt with only two men? We need more hunters to be effective. Where will we look for another clan? If we go to the plains, or farther north into reindeer country, we might run into Agar. If we stay near the bison hunting grounds and manage to avoid Agar, perhaps we can find another clan. Perhaps we can find the clan that we saw at the hot springs. No, that wouldn't do. They speak a strange tongue and I could never learn that. Dorik will know what to do. With him here, I won't have to worry, and I'm so very, very sleepy.

Just as his mind was released to the numbness of sleep, he thought he heard the long sustained call of a wolf.

Dorik lay awake a long time pondering his own decision to leave the clan. Since his defeat by Agar years earlier, life had lost much of its meaning. The years of his clan leadership had been exciting and he had taken pride in his management of the hunting families. He painfully recalled the humiliation that followed his defeat by Agar. Amalee and his son had been taken from him. A year passed before Agar assigned him the mate and children of a fellow hunter who had been killed by a wounded black bear.

I've never liked that woman, he reminded himself. I'm certain Agar assigned her to me because of his hatred for me. He wanted to force me to supply food to a woman for whom I had no interest.

Many times during the following years Dorik had considered leaving the clan but had also known that his survival alone would be doubtful. Even his decision of the previous day offered small chance for success, but his love for his son and Amalee left him no choice. Life in the clan without his son nearby would have no meaning. He could at least hope to improve the survival chances of his loved ones.

Dorik slept lightly that night, often reaching out to touch the flint-tipped spear that lay near the bed. Without the campfire as a deterrent, he knew they were vulnerable to a night prowling tiger, or even a wolf pack if the animals were hungry enough. He had seen no signs of tiger, and the wolf howl that had startled him the previous night was probably one of the old camp wolves that had scavenged the carcass of the long-horned cow. Bears could also be a nuisance during mating season, or when fresh out of hibernation, but they were more apt to do their feeding during daylight.

When dawn arrived, exposing a cloudless sky, Dorik urged the small group out of bed.

"We'd better move on to where we have water," he suggested. "I don't see many signs of game here and we're going to need meat soon."

Nomi assisted Amalee to her feet and added the woman's bed robe to her own bundle. "How do you feel this morning, Amalee?" the young woman asked.

The older woman smiled weakly. "I do think I feel a little stronger. I should be carrying my own pack. It isn't fair for you to carry the extra burden."

"Someday I'll let you carry my pack," Nomi joked as the small band formed into a column behind Dorik and Orin.

There was no defined trail and their progress was slow as they made their way around fallen logs or dense thickets of underbrush. Dorik continued on a generally westerly course, staying parallel to the mountain range to their left. Upon reaching a small stream, they paused for a short rest and, lowering their packs, knelt to drink of the refreshing cool liquid.

Their route took them near a thicket from which a game hen fluttered noisily into the air. They immediately made a successful search for the nest where, after shedding their packs, they cracked and sucked the nourishment from the eggs.

Dorik continually scanned the horizon, searching for any wisp of smoke that might signal either another clan or a fire from the previous day's lightning storm.

The sun was still climbing when Dorik signaled a stop. After listening carefully for a few moments, he informed his followers, "I think I hear a stream up ahead. It sounds fairly large."

As they neared the sound of tumbling water, they quickened their pace. Dorik halted at the bank of a shallow ravine to study the swift flow of water cascading around the large boulders below. He then examined the well worn game trail that paralleled the creek. "I think we'll follow the stream for a while. We're more apt to see animals near the water."

The trail often detoured well away from the stream, impeding their progress. Shortly after noon they heard the turbulent sound of a waterfall, and after descending to the lower level of the stream, paused to enjoy the beauty of the display.

"Oh, Orin," Nomi said, raising her voice to be heard above the noise. "Isn't it beautiful. I'm so thrilled. I'm sure it's an omen of good fortune. The spirits must be telling us that everything is going to be all right."

Orin put his arm around the excited girl. "Yes, Nomi, everything is going to be all right. I'm sure of it."

The small group continued only a short distance before the trail left the stream to cross a small ridge through which the water had cut a deep gorge. As Dorik reached the summit, he paused to motion his followers to his side. They looked out across a broad, grassy meadow through which the stream flowed in long, curved loops. The woods, adorning the slopes on either side of the valley, abruptly ended at the edge of the large meadow. At the far end of the valley could be seen the reflected light from the surface of a small lake. They each remained silent while absorbing the beauty of the landscape below.

Dorik finally raised his arm to point at a herd of long-horned cattle. "This is what we've been looking for. Do you see the herd of aurochs near the far edge of the meadow? Do you see the beaver dams in the stream? The pine forests must be filled with deer that come down to the meadow at night to graze. There will be plenty of firewood for our camp and the women should be able to find plenty of plants and roots along that beautiful stream. We'll make camp near that lake, and if the spirits favor us, we might stay here most of the summer."

Amalee said nothing, but offered her silent gratitude to the spirits for supplying a resting place for her tired and aching body.

With the sun still high in the sky, the enthusiastic column continued across the meadow to the lakeshore near the timbered north slope.

"This is a beautiful place," Orin said to his companions. "I just hope we're far enough off the main trail."

The travelers lowered their packs to the ground a short distance from the lake. The grassy area was flanked on the upper side by a sharp earthen bank, twice the height of a man's head. The mountain side above was heavily wooded. The roots of a large pine that had once towered skyward from the upper edge of the bank had subsequently yielded to wind and erosion, allowing the tree to fall toward the lakeshore. The roots still clung tenaciously to the soil above the bank, forming a horizontal tree bridge under which a man could stand with considerable head clearance.

Dorik surveyed the fallen log. "We should be able to make a very comfortable shelter here, but first things first."

Orin and the others waited near the older man who was scanning the surrounding terrain.

"We need a fire badly," he stated. "I've heard of clans who start fires with a whirling stick, but I've never seen it done. I remember Tomar experimenting day after day. I even saw smoke come from the wood that turned black from the heat, but never any fire. I hate to waste time trying such a thing when Orin and I should be out hunting, but we need the fire so badly that I think we should try. You women should start collecting roots and dandelions. I noticed cattails and water lilies at the edge of the lake, and we all saw the watercress bed just above the lake inlet."

Without questioning Dorik, the women took their gathering pouches and departed in search of food.

Dorik turned his attention back to Orin. "If we're going to try to build a fire the way Tomar tried, we need at least one good dry willow the size of your thumb and a couple of larger dry pine limbs. We also need to collect some very small dry twigs and moss."

The two men quickly gathered the necessary supplies, including mounds of dry tree moss gleaned from pine boughs. When ready, they knelt to pursue the task. Orin watched eagerly as Dorik, using his sharp cutting flint, shaved pointed ends onto the foot-long length of dry willow.

"I think I remember how Tomar tried it," he explained. "We'll hold the willow vertical with the lower point against this pine limb on the ground and I'll have you hold this other short limb against the point on top. There, just like that. Now hold the top limb steady and press down slightly while I whirl the willow between my palms."

Dorik vigorously moved the palms of his hands back and forth, spinning the willow first one direction and then the other. He worked at fever pitch with no apparent results.

"Do you think it's getting hot?" Orin inquired.

"I don't know but my hands are sure getting sore. Here, let me hold the limb and you spin the willow."

The two men reversed roles and worked until sweat dripped from the brow of the young man. They finally sat back in defeat.

"I'm not sure it can even be done," Dorik conceded. "It may have been a false story, told and believed by wishful thinking."

Orin shrugged his shoulders. "The point of the willow did char a little. If we could just spin it a little faster perhaps it might start burning."

"I don't know how we could spin it any faster," was his father's reply. "There's no way I could spin it faster and I don't think you could either."

The men sat silently for a short while, pondering the problem, before Orin jumped to his feet. "I have an idea," he said. "It might not work, but it wouldn't hurt to try."

Dorik watched with avid curiosity as his son ran to his bed robe and returned with the thong he had used as binding.

"Hold the willow between the pine pieces again and let me try something," Orin suggested. "I'll wrap this thong around the willow and have you pull one end toward you after which I'll pull the other end back."

They experimented with the thong several times, but although it was occasionally successful in spinning the dry stick, it was ineffective.

"We have to keep steady back pressure on the thong," Dorik observed, "otherwise it slips."

Again they experimented until they finally developed a rhythm that seldom failed to twirl the willow. After working vigorously for a short time, they were rewarded with small wisps of smoke and a faint smell of burning wood.

Dorik finally shook his head in defeat. "We're so close to getting a fire, but it just isn't enough. If we could just press down a little harder, or spin the willow a little faster, I think we could get a fire started."

Orin jumped up, and without comment, ran toward the lake-shore. Dorik watched as the young man finally cut through a long green willow with his flint knife.

Upon Orin's return, Dorik displayed a critical frown. "I told you the wood has to be dry. That green willow wouldn't burn, even if we already had a fire going."

Orin, ignoring the remark, continued his activity. He tied the end of the thong to one end of the three-foot-long green willow before bending the willow slightly and tying the other end of the thong to the other end of the willow. He called loudly to Nomi who was returning with an arm full of dripping watercress, signaling her to his side. When she arrived, he bent the green willow to produce enough slack to form a single loop of the thong around the dry pointed willow. With the green willow holding the thong uniformly taunt, he reseated the points in the charred holes. A broad smile developed on Dorik's face as he recognized the significance of the design.

"Nomi, you hold that end of the bowed stick," Orin ordered, "and I'll hold this end. We'll pull back and forth to see how it works. Dorik, you hold the pointed willow steady between the pine sticks."

Orin and Nomi, awkwardly at first, and then smoothly, developed a rhythm that kept the pointed dry stick spinning much faster than before. As they developed a faster rhythm, the wood squealed in protest. Smoke curled from both ends of the whirling stick, generating increased enthusiasm. Orin reached with one hand to nestle a small mound of dry tree moss snugly against the smoking willow. Furiously they maintained the beat until their arms ached. Dorik increased the downward pressure until suddenly a red glow appeared in the moss near the stick.

"Keep going, faster," Dorik urged. "It looks like it's about to start any moment now."

Orin lowered one hand to adjust the moss from which heavy plumes of smoke curled. As he repositioned the small mound of moss, air gave life to the glowing spark, generating a flame which grew and quickly spread through the dry tinder. Dorik quickly added additional moss and twigs. With a bright fire burning at their feet, the men relaxed their effort.

While Nomi and Orin were exchanging expressions of gratitude, Dorik and Amalee both closed their eyes, offering thanks to the generous God of Fire.

"Carma and Retta should start hauling firewood in from the forest," Orin suggested. "We're going to need a lot of it in the next few days."

The fire offered not only warmth and security, but enabled the women to provide a variation from the diet of the past day. Nomi and the sisters were sent to the marsh end of the lake to retrieve cattail and water lily roots which were roasted on the hot stones that surrounded the fire. Arrowroot tubers and wild onions accompanied the mounds of watercress. Although they would also have enjoyed the taste of meat, there were no complaints. Darkness deepened with the small group of grateful people sitting silently watching the dancing embers of the fire.

Orin's arm encircled the shoulders of Nomi as she nestled her head comfortably against his chest.

Dorik reached for the hand of the frail woman who had shared his hearth many years earlier. "We'll maintain our camp here until you have your full strength back. With only two men, we'll have to change our hunting style, but with our fire, I think we should at least be safe."

- 15 -

As darkness settled over the valley, Orin conferred with Dorik to explain the problem that had often occupied his mind since leaving the clan. "If it wasn't for my trouble with Agar, and if I had been accepted as a hunter in the Ceremony of the Hunt, I could have then claimed Nomi as my mate. Do the spirits require that I wait until we join another clan to perform the ceremony? That might be a long time."

Dorik appeared very serious as he stood up. "Orin, you told me last night that you wanted me to be the leader of this little clan. I accept that responsibility and honor. As a past clan leader, the spirits will accept my authority, so I want you to now stand here before me."

The flames of the freshly stoked fire danced brightly, casting flickering shadows on the nearby landscape. Orin moved into position before the once powerful clan leader. The women watched from the far side of the fire, engrossed by the proceedings.

Dorik raised his left hand in the air and placed his right hand on the shoulder of his son. His voice was solemn as he spoke. "I, Dorik, leader of the clan of Dorik, with all the authority as clan leader, do hereby award to you, Orin, the full status of Clan Hunter."

He then paused, drawing the hunting axe from his robe binding. He then continued, extending the weapon to Orin. "In recognition of your new status, I now present to you this hunting axe as a symbol of your new responsibility. It is to be carried with pride and courage to the everlasting honor of this clan."

Orin's eyes moved from the hunting axe to the face of the leader. "But Dorik, this is your hunting axe. You shouldn't give it to me."

The older man pulled his face into a mock frown. "You must never question the actions of your leader. You've been a hunter of full status only moments, and already you are breaking the prime clan rule."

Orin slid the handle of the axe into his waist binding and waited silently for Dorik to continue.

"As a new member of the Order of the Hunt, in the Clan of Dorik, you now have privileges and responsibilities. One of the new privileges that I now bestow upon you is the selection of a mate. Have you, Orin, made that selection?"

Orin had a slightly uneasy feeling. Considering the nature and size of the group, he wondered whether the spirits might not condone such a ceremony. Dorik was clan leader for many years, he reasoned. He assigned many mates to the hunters of the clan. Surely the spirits will sanction and honor his authority. The young hunter allowed his enthusiasm to crowd any doubts far back into the recesses of his mind.

"I have," he responded.

"And who have you selected?" Dorik continued.

Orin looked across the fire and returned the smile that the young woman displayed. "I have selected Nomi as my mate," he proudly answered.

The eyes of the other members of the group focused on the girl as Dorik continued. "Nomi, you are to stand behind Orin."

When the slightly nervous girl was in position, standing behind and a little to the side of Orin, the older man proceeded. "Orin, do you, as a hunter in the Clan of Dorik, accept this woman as your mate?"

The young man glanced back over his shoulder before responding. "Yes, I do."

Dorik then turned his attention to the girl. "Nomi, you have been chosen as the mate of a hunter in the Clan of Dorik. By my authority as the leader of this clan, I hereby award you to this man as his mate and order you to serve and obey him to the extent of your ability, to never question his orders, but to devote your life to his comfort and happiness. Is that understood?"

The firelight reflected the joy in her deep blue eyes and on her face. "Yes, oh yes," she replied, stepping to Orin's side to grasp his arm.

The serious look on Dorik's face became a smile as he rested his hand on his son's shoulder. "Congratulations, hunter. You now have a mate, and may the Spirit of Fertility bless you with many sons."

That night Orin and Nomi shared their sleeping robes, placing them back a distance from the other clan members.

On the following day, Dorik and Orin scouted the nearby forest. They had penetrated the wooded slopes only a short distance when Dorik pointed to the still moist deer droppings. "This is a good sign," he explained. "I suspect the woods are full of deer that feed at the meadow during the night."

By looking for disturbed leaves or needles, they easily and quietly followed the path of the deer.

"I would judge there are four or five of them," the older man whispered. "We're probably wasting our time, but let's follow their trail for a short distance. We'd need at least six hunters to set up an effective ambush."

The trail joined the tracks of other deer before entering a path that displayed countless hoof prints.

"That's odd," Dorik observed. "It's more like the well-worn trail of cattle or bison. Look here. These are the tracks of the long-horned cows."

Orin appeared puzzled as he questioned his father. "Why would the cattle leave the meadow where the grass is so good?"

Dorik thought a moment before answering. "A couple of years ago, I saw a path like this that led to a salt lick. Do you remember? We were out on the plains."

"Yes, I do remember," Orin affirmed. "Those trails were even wider and deeper than this, but of course it was traveled by large herds of bison. Do you think this might lead to a salt bed? Wouldn't we be lucky?"

The two men abandoned their stalking pace to begin jogging along the trail where other paths merged with the earlier hoof prints. After turning a corner, they arrived at a clearing near the base of a barren, red knoll. A full antlered buck bobbed his head up, staring at the intruders. The alert stag snorted a warning before whirling to lead five other deer bounding into the woods beyond the clearing.

Any thought of the deer was soon forgotten. The two hunters ran to the face of the outcropping where they peeled small white crystals of salt from the face of the stones. The salt, from an ancient seabed that millions of years earlier had been pushed up to become a mountain ridge, had been slowly dissolved by seeping rain water and again crystallized by evaporation upon reaching the air.

"We're very lucky indeed. The spirits have truly bestowed their favors on us," was Dorik's observation as he licked his fingers to taste of the mineral they had missed for so long.

* * *

The two men busily peeled slivers of the white crystals from the rocks, storing them in their traveling bags. Even the mud below their feet showed small crystals where the moisture had evaporated.

"We've collected quite a bit," Dorik suggested. "We'll come back someday with the women and let them collect a larger supply. If we locate another clan, we can always barter the salt for flint. We could surely use a new supply."

As the possessor of the only flint hand axe in their small clan, the remark produced a guilt feeling in the younger man.

Upon returning to the campsite, the men handed their supply of salt to Amalee who doled out small pinches to the girls and herself. She then carefully stored the balance in a leather pouch, hanging it from a limb to deter pilfering by the numerous ground squirrels or mice near the camp.

"This is also a good omen," Amalee said to Nomi. "The spirits have selected us to share the pleasures and benefits of their gift. With this salt, we'll be able to cure and preserve any surplus meat the men kill and we'll have fewer hungry days."

The two hunters returned to the nearby forest, searching for game. They located and easily killed a large, fat porcupine.

"If we plan to stay at this camp for a long time," Dorik commented, "we'd probably be wise to not kill too many porcupines unless we need them badly. They usually stay in the same area and would always be available for an emergency. If we know they're nearby, we can always hunt them when the other game is scarce." He then added with a smile, "However, we'll consider this an emergency. I will sure enjoy some roasted meat."

The quills were singed and the skin removed, exposing layers of delicious fat. Forked sticks were driven into the ground and the porcupine was skewered above the hot glowing, coals. As the outer layers browned over the fire, the eager clansmen peeled juicy strips of succulent flesh from the carcass to begin their feast. They silently offered their thanks to the generous Spirit of the Hunt.

With stomachs full, the contented clansmen sat near the fire, singing the ancient lyrics they had learned as small children. They sang only the happier songs for on that occasion they felt secure and comfortable.

As their voices faded at the end of a lyric, Orin's attention was suddenly diverted to the shadows at the outer edge of the firelight. All eyes caught his concern and they all turned to stare into the darkness.

"What was it, Orin? Did you see something?" Nomi asked.

"I'm not sure," he answered, pointing. "I think I saw a pair of eyes just beyond that tree there."

Dorik rose to his feet, and carrying his spear, moved to the edge of the firelight. "It could be some small scavenger that smelled our meat," he suggested. "We'll have to be careful to hang the rest of it well out of reach on this limb near the fire. I'm in no mood to share our food."

Although there was little concern, the fire was maintained considerably brighter during the night. The clansmen slept soundly except for Dorik who occasionally awakened to place additional wood on the fire.

As the darkness of night gave way to the first light of dawn, Dorik called softly to his son. "Orin, take a look over there. I think those were the eyes you saw last night."

Orin rubbed the sleep from his eyes, searching for the object of Dorik's comment. Two wolves, approximately a hundred paces away, sat watching the camp.

"Those are the camp wolves we saw the other day," Orin remarked. "They must have followed us all the way here."

"I don't think they'll be any real threat," Dorik suggested. "We'll just have to be careful to not leave Retta or Carma alone." As the two men watched the motionless animals, Dorik added, "I hate to give up any of our food, but the girls will be safer if the wolves have full stomachs." He then went to the tree cache to tear part of the carcass from the hanging porcupine which he threw in the direction of the animals. Within a few moments the female advanced cautiously to retrieve the morsel. The two wolves then trotted some distance away with their booty before stopping to devour it.

The women were all up when the men returned from watching the wolves consume the meat. He cautioned the girls to not leave the camp alone and to always carry a club.

136

"I don't think we have any great worry, but we shouldn't take chances," Dorik cautioned. "I wish we could have found a cave near here. A cave would be a safer place for the women and would have made this valley a paradise."

"If there had been a good cave here," Amalee said, shaking her head, "some other clan would have found it and all the game would be gone."

"Do you remember that Nordo woman with the clan we saw by the hot springs?" Orin asked, his words directed at Dorik. "She told of people in a far land who lived in wooden caves. What did she mean?"

"I don't know," Dorik answered. "Maybe they lean poles against the cave entrance to support the robes like we do at the grotto."

Orin pondered the thought a few moments. "I don't think so. I think they just piled logs on top of each other, something like a big beaver dam, and then lived under them."

"Do you mean the way we tie poles together and hang robes on them to get out of the rain when we're on the trail?"

Orin was lost in thought for a few moments before answering. "No, I don't think so. I know it would be a big job, but I believe we could build us a shelter without robes that would not only keep the wind and rain out, but would also keep the wolves and other scavengers out."

With the women avidly following his every word, Orin explained to Dorik the idea that was forming in his mind. "If we lean smaller poles side by side against a horizontal pole such as that big old tree that fell over, maybe we could cover it with something that would divert the rain and wind."

Although the leader couldn't completely comprehend the plan, with a desire to please his son, he consented to the group effort. Orin took charge and together the clansmen searched the nearby forest for standing, dead, pine poles. The small slender trees, that had died from lack of sunlight, but had not yet suffered decay, could easily be toppled by group effort. The root structure, having decayed from continuous exposure to soil and moisture, would easily yield to a rocking effort by the workers. Poles were selected that were about as thick as a man's arm which could easily be carried or dragged into camp. The root ends of the poles were placed in the fire to be burned away and were then placed, charred end down, against the large fallen log that wind and erosion had so generously supplied.

The task, which took many days, was interrupted often to hunt or to gather nature's bounty of roots and bulbs. Strawberry plants that flourished along the creek banks of the meadow began to ripen and yield their sweet fruit to the happy women.

"We're going to need longer and better thongs for trapping game," Dorik announced one day. "Those swamp reeds should be good to weave into strong ropes that we can use for hunting."

He had the girls collect bundles of the long reeds that grew from the shallow water near the upper end of the lake. The reeds were stripped into long fibers which were held at one end while the other end was rolled into long twisted strands. While continuously twisting the individual strands, three of those strands were then allowed to intertwine. To the amazement and fascination of the young girls, the intertwining fibers formed into a stout rope. By carefully adding additional fibers to the strands while being twisted, they could be extended to become any length of rope desired. Ropes of various sizes and lengths were made and used both at camp and for hunting.

Small ropes or leather thongs were made into snares that were set out along the rabbit trails. It became necessary to check the traps frequently after the camp wolves learned the snare locations.

On one occasion, as Orin returned to camp after checking his snares, he complained, "Those lazy wolves stole another free meal from one of my snares. They're becoming a real nuisance."

Nomi sympathized with him, adding her own comment. "I guess they're just getting even with you. Remember when the clan took the cow away from the wolves. The spirits just might be giving them some food in return."

After four days of hard labor, collecting logs for their shelter, Dorik and Orin took time to build and set a few large snares along the well-worn trail to the salt lick. Ropes were formed with a small loop at one end. The other end of the ropes were passed through the loop, forming a larger loop. The large loop was adjusted and hung very carefully across the trail in such a way that the lower part of the loop was at chest level to a deer, leaving the top portion well above the animal's head.

"With a little luck," Dorik commented, "we should get us one of the deer we saw at the salt-lick."

"We also saw tracks of the long-horned cows," Orin said. "How would we handle it if one of those got in our snare?"

"I'm afraid the rope isn't strong enough for a fully grown cow," Dorik answered. "We'd probably lose our snare."

After three such snares were set, the hunters moved away from the trail on the downwind side. The two men sat quietly and motionless, concealed behind a growth of dense shrubbery. They waited, silently watching as the sun settled lower toward the western horizon.

"I'm afraid this isn't our lucky day," Orin at last whispered.

Dorik looked critically at his son. "Patience is just as important as strength or cunning. We can't hope for success every day."

The sun settled below the western horizon, bathing only the higher peaks with its red glow. The two men waited quietly. Dorik reached slowly out to touch Orin's arm before moving his finger to his lips to signal silence. An occasional faint snapping sound was heard above the whisper of the light breeze. The two men grew excited as they watched three does and two yearling fawns walking at a steady gait along the trail. At a signal from Dorik, the two men moved quietly back onto the trail, well behind the deer. When in position, Dorik signaled and they began shouting loudly while running toward the deer. The startled animals bolted, racing along the path away from the hunters. The men passed the first snare, noting that it had been dislodged and was hanging uselessly in a shrub. As they neared the second snare, they heard a thrashing sound and ran on to find a doe with her head and one leg entangled in the stout rope. Orin reached the floundering animal first, and with his hunting axe, delivered a stunning blow to the doe's head. He then reached into his pouch, and with his sharp-edged flint knife, opened the throat of the still feebly struggling animal.

The excited women, expressing their praise, met the two hunters as they entered camp carrying the deer hung from a pole supported on their shoulders.

After the carcass was skinned and hung from a nearby tree, the hide was spread to dry on poles near the fire.

That night the clan feasted on the liver and heart of the animal. The head and entrails were delivered to the waiting pair of hungry wolves that came to within a few paces to receive the welcome gift. Orin watched as the animals feasted, and they, in turn, maintained wary eyes on him while gnawing on their unearned supper.

The following morning, Amalee, Nomi and the two sisters went about the task of cutting the deer meat into long, thin strips. The meat was then soaked in a saltwater brine for a short time before being hung near the fire to dry.

Orin and Dorik resumed the task of collecting poles for the shelter. A shallow trench was dug, parallel to and a few feet away from the large fallen tree that served as a ridge beam for the new shelter. The ends of the poles were burned away to adjust the length and were then stacked against each other with one end in the trench and the other against the fallen tree. Soon a broad span was completed.

Dorik carefully studied the structure. "It's very interesting, to say the least, but what's going to keep the rain from leaking through? A cave would be much better."

"Of course, a cave would be better," Orin said, defensively, "but we don't have a cave. We'll build it like a cave though. I plan to collect mud and sod from the lakeshore and pile it on the poles. I think that should keep the rain from falling though."

The older man remained dubious. "How are you going to close the ends of your wooden cave?"

"We'll stack poles across one end, and on the other end we'll hang deer hides to keep the wind from blowing through."

Dorik harbored considerable doubt but labored hard to please both his son and the boy's mother, who eagerly watched the progress. When the project was partially completed, Orin decided to apply mud to the roof. Moist, heavy clay was located and piled on a deerskin which was then carried or dragged to the project. The first effort was disappointing. Some of the mud held in position but much of it oozed between the poles, falling to the ground below.

"What if we piled a layer of willows over the poles?" Dorik asked. "Wouldn't that help hold the mud in position."

"I'm willing to try anything," Orin responded. "We'll try it to see if it works any better."

The women were assigned the task of stripping small willow branches from the bushes nearby which the men carefully placed in layers across the poles. Again they applied the mud with marginal success. Orin then decided to mix marsh grass with the mud to aid in holding it in position. Trying again, the two men became encouraged and soon had a broad area of roof covered. After a couple of days of steady progress their effort was tested by a steady rain that lasted throughout the day. A small fire was moved into the shelter and easily maintained from a wood supply stored beneath the poles. The clan members were encouraged to note that no rain had dripped through the layer of mud, but observed a considerable amount had washed off the surface of the roof.

"In the future, we may have to add more mud," Orin explained. "That can be added at any time."

The storm moved on and the men continued the project with an occasional interruption for hunting. After resetting their snares, they again attempted to drive deer into the traps, but were often forced to return to camp empty-handed. The traps had either been avoided by the deer or the animals managed to slip through the noose and escape. It was only after several unsuccessful days of hunting that a large buck, that had tangled his velvet-covered horns in the stout rope loop, was caught and killed. Again the women were put to work cutting and drying the meat.

After the shelter project was completed, a new problem appeared, adding frustration to Orin's hopes. The late spring sun beat down on the mud, drying and cracking the surface. A passing thunderstorm crossed the valley, again testing the roof. Orin watched helplessly as muddy water dripped from several of the poles inside the shelter. Amalee attempted to console her son by emphasizing that she considered even the leaking shelter a tremendous improvement over the wet and cold they had experienced on the trail.

- 16 -

Every passing day seemed to restore to Amalee some of the strength that her illness had stolen. She gradually gained a little weight and the darkness around her eyes disappeared. She smiled more often and took a greater interest in teaching her daughters the crafts of the clan.

"It's time you girls learn how to weave baskets," Amalee told her daughters. "If we're to stay here at the meadow for a while, we're going to need storage containers."

"I'd like to watch also," Nomi volunteered. "I never learned to weave them like my mother did."

Nomi and the sisters watched as the older woman selected choice reeds from the marsh, and with deft hands, wove the reeds into crude baskets for gathering food. The girls were soon emulating their tutor and accumulated an assortment of strong reed baskets which were hung from the ceiling of the shelter.

"I also want you to learn how to prepare skins into soft leather for making garments," Amalee told her daughters.

The women constructed a pit in the clay mud near the lakeshore which was filled with wood ashes and water which would form a lye solution. After the dried deerskin had then soaked in the lye solution sufficiently, the coarse hair could easily be pulled free. The skin could then be scraped, rubbed and worked until it was soft and pliable. The tanned hides could then be cut and shaped into body garments and boots. Leather thongs could be used to sew together the pieces of soft leather. Sharp pointed tips of deer horn served as awls to puncture the holes in the leather through which the thongs were laced.

"This deerskin will make a fine summer body jacket," Amalee explained. "We'll leave the hair on the ones we prepare for winter use."

* * *

On one of the women's food-gathering excursions, Amalee stopped to examine the bank of the stream below the lake. With her stick, she pried loose samples of the heavy clay and tested the texture with her fingers.

"This looks very much like the clay we use to make our pottery back at the winter cave," she explained. "We could sure use some cooking pots."

"I remember seeing clay bowls baking in the fires back at the cave," Nomi stated. "Can you make those kind of pots from this heavy mud?"

"I'm not sure this is the right kind of clay, but it's worth a try," Amalee answered. "We'll select only the smooth pliable type."

Each of the girls carried a basket full of the heavy clay back to the camp. The women returned to the stream to locate rocks of various sizes, selecting those which were rounded and smooth. After carrying the rocks to the camp, and following Amalee's instructions, they worked the damp clay into a firm, pliable texture and carefully molded a layer to the rounded portion of the rock. A flattened section on top would later serve as the base of the bowl. Extra fires were established surrounding the clay molds. The heat was applied slowly at first, and then gradually increased until glowing hot coals surrounded the molds. As the clay baked and hardened, the mold would loosen from the rock. Those that didn't crack were then allowed to cool slowly by the fire. Failures far outnumbered the few successes, but eventually the proud women displayed several clay pots that could be used for cooking or storing liquids.

The small camp in the remote valley was beginning to enjoy some of the comforts and conveniences of the winter cave which seemed to them very far away.

One evening, the women prepared a meal of stewed deer meat, water lily and cattail roots, flavored with burdock and dandelion roots. The mixture bubbled in a large clay pot near the fire with mouth watering aromas teasing the nostrils of the men who waited anxiously nearby.

"We've got all the comforts of the grotto," Dorik said.

* * *

After the meal of venison stew, the six clansmen sat comfortably on the logs that were situated at the fire's edge. The sun had finished its daily journey, and as it sank behind the low western hills, it cast a reddish hue on the billowing clouds high overhead.

"What a beautiful sunset," Amalee observed. "The Sun God is reminding us of his power and that he will return tomorrow."

Retta moved to Amalee's side to affectionately embrace her mother. "Where does the Sun God go at night?"

"I've told you many times," her mother replied. "The fire goes out, and then during the night the sun creeps back across the sky and rebuilds its fire so it can rise again and warm us during the day."

The small girl's face displayed a puzzled frown. "If the sun follows us when we take our long trips, how do the clans at the seashore get along without the light while it's up here with us?"

Amalee patted the girl on the shoulder. "Goodness sakes, child. You ask too many questions. There are some things the Gods want to keep secret. We just have to trust the Gods and not question the wisdom of their actions."

"I like the part you tell about the stars being the spirits of all the brave hunters who died. I just love to look at the stars at night. Sometimes I think I can hear the spirits talking."

Orin added his own thoughts to the conversation. "I like to think that I've located which of those stars are the spirits of our ancestors. I believe our ancestral spirits control our luck and keep us safe during the hunt. I also think those spirits follow and protect us, both night and day."

Dorik looked at his son and then at Amalee. "I think that sometimes our enemies have even stronger spirits looking after them." The comment brought silence to the small group and they sat for a long time without talking. At last the older man again spoke. "We've got to think about moving on if we're ever going to join another clan."

"Do we have to?" Orin asked. "The hunting is still good here and we don't know what kind of clan we might find.

144

We might accidentally encounter Agar and I know he'd try to kill me and take Nomi back with him."

"In any event, we'll have to go south before winter when the heavy snow arrives," Dorik argued. "Maybe we can get back before Agar does and we can find another clan farther down the river to join up with."

"Why do we even have to go back south?" Orin protested. "Why can't we spend the winter here?"

Dorik studied his son, shaking his head negatively. "You're not thinking clearly," he said. "No one could ever survive the winter up in this country. The snow gets very deep. On some of our early spring trips, I've seen snow on the north slopes that was as deep as a man's head. No, lad, it's out of the question. No one has ever survived a winter up here."

"Where do the deer and cattle go in the winter?" the desperate young man questioned.

"I don't know," Dorik admitted. "The reindeer and bison migrate to some far-off land. I don't know where the deer and cattle go, but I'm sure that it gets so cold here that we could never survive."

"I don't want to take Nomi back to any place near our old winter cave," Orin objected. "I'd rather die here than lose Nomi to that evil monster." His emotional words produced worried expressions on the faces of the women.

Dorik again shook his head negatively. "I can understand your concern, and of course I can never return to the old clan either, but there are other lives here for us to consider. Your mother and your sisters would perish here. Maybe we can find a clan that spends the winters farther south at some grotto far from the clan of Agar. Maybe we can find a grotto near the sea just for the six of us. We should now be concerned with drying as much meat as possible for our future journey."

The conversation ceased but their thoughts dwelled on the implications of their situation and possible solutions.

The next day, Orin made his familiar trek, examining and resetting his snares. It had been a couple of days since his last success. The previous day he had found only a small ball of soft fur in the tightened noose, evidence that the camp wolves had eaten his catch. He was approaching the site of the earlier loss when he was alerted by a deep growl. Raising his spear to a stalking position, he advanced slowly. As he passed a shrub, it became immediately clear what had happened. The male wolf had returned to the scene of his earlier meal and had become caught in the same rope snare. The wolf growled savagely and drew back, tightening the loop ever tighter around his neck.

He must have become caught just a few moments ago, Orin reasoned. A wolf would be smart enough to chew through the rope and escape.

As Orin advanced to within a few feet of the snarling animal, the wolf bared his teeth and lunged. With an automatic reaction, Orin drove the spear deep into the shoulder of the wolf and saw it crumble to the ground in a series of death spasms.

"Now maybe I won't have my rabbits stolen from my snares," the young hunter said aloud. "You've stolen your last rabbit."

After resetting his snare, Orin dragged the carcass back to camp where the skin was removed and hung to dry. The canine fangs were broken from the jaw to serve as trophies and the carcass was thrown to the outer edge of the camp for ravens to scavenge.

- 17 -

While the two men stood watching the cattle grazing at the far side of the meadow, Dorik remarked to his son, "If we just had all the hunters of the clan here with us, we could probably kill one of those cows. They're getting quite fat and just one would give us enough meat to last for several moons."

"Do you see that cow grazing away from the others over near the edge of the meadow?" Orin asked.

"Yes. What are you thinking?"

Orin pointed to the wooded area across the meadow. "I would guess that she has a new calf bedded down in the brush near the woods. Why don't we go looking for it?"

"A good observation, son," Dorik proudly commented. "Maybe this is our lucky day."

The two hunters, to avoid alerting the grazing cattle, circled far around them. They searched for a long time exploring each shrub along the meadow's edge. Dorik finally offered a suggestion. "I'm afraid that, if there is a calf, it's too well hidden. I suggest we climb a tree where we can see a larger area and then wait for the cow to show us the location. Sooner or later she'll return to nurse the calf."

The two men selected trees some distance apart near the edge of the timbered slope. Orin selected a large pine with sparse foliage and, after climbing to a large limb, seated himself.

As the sun advanced into afternoon, Orin became increasingly uncomfortable and was convinced they had misjudged the cow. Perhaps she hasn't calved yet and we're only wasting our time, he reasoned. Or perhaps she's already calved and lost it to a predator. There's also the possibility that she isn't even going to calve.

Orin was about to admit defeat and locate his father when he noticed the cow turn and face his direction. He waited and again was about to give up when the cow began moving toward the wooded area. He waited quietly, watching the cow move through a brushy area and was then delighted to see the well concealed calf struggle to its feet to instinctively probe the underside of the cow, searching for milk. The young hunter impatiently waited for the calf to nurse. When at last it finished, and was again bedded down, he saw the cow return to the meadow to continue grazing.

Dorik, who had also witnessed the location, joined his son at the site of the young calf. The newborn animal lay motionless with his head resting flat against the ground. The color blended so well with the surrounding tall grass that the men understood why they had missed it on their earlier search. Rushing forward together, they grasped the neck of the calf and tied its legs together with a stout leather thong.

"I'd like to try something different," Dorik suggested. "If we keep the calf alive and tie it to a log at the edge of the meadow, and then keep moving the log and calf toward our camp, perhaps we can entice the cow away from the other cattle and can then somehow kill her."

"That sounds like a great idea," Orin agreed, "but how can two of us kill a big cow, even if we get her all alone?"

"I don't know yet, but we'll figure something out. Maybe we can lure her out into the marsh where she'll have trouble maneuvering in the deep mud."

"If the calf is tied, won't some large hunting animal kill it?" Orin asked.

"The cow should be able to protect her calf from most attackers," Dorik suggested. "The chance of getting all that meat is worth the risk."

Dorik and Orin moved the calf a short distance toward camp where, with a long rope, they tied it to a small log they had dragged onto the meadow. The movement of the two men and struggling calf caught the attention of the grazing herd of cattle. The bellowing cow was the first to run toward her offspring, followed by the remaining cattle.

"Here they come," Orin shouted as he began running toward the edge of the meadow.

The men quickly retreated to the forest and were prepared to quickly climb a tree. The cattle lingered near the calf, taking turns sniffing or bawling their call of distress. The old dominant bull, with a couple of younger bulls, took up defensive positions between the cows and the two hunters who waited at a safe distance. Orin wondered whether the slim chance of killing a cow was worth the risk of losing the calf but was willing to give his father's plan a chance.

"What if the cattle stay close to the calf?" Orin asked.

"If we worry about all the things that might happen in this life," Dorik cautioned, "we would never accomplish anything. Sooner or later the animals will have to leave the calf to graze."

For the balance of the day the hunters watched the cow nervously guarding her calf. As the other grazing cattle moved farther from the calf, the frustrated cow trotted back and forth in a display of divided emotions. Each time the cow left the calf to rejoin the herd, the two men ran to drag both calf and log a few paces closer to camp. And as before, each time the cow ran to protect the calf, the men quickly retreated to the safety of the woods. The sun was disappearing below the horizon when the two men decided to return to camp.

"We can't do much more before dark," the older man reasoned. "It would be too dangerous. We'll come back tomorrow."

The two men arose early the next morning and proceeded toward the location of the calf. As they approached, they saw the mother cow standing defiantly near her offspring while watching the female camp wolf that waited a safe distance away.

"That cursed wolf is going to ruin our plans," the older man muttered. "I had hoped that when you killed her mate she would leave the area."

Orin studied the wolf as she retreated a short distance from the two hunters. "Look at her belly," he observed. "I think she's had pups. That's why she hasn't left the area. If we locate the den, we can kill the pups and maybe then she'll leave us alone."

Dorik smiled at the thought. "Good luck. You might also catch a cloud. You have about the same chance."

The ridicule bothered Orin and he quietly resolved to try to locate the den to vindicate his reasoning.

As long as the wolf was visible, the cow remained close to the calf, depriving the men of the opportunity of moving the calf and log. Dorik became impatient and returned to camp, but Orin watched from a distance, determined to monitor the situation. The wolf, after waiting nearby for a considerable time, finally decided to abandon the calf. She turned and trotted slowly toward the woods.

Orin followed at a distance he judged would not alert the wolf, but after entering the forest area, the young hunter was unable to follow the animal's track. Dorik was right, he begrudgingly admitted to himself. With the entire forest to search, I have very little chance of finding the den.

Orin wandered aimlessly through the unfamiliar wooded area, exploring for game and for future hunting locations. A startled doe with young fawns bounded over fallen logs before disappearing into the brushy area. The young hunter quietly followed the deer tracks, knowing the futility of pursuit. As he stepped over a large, fallen, decaying log, his attention was drawn to the vivid contrast of a few still damp overturned leaves. He examined the ground further before discovering a shallow opening beneath the log. On hands and knees he peered into the darkness of the den and saw several small pups huddled together.

"So this is where you hid your litter," he mumbled half aloud. "I did catch that cloud that Dorik thought impossible."

He nervously looked back across his shoulder, expecting an imminent, furious attack from the mother wolf. She is apparently searching elsewhere for food, he reasoned while continuing to cautiously study the area. Lying prone near the den opening, and after placing his hunting axe where he could quickly grab it, he reached in to pull the five small, furry creatures to the surface near his shoulder. After placing them in his leather game pouch, and keeping his spear in ready position, he walked rapidly back to camp.

As he approached the shelter, he called to his sisters who were weaving baskets near the fire. "Come see what I have."

The two young girls dropped their unfinished baskets to run to his side. "What is it?" they begged. "What do you have in there?"

Orin lowered the pouch to the ground, loosening the cord to expose the squirming pups.

"Oh, Orin, they're darling. They're so cute. Can I have them?" Retta pleaded. "Oh please, Orin, please."

"No, Retta," he answered. "I'm sorry, but I'm going to kill them so the mother wolf will go away. I just wanted you to see them first."

The young girl ran crying toward her mother who emerged from the shelter. "Mama, please don't let Orin kill the wolf pups. Please, Mama."

Amalee walked to where the small creatures tumbled across each other in awkward efforts to walk. She smiled as she watched the animals and then her expression became serious. "You shouldn't have brought them back, Orin. You should have killed them at the den. Your sister is now upset and doesn't understand that they won't survive anyway."

Orin looked sympathetically at his younger sister who sobbed at her mother's side. "She could play with them for a little while. I can always destroy them tomorrow."

"If the mother wolf finds them here, it could be very dangerous," the woman reasoned. "You know how vicious a wolf can be when defending her young."

"All right, I'll get rid of them." Orin realized he had made a mistake in letting his sisters see the small creatures. Even if the mother wolf abandons her pups, he reasoned, the girls are bound to be disappointed when the animals die from lack of milk. Before departing he allowed the girls to play with the pups for a short while and then, over the protests of his two half sisters, he placed them in a basket and proceeded back toward the woods.

As he carried the young wolf pups away from camp an interesting thought crept into his mind. Maybe I can use the pups to lure the mother wolf into a trap and get rid of her also.

As he entered the forest area near the den, his mind experimented with ideas of how to accomplish the task. There was no doubt in his mind that, with his spear, he could successfully meet the savage rush of the wolf, but there was always a chance that he could get hurt by her slashing fangs. He considered the technique that was often used to kill a doe, whereby the hunters would tie the newborn fawn at the foot of a large tree, where, while waiting in the heavy branches above, they could drop onto the unsuspecting doe as she approached her fawn.

How dumb can a deer be? he pondered. The stupid animals will never look up into a tree above them. A wolf, however, would see me in the tree and try to attack me. Maybe I can use that to my advantage. I'll be ready for her.

He placed the basket containing the sleeping pups against a tree near the den before climbing onto a large limb that extended horizontally a little more than a man's height above the ground. As he waited with spear poised, his thoughts became occupied with the disappointment of his two sisters.

If we could keep the mother wolf alive for a few days, he reasoned, she could nurse the pups until they're weaned. He considered some of the problems. I could always make a snare and catch her, but I wouldn't be able to handle her without her attacking me. If I leave her in the snare, she would soon chew away the rope.

Orin finally thought of a possible solution. While setting a snare over the basket, he worked nervously, knowing that the wolf might return momentarily. After securing the rope to a limb, he descended from the tree to set the loop.

Although anticipating the return of the wolf, he was startled to hear the rushing sound of the animal. Turning quickly, he saw the female wolf racing toward him with fangs bared. As he jumped to pull himself onto the limb the wolf also leaped. Orin, by grasping a higher limb, barely managed to avoid the slashing teeth of the aggrieved animal. After several more futile leaps, the wolf abandoned the hunter, turning her attention to the pups. Orin reached down to grasp the end of the snare line that was still attached to the limb below. Waiting until the mother wolf reached her head into the basket to retrieve a pup, Orin pulled sharply on the rope, tightening the loop around the animal's neck and one leg. By pulling aggressively on the rope, he held the wolf suspended above the basket of pups. After tying the rope to a higher limb, and carefully avoiding the teeth of the snarling animal, he jumped safely to the ground. The wolf struggled to the limit of the rope restraint.

There must be some way to tie her and hold her beyond the range of those teeth, Orin reasoned. As he pondered the problem, the solution became apparent. He first located a ten-foot-long pole about the size of his wrist. He then removed a heavy leather thong from his carrying pouch, both ends of which he tied to the end of the pole, forming a loop of about a foot diameter. Several times he attempted to slip the loop over the head of the wolf, but with each attempt the wolf snapped her bared teeth at the pole. Continuing his effort until the animal relaxed from exhaustion, Orin then managed to successfully maneuver the loop over the wolf's head. By rotating the pole, the thong became twisted tighter and tighter until it gripped the animal's neck snugly. With his free hand, he then loosened the rope that had earlier held the wolf suspended. When the wolf was lowered to the ground, she again tried to attack her captor but was easily restrained at a safe distance by the pole and leather thong. By occasionally twisting or untwisting the pole, a snug loop was maintained around the uncooperative animal's neck. Slowly, while carrying the basket and spear, Orin managed to drag the uncooperative wolf toward camp.

When within shouting distance, he called for help. "Nomi, Carma," he shouted. "Someone come help me."

The two younger girls ran along the lakeshore to meet Orin as he struggled to move the animal in the desired direction.

"Stay away from the wolf," he cautioned. "I'm trying to take her to our camp. You carry the basket of pups."

Carma carried the basket while Retta showered her brother with questions. "Can we keep the pups, Orin? Will the puppies be able to nurse the mama wolf? Can I have one all for myself? Please, Orin, please."

"You ask too many questions, sister dear," he replied. "I don't know whether the mother wolf will live or not, and even if she does, I don't know whether Dorik will allow us keep her."

Upon reaching camp, Amalee and Nomi emerged from the shelter to witness the excitement.

Dorik, returning from a scouting foray, approached the group. He listened to the details of the capture, and after being questioned by the girls, he consented. "It's up to Orin. If he's willing to look after the wolf, and if you girls stay completely away from where she's tied, I guess it should be all right for a while. We probably have enough meat scraps to keep her alive, but if we run short of meat, we'll have to get rid of her."

The girls were thrilled, and Retta, who was usually a little cool to Dorik, ran to his side to throw her arms around his waist. "Oh, thank you, thank you. I'll take good care of the puppies. Can I have one, just for me?"

Dorik, yielding to the unaccustomed display of affection, responded, "Yes, you can have one, but only until they get big enough to become wild. They'll probably leave camp by then, or become vicious, in which case we'll have to get rid of them anyway."

The girls joyfully played with the pups while Orin tied the wooden pole and wolf to a nearby tree. Orin later carried the pups to the mother wolf and also left a supply of meat and water within reach of her.

The following morning, upon inspecting the wolf, Orin discovered she had chewed partially through the wooden pole. She had eaten the meat and apparently taken some water. He improvised a second pole and loop, and, with Dorik's help, replaced the first. When left alone, the mother wolf accepted her pups for nursing, but remained aggressive if anyone approached.

Nomi met Orin as he later delivered the pups to his sisters. "The girls are so happy," she said. "I'm so glad that Dorik let them keep the pups. I wonder how the girls will react when we have a new baby in the clan?"

Orin stopped to stare at the girl. "What do you mean? Are you telling me something?"

Nomi's smile became a little more serious. "I don't know for sure, but I haven't had the moon curse for a long time. My mother said it was a sign that a baby is growing in a woman. I hope you're pleased."

Orin lowered the basket of pups to the ground and took her in his arms. "Of course, I'm pleased. How wonderful. Someday he'll become a great hunter."

"Maybe he'll be a she," Nomi countered. "Perhaps it was a female spirit that entered my body."

Orin pondered the thought for a moment before replying. "It's going to be a boy. I just know it will." He allowed his mind to imagine the hunting games that he would someday play with his son.

Later in the day, the log and calf were again moved closer to camp and the long leather thong was untangled to permit the calf greater freedom. As she had done earlier, the cow periodically left the other cattle to be near the calf, allowing it to nurse.

Dorik explained his plan to Orin on how he hoped to kill the cow. "If we move the calf out on the marsh near the lake, the cow will probably wade out into the deep mud to be near her calf. A heavy cow should sink in deeper than we would so maybe we can get close enough to use our spears."

It was still dark when Orin was aroused from sleep by the distant distressed bellowing of the cattle on the meadow. The sound was closer than he would have expected, and as he climbed from his sleeping robe, he saw the outline of Dorik, silhouetted against the glowing coals of the fire.

As Dorik added wood to the embers, he commented, "There's something out there that has really upset the cattle. I wish we had some moonlight. I can't see anything."

"Could the cows be upset because of the calf?" Orin asked.

"No, I don't think so. They've already accepted that situation. I wonder if a bear or a pack of wolves might be after the calf."

"The position of the stars indicate that it should be morning soon," Orin said. "We'll find out then."

After Nomi and Amalee awakened, the adults all sat near the fire, waiting for the first glow of daylight and speculating on the cause of the disturbance.

As the first morning light penetrated the valley, the two men took their spears and cautiously advanced a short distance toward the meadow. "I think I can see the cattle over where we left the calf," Orin said, pointing.

They waited, until, with increased light, they saw the mother of the captured calf lying motionless on the meadow. The other animals nervously milled around the downed cow, bellowing their alarm and directing their attention toward the wooded area.

"Something killed our cow before we could," Dorik observed. "Let's move to where we can see better."

The men advanced cautiously through the brush, following the lake shore in an effort to not distract the cattle herd. As they moved to a favorable position, Dorik stopped abruptly, pointing his spear in the direction dominating the cattle's attention. "Look over by that willow bush," he whispered. "It's a large tiger. It must have killed the cow and was then driven away by the bulls. I suppose the tiger is waiting until the cattle leave so he can have his meal."

Orin studied the huge cat whose attention remained directed toward the nearest large bull. "I should think the tigers would be out on the plains, following the bison herds," he commented. "I was hoping they wouldn't come into this valley."

"I'm afraid we have a problem," the older man said. "So long as there are cattle here in the valley, the tiger will probably also stay. We should be very careful. Tigers don't usually stalk people, but you never know. We can't take any chances."

The hunters watched and waited from their concealed position until, as expected, the cattle finally accepted the death of the cow and ceased their vigil. Within moments after the old bull led the other cattle away from the dead cow, the tiger moved to claim his prize. The two men watched as the large cat, ignoring the calf, ripped open the stomach of the cow to feast on the liver and other viscera of its victim.

Later in the day the tiger dragged the uneaten remains of the carcass into the woods, providing an opportunity for the two hunters to salvage what was left of their great plans. They cautiously moved out and quickly returned to camp with the calf, the fate of which had earlier been determined by the death of its mother.

An increased degree of nervousness gripped the small group on the shore of the lake. Extra wood was stockpiled near the fire, and for the next few nights the flames were maintained at a higher than normal level. The women were instructed to leave camp only during the middle of the day and to stay together when gathering food. The two hunters also walked together while setting and inspecting their snares.

After several days, the absence of any new signs of the tiger allowed tensions to ease.

"I think our tiger may have moved out to the plains," Orin observed.

"I wouldn't count on it," Dorik cautioned. "Even if it moved on, it might return if it becomes hungry. We should still maintain our precautions."

The summer days passed with increased activity by all the members of the small clan. Ripened berries were gathered by the women for the pleasure of all. Hunting continued successfully with an ever increasing stockpile of dried meat. The pups were growing at an amazing rate and were following the girls on most of their activities. The mother wolf remained sullen, but when left alone, continued to allow the pups to nurse. Retta began offering small scraps of meat to the pups and was pleased to watch the small playful creatures chew on the morsels. The girls, when not gathering food, often romped and tumbled with the pups as they begged for attention.

"This boy puppy is mine," Retta announced to Carma. "He's my very own and I'm going to give him a name."

"I don't care," responded the older sister. "Mother said they'll all run away someday so we shouldn't be unhappy when it happens."

"Mine won't. Mine will stay with me forever. I just know he will. I'm going to name him Dorg."

"What kind of a name is that?" Carma teased. "That's a man's name. I'm going to name mine Fluffy."

Amalee overheard the bickering and said, "I'm going to name them Trouble. You girls have been neglecting your work ever since Orin brought those pups into camp."

As the two men returned from inspecting their snares, they paused to look out across the meadow.

"I can't tell for sure," Dorik commented, "but I think another one of the cows is missing from the herd. I suspect the tiger is still in the area."

"I haven't seen any tracks or spoor," Orin remarked. "Maybe when winter approaches, he'll move on."

"And that's what we should do also," Dorik added. "I know you'd like to stay here all winter, but I get nervous just thinking about it."

"And it makes me very nervous thinking about losing Nomi," argued the younger man. "I'd rather gamble on staying here than take a chance of meeting Agar."

"I agree that we want to avoid him, and I've given it a lot of thought. Life has been pretty good here in the valley. I don't know whether we could survive the entire winter here, but if we stockpile enough food and wood, and have the women make us extra heavy garments from the deer hides, we might have a chance."

Orin looked surprised and pleased. "Then you'll agree to us staying?"

Dorik didn't answer for a considerable time. "We'll prepare and plan for it, but if the situation looks bad when the leaves begin to fall, we'll depart and look for a new home down near the sea."

Orin couldn't conceal his pleasure. "I'm sure we can survive the snow. Everything will work out fine."

With the decision made and announced, the little band of adventurers increased their efforts at gathering and storing the food that would probably be badly needed during the coming moons. A large supply of firewood was gathered and piled near the shelter entrance. After Dorik made a mental inventory of the stockpiled food and supplies, they all felt a little more secure facing the unknown.

Orin and Dorik were met by the girls as the two men returned from inspecting their snares. Carma outdistanced her sister as they ran to meet the men. "The old mother wolf is gone," she announced. "I think she chewed through the pole."

The men accompanied the girls to verify the loss. Dorik examined the gnawed stub of the pole. "Maybe it's just as well." He then looked down at the five wolf pups that played near his feet. "If we spend the winter here, we'll need to reduce the number of mouths to feed. I'm surprised the pups didn't follow the old mother wolf."

"Please, Dorik," the younger sister pleaded. "They won't eat much. I'll eat less if you'll just let them stay."

"They'll probably leave anyway when they get a little older. They can only stay so long as they can live on the waste scraps and bones. When we have to feed them our dried meat, we'll have to get rid of them."

- 18 -

As summer advanced into fall, each morning brought an increased chill to the air. Dorik and Orin were pleased to observe the ever mounting supply of dried meat that was stored in pouches and hung from the ceiling of the shelter. Baskets of roots rested along the wall and pottery containers held a supply of seeds that had been stripped from the grasses that bordered the lake. The seeds could be ground into meal that, when added to water and cooked in a pottery container, became quite palatable. Several apple trees were located that produced a generous supply of small, tart fruit that lasted many moons in storage. The numerous black walnut trees that grew along the boundary of the meadow yielded vast quantities of nuts. They all agreed the spirits had been generous and believed the harvest to be a good omen of the future.

"The Sun God is moving farther south on his daily journey across the sky," the clan leader noted. "I hope he won't leave us to follow the other clans back to the caves."

"If the animals can survive here, we should, also," was Orin's defense.

Dorik harbored considerable doubt as each day brought them closer to the test.

The two hunters were in the timber, setting snares, while the women remained busy with the task of tanning and conditioning the many hides that had accumulated during the summer.

Amalee and Nomi were suddenly alerted by the growling and snapping jaws of the young wolf pups. Upon leaving the shelter, the women were startled and frightened to see a small black bear engaged in dragging down the line where meat had been hung to dry. The women began shouting loudly while throwing sticks at the preoccupied beast, and the young wolves continued their ineffective attack until, with a swipe of its powerful paw, the bear sent one of the pups catapulting across the ground. The continued attack by the women and remaining young wolves finally convinced the bear that it was in hostile territory. Glancing back at his attackers, the small bear loped off toward the forest with the remaining pups nipping at his legs.

When the two hunters returned and learned of the problem, they expressed their concern and their gratitude for the part played by the young pups.

"There may be some merit in having some friendly wolves around camp," Dorik remarked. "I've noticed we haven't been troubled by many small scavengers. Maybe the pups will earn their keep."

The injured pup was put in the care of Retta to be nursed back to health. No bones appeared to be broken and the child was delighted and proud to play nurse to the bruised animal.

The remaining leaves had fallen from the deciduous plants, and each day Dorik nervously watched large formations of geese moving south. The sky had taken on a gray mood with a cold wind sending occasional shivers through the body of the older hunter. As he studied the sky, strong doubts lingered about the earlier decision, although he felt the time had passed to even consider leaving the valley. The greatest worry was the unknown. He had never heard of anyone staying all winter in the north country. If the friendly spirits that controlled their lives should desert them now, he felt, how could they ever survive? What awesome and powerful creatures would possess these mountains and valleys once the snow began to fall?

Dorik tried to reconcile his fears, accepting what he felt was the lesser of evils. He knew that another encounter with Agar would precipitate the loss of Nomi and the girls as well as the probable death or mutilation of his son. Even if they had departed earlier in the year to search for a new clan or cave near the sea, the chances of survival were no more than marginal.

Whatever happens, will happen, Dorik thought. We'll just try to make the best of whatever the future brings.

An attempt was made to improve the shelter. After experimenting, an effort was made to reduce the erosion of soil from the roof. Orin supervised a project of collecting green pine needle boughs that were then layered over the dirt slope of the shelter. By starting at the bottom and piling layers of pine boughs with the needle tips sloped downward, it was discovered that the rainwater was carried down the roof without reaching the dirt below. Layers of the green limbs were also stacked against the unused end of the shelter, and deer hides were laced together and hung from the open end as protection against the cold wind. There was adequate ventilation for the use of a small fire inside.

The women fashioned boots from deer hides and made additional warm and comfortable garments which were laced together with deerskin thongs.

Several storms arrived from the northwest, depositing shallow layers of fresh snow. The men found the new snow a distinct advantage. They could easily locate the frequently travelled routes of rabbits and deer. Often they could follow a fresh set of rabbit tracks that terminated in a shallow burrow where, with spears, they could easily extract a fresh meal for the small clan.

"That last storm was no worse than the ones we often have near the winter cave," Orin commented to his father. "Perhaps a little colder, but about the same amount of snow."

"Just you wait," his father chided. "I suspect that before this winter is over you'll see all the snow you'll ever want to see. I don't think we're really into winter yet."

As the days passed, the hunters became increasingly successful at snaring deer on the path to the salt lick.

Dorik had been watching the cattle forage for grass on the meadow. "I'd still like to get us one of those big cows," the older man remarked. "We'd then have meat enough to last well into the winter."

"I've also thought about that," Orin agreed, "but until a cow gives birth to a calf, I can't see any way to isolate one of them."

The members of the small clan often sat at night near the small fire inside the shelter. The five wolf pups, fully grown but still awkward, shared the shelter and loved to be petted as they rested their heads on the laps of the clansmen. With the passing days, the hunters became increasingly aware of a change in the young wolves. The animals were constantly challenging each other for dominance, and occasionally growled at any clansman who might be chewing on a strip of dried deer meat.

Dorik became concerned with the change. "I was afraid this would happen," he commented. "It seems as though they're becoming more aggressive as they grow older. We'll either have to get rid of them soon or do something to change their attitude. I want everyone to keep a willow handy and if a pup growls at you I want you to give him a good, sharp whack. Perhaps we can teach them who their masters are."

The discipline appeared to work. Each time a clansmen was challenged, a willow would be sharply administered to the rump of the aggressive pup. The offended young wolf would usually whimper and cower in the shelter corner for a short time before emerging in a more cooperative and playful mood.

The winter weather intensified. A new storm moved in and by nightfall the snow was falling steadily. The clansmen banked the fire inside their shelter before nestling comfortably in their sleeping robes. When morning delivered the first light, Orin glanced out through the shelter opening. He arose from his sleeping robe to gain a better view of the strange scenery outside. The snow was three feet deep and still falling. Adding wood to the fire, he waited for the other clansmen to awaken so as to share the spectacular sight. When all were awake, the girls became enthused about playing outside. They threw themselves into the snow and made snowballs to throw at each other. The wolf pups also joined them in play, pouncing on the girls in mock attack. Nomi and Amalee were pleased to see the girls enjoying themselves, but Orin and Dorik pondered the consequence of such a depth of snow.

As the sky brightened later in the day, the temperature turned sharply colder with an increasing wind. Orin and Dorik laced on extra robes before emerging to explore the new and different world. An effort was made to search for the snares that had earlier been set, but they soon abandoned the effort. Returning to the shelter, they accepted the situation and decided to enjoy the comfort of the fire.

The children persuaded Dorik and Amalee to repeat the stories that had been told for generations. Retta occasionally corrected the storyteller if the narration varied slightly from what she remembered.

When the adults became bored with reciting the old familiar tales, Dorik and Orin engaged each other in a challenging game that was traditionally popular with the hunters during the long winter moons in the cave. Two parallel rows of shallow holes were dug in the soil with a larger hole at each end. Small pebbles were placed in the larger holes and the players took turns advancing their pebbles down and back the parallel row of holes. Each player would hold one, two, or three pebbles in the closed palm of his hand and the total stones of the two players would determine how many holes the player must advance the pebble of his choice. Whenever a player's pebble would fall in a hole occupied by the opponents pebble, that pebble would be captured. Eventually a player would capture all of his opponent's pebbles. The game became a test of wits. The two men played and laughed while the two sisters lay on the ground, watching. Finally the men tired of the game, allowing the young girls to play.

"The deep snow has helped us in one respect," observed Amalee. "We don't get that draft of cold air that often blew through the bottom of the shelter."

Orin agreed, adding a suggestion. "Maybe we could pile the snow even deeper and cover the other holes."

The two men began a project of packing additional snow against the few remaining cracks, returning often to the interior of the shelter to warm themselves at the fires's edge.

The following morning the clansmen awakened early and nestled in their bed robes waiting for the light of day.

"It seems the winter nights are longer than I remember at the cave," Amalee commented to Dorik, "and the sun travels lower across the sky. Maybe it's traveling south a little more each day and will eventually leave us to go back to the valley of the caves."

Dorik responded by reaching out to rest a hand on his son's shoulder. "Orin said something once that makes sense. He said that, if the animals in this valley can survive through the winter, we should be able to do the same."

When the sun at last climbed above the horizon, it shone brightly through a cloudless sky. Although the air was crisp and cold, the clansmen were all anxious to get out of the shelter. They tied on the heavy boots and garments the women had created earlier, finding the clothes warm but cumbersome.

Amalee, Nomi, and the girls decided to try making their way to the watercress spring. Orin and Dorik accompanied them while on their way to check their snares. The men took turns breaking trail through the deep snow and they all laughed and joked about the strange new world through which they struggled. The young wolves romped and played, lunging ahead of their masters. Upon reaching the watercress spring, everyone was amazed that the crystal clear water was not frozen.

"I thought we'd have to dig through the snow to find the watercress," Amalee remarked. "The Storm God must have protected this small area."

Orin pointed to the several hoof prints leading to and from the watercress bed. "Look at the tracks," he remarked. "Perhaps the Storm God saved this pond as a winter feeding place for the deer."

"Or saved it for us," Dorik countered.

Orin stooped to dip his hand in the spring. "Feel how warm the water is," he remarked. "Last summer this was the coldest water in the valley, and now that the lake and stream have frozen over, this water feels warmer. That must be why there is no snow. I think it melts as fast as it falls into the water."

Leaving the women to fill their gathering baskets with the watercress, the men began following the fresh deer tracks into the woods. The young wolves accompanied the men, occasionally lunging out in front of the struggling hunters.

"We could never surprise a deer with these pesky pups running ahead of us," Dorik complained.

After they entered the woods, and had struggled through the snow for only a short distance, they heard the commotion of a small herd of startled deer. The hunters, struggling toward the sound, watched the five young, excited wolves lunging ahead of them in pursuit of the quarry.

"We'll never catch the deer now," Dorik grumbled. "The troublesome wolf pups will scare all the game completely out of the valley."

"Look over there," Orin shouted, pointing his spear toward a large buck that had turned to challenge the five aggressive wolves.

The does and half-grown fawns had continued a safe distance beyond before stopping to watch their leader. The buck, supporting a broad spread of polished antlers, had little difficulty keeping the inexperienced pups away from the vulnerable tendons of his rear legs. As the two hunters approached with raised spears, the buck again lunged into the deep snow to escape his attackers. The wolves managed to overtake the struggling buck which again turned to fend off their gnashing teeth. After each escape effort, the beleaguered stag would stop and turn, trying to defend his rear legs from the relentless siege. As the buck became tired he became less and less aware of, or concerned with, the two hunters who cautiously advanced to within a few feet of the preoccupied animal. The buck momentarily turned his attention from the hunters to defend himself from one of the wolves. Orin sensed an opportunity, and wading forward a few steps, drove his spear into the rib cage of the bewildered stag. As the buck swung his antlered head back toward the men, his front legs collapsed, allowering his body to settle into the snow. As the struggles of the buck ceased, Dorik offered his congratulations to Orin.

With the excitement of the kill, and the smell of blood, the dominant wolf pup moved toward the carcass, baring his teeth in a growling challenge to Dorik. Orin swung his spear, delivering a sharp stinging whack to the rump of the snarling animal. The wolf emitted several yelps before retreating a few feet to cower timidly.

"I think the beast needs an occasional reminder to show him who his masters are," Orin said to his father.

"I think your spear just accomplished that," Dorik responded. "I just hope the wolves never challenge us as a group. We might lose such an encounter."

Orin looked at the submissive pup. "I don't think they would. When he challenged you the other wolves just stood watching. I think they consider us as one of them and we were merely being tested to see who was master. It was the type of challenge they constantly make against each other to determine which one is pack leader."

"I do have a new appreciation for them," Dorik observed. "Without the wolf pups we could never have gotten close enough to the buck to make the kill. I believe they'll turn out to be worth their weight in salt."

The deer carcass was opened and the eager pups rewarded with some of the viscera. The two men then tied the dead buck to a pole, and, shouldering their prize, began the difficult trek back along the snow trail toward camp.

At the shelter, Retta and Carma listened wide-eyed with excitement when Orin related the story of the hunt and the part played by the young wolves.

Dorik, noting the women's preoccupation with repairing the hunter's garments, said, "I think we'll hang the buck up in the big pine tree and you women can wait until tomorrow to cut it up for drying. You can cook the heart and liver for our meal today."

The carcass was suspended high on a limb, well above the reach of the young wolves. After the men completed the task, Orin commented to his father, "At least we don't have to worry about flies. I wonder where all the flies and mosquitoes go in the winter?"

"That reminds me," the older man said, ignoring the question. "Last summer, I saw lots of bees flying in and out of an old hollow tree up on the south slope. Now that the weather is cold and the bees are asleep, I think we should go exploring that area for honey."

The following morning arrived with a low overcast obscuring the mountain tops on either side of the valley. The two men, followed by the wolf pack, started their search for the honey tree, but the struggle of wading through the deep snow soon became exhausting.

Dorik decided to cancel the search. "It's too far away," he rationalized, "and I'm not even sure I could find it in this deep snow. There may not be any honey there anyway. We should have looked for it right after it turned cold, before the snow got so deep."

"If we had big, wide feet like some of the rabbits, "Orin commented, "we wouldn't sink into the snow so far. I wonder if we could build something out of willows to tie to our feet that would support us on the soft snow."

Dorik looked quizzically at his son. "I can't imagine what you have in mind, but I'm willing to try anything."

After returning to camp, Orin rushed into the shelter to grab one of Amalee's largest baskets. He emptied the dried meat into other smaller baskets before taking the container to a snow area that was undisturbed. After setting the basket on the snow, he carefully placed one foot inside. Shifting his weight onto the basket, he noted how little it sank into the snow. The test confirmed what he had hoped. The two men then gathered an armful of willows of various sizes. After experimenting with several plans, Orin selected a design and began assembling the device. He tied a pair of three-foot-long green willows together at the ends after which he began weaving smaller, long, green saplings between them.

With the woven pattern resembling one of Amalee's baskets, Orin called on his mother for help and advice. "I can't weave these willows the way you do with baskets. I never learned how. Anyway, weaving baskets is women's work. Maybe you could help me finish this frame."

"Of course," Amalee agreed. "You shouldn't be doing that kind of work. After all, women could never hunt animals the way you men do."

With the frame completed, Orin tested his theory and was pleased to discover that the device, which he called a "snow walker" could support his entire weight without sinking very far into the snow. After building a duplicate frame, he then laced leather straps through the woven material which were then tied to his deerskin-covered feet. To test the devices, he waddled out onto the snow while Dorik and the women watched. His manner of walking generated a few chuckles from the observers with a reference by Dorik regarding a duck. To Orin's delight he was able to walk effortlessly on the deep powdery snow. Dorik was amazed and soon persuaded his son to let him try the new devices.

"If we can walk on the snow," Dorik reasoned, "we'll be able to continue hunting regardless of the weather."

After the short, successful test, the older man persuaded Amalee to construct a similar pair for his use.

The following day the two men, wearing their snow walkers, departed with their spears and baskets in search of the honey tree. The wolves had difficulty keeping up. Dorik, after watching the struggling animals, repeated a stern command several times which finally sent the pups back toward the shelter. "We don't need their help to gather honey," the older man commented.

After a short period of experimentation, the men developed a walking technique which allowed them to increase their speed to an awkward jog.

Orin became excited about the new possibilities. "With these snow walkers, I'll bet we could stay on the heels of a deer until it falls from exhaustion. I think the Storm God has favored us with the deep snow. With these snow walkers, and the wolves to help us, we should be able to get all the game we ever want."

"So long as the snow is deep," agreed the older man. He then paused before adding, "That honey tree must be farther than I remembered. I think it's up on that wooded slope."

A worried look appeared on the face of the older man as he slowed to a halt near the edge of a deep set of tracks. "Are you thinking what I am?" Dorik asked.

The young man scratched his short, red beard. "They're too big for bear tracks," he observed, "and anyway, a bear would probably be asleep in this weather."

Dorik nervously scanned the area around them. "There's only one thing it can be. Look at the distance between the footprints. It has to be that tiger and it has crossed here since this snow fell. I was hoping it had left the valley."

"We should always take the young wolves with us when we're hunting," Orin nervously suggested. "The pups wouldn't be much more than a nuisance to a tiger, but if we kill a deer and the beast is attracted to the blood, perhaps the wolf pups would distract it until we escape."

The older man pondered the thought as they continued the search. Dorik finally located the honey tree and, as suspected, the cold had demobilized the bees. After removing large pieces of rotten wood surrounding the hive entrance, the men sampled the honey, eagerly sucking it from the wax comb. After filling their baskets, they began their trek back to camp.

"We're lucky that a bear didn't find this last summer," Dorik commented. "There wouldn't be any honey left. This calls for a celebration tonight."

Nothing was said as the two hunters again crossed the tracks of the tiger, but each man glanced nervously around and increased his pace. They crossed several rabbit tracks and once stopped to watch a red fox that was intently pursuing his quarry.

At the shelter, they were greeted with joyous enthusiasm at the sight of the honey, and a celebration quickly began.

* * *

The early winter passed with fewer hardships than had been expected. Using their snow walkers, and with the help of the fully developed wolves, the men were occasionally successful in stalking and killing a deer. The animals became a valuable tool in the process. Upon locating fresh deer tracks in the deep snow, the men would track the animals, encouraging the pups to follow. The wolves soon learned the technique of distracting and holding the prey at bay by attacking from all sides. The hunters could then wait nearby until the preoccupied deer became exhausted and unaware of their approach. With the aid of their snow walkers, the men became adept at spearing the distracted animal and agreed that the wolves earned more than the few meat scraps offered to them daily.

"We can thank the Storm God for this deep snow," Dorik often said to his son.

Orin noted that rabbits usually established and followed well worn paths in the snow, offering good opportunities for setting small snares under brush or low limbs. Success required constant checking of the sites to prevent the loss of their catch to a fox or other scavenger.

As winter progressed, the days became noticeably longer and the deep snow began shrinking from evaporation and melting. The men noticed and repeatedly discussed the higher path in the sky travelled by the Sun God. With the passing days, the snow pack diminished faster than it was replenished. Game that had earlier been plentiful became scarce and hunting, more difficult.

As the days lengthened, the hunting advantage of the snow walkers diminished. The devices that had served them so well earlier, were discarded.

"They're great in deep snow," Dorik observed, "but they're not worth a hoot now."

The hoard of dried meat, nuts, and roots from the previous fall, was consumed and badly missed. Watercress flourished and remained plentiful although it did little to allay their hunger on the days following unsuccessful hunts.

The two men began watching the cattle herd that foraged on dormant grass beneath the diminishing snow cover. The animals occasionally grazed at the very edge of the stream, nibbling the small tender shoots of new growth. The two men were never certain of the count, but both agreed that a few cows and calves appeared to be missing from the herd.

Nomi sat near the fire with her hands resting on her enlarged stomach. "Amalee, I'm terribly worried. I think something is terribly wrong."

"What do you mean?" the older woman asked. "Do you have any pain?"

"No, but every once in a while, I feel a thump in my belly. I've never had that happen before in my whole life."

Amalee laughed and seated herself near Nomi. Placing her arm around the shoulders of the worried girl, she said, "You've never been pregnant before. Don't you know what that is? Didn't your mother ever talk about such things?"

"I knew I was pregnant, of course. But what is it that I feel?"

"You dear girl," Amalee explained. "That is the baby kicking his feet. You'll feel a lot of that before he's born."

Nomi was delighted and called to Carma and Retta to feel. They all laughed and speculated as to when the new clan member would arrive.

The snow continued to melt, and on the bare, southern facing slopes, new shoots of tender grass emerged. Bulbs pushed early slender shoots through the grass in a race for the precious sunshine. Hunting became difficult. Walking through the slippery mud became a difficult chore, limiting the hunter's scouting range. The supply of stored food had become exhausted, forcing the women to forage on the melted slopes or to wade in icy water searching for cattail or water lily roots.

The young wolves also suffered from the reduced meat supply. Dorik had become fond of the animals and fully appreciated their value on the hunt.

The two men futilely searched for one of the porcupines that had been reserved for such an emergency. Even the deer seemed to be leaving the area, moving to higher elevations.

Morning arrived with a steady, cold rain that turned the area around the shelter into an ankle-deep quagmire. Water seeped between the poles and entered the shelter, creating mud pools over much of the floor. While the men worked in the cold rain, digging diversion ditches away from the shelter, the women gathered green pine boughs which were stacked inside to hold the bed robes above the mud and water. They all returned to the fire periodically, numbed and shivering from the cold.

The remaining meager wood supply had become soaked, making it difficult to sustain a fire. Concerned about the possible loss of the fire, Dorik sent the women into the woods to search for suitable fire material. They returned soaked and cold. Retta cried and complained as she struggled through mud with her armful of dripping twigs and small branches. The five grown wolf pups occupied the small corners of the shelter, often defending their territory by snarling or snapping at each other.

The rain continued relentlessly for several days, afflicting Amalee with a severe cough and low fever that consumed much of her remaining strength. Insisting that the older woman stay in her bed robe to conserve her strength, Nomi took Carma with her to search the banks of the stream for edible roots.

"I'm cold and awfully wet," the child complained. "Can't we go back to the shelter?"

"I'm sorry, Carma. I wish we could," Nomi said, "but we have to find food for Retta and your mother." After returning with the meager supply, Nomi boiled and crushed the roots into a thick soup for the ailing woman.

"I thought winter and the deep snow would be our main problem," Dorik commented to Orin while out hunting. "The snow was a pleasure. I think the Storm God must now be very angry with us. Won't this rain ever stop?"

"I'm sure it will, but we can't wait," was Orin's reply. "We have to find some game soon. I'm worried about both mother and Nomi."

The old hunter scratched his graying beard. "I've been watching and thinking a lot about the cattle," he said. "The cows will start calving soon and we should at least be able to get us a calf or two. Of course, I'd still like to catch one of those cows, but I'm not sure our scheme of luring one out into the mud would succeed. Even if we could build a snare strong enough to hold a cow, there's no place on the meadow to hang it."

The conversation nourished a line of thought in the mind of the younger hunter. He considered and abandoned one idea after another as he probed for a solution to the challenge posed by his father. Before returning to the shelter, Orin sloshed through mud to the willow grove at the edge of the lake to gather an armful of small, dead willow twigs the diameter of his small finger.

Nomi turned from her task of scraping and softening a deerskin. "You don't have to gather firewood. The sisters and I will do it. I was just waiting, hoping the rain would ease up a little."

"This is for an experiment," Orin explained. "I want to try something. We can use it for firewood later." After breaking the twigs into various lengths, the young man stacked twig on twig at various angles and designs. "This is just a toy size of what I have in mind," he explained to his father who was watching with avid curiosity. "If we could stack several poles on top of each other and secure the corners, we could build a pole trap strong enough to hold a cow." After testing various designs, Orin again turned to his father. "If we gather poles like we did for the shelter, and stack them across each other to build three sides of the trap, maybe we could lure the cow in by tying her calf inside."

"But what would keep the cow inside?" his father asked, pointing to the open end of the toy trap.

"We'll build a frame just the size of the open end. We'll tie one end of the frame to the top of the trap so the other end can swing down to the ground. We'll support the swinging end of the frame up out of the way to keep the trap open and figure out some way to release it after the cow goes inside."

After the rain diminished, the two men, who were temporarily discouraged with hunting, turned to the construction of the trap as proposed by the young hunter.

"We should build it near the meadow," Orin suggested, "but it should be away far enough from our shelter so the cow won't be suspicious. If we build it in the edge of the woods, we'll have less distance to carry the poles."

The two men explored the forest near the meadow where pine trees grew in abundance. Orin was delighted to locate a site with several trees growing closely together that were ideal for his plan. Twin trees, each about half a foot in diameter, grew about two feet apart and about six feet from two other trees similarly situated. Other trees would support the walls at the open end of the trap. Fire was carried from the shelter and used to burn poles to the critical length that were then placed between the twin trees with every alternate course spanning the six-foot gap across the far end of the trap. As the work progressed, the men became increasingly enthusiastic with the project. After the walls had been completed, reaching well above a man's head, the two men secured a layer of poles across the top of the structure.

The two hunters stepped back to admire their work. "Now all we have to do is build the entrance frame," Orin proposed. "That will be the difficult part. One end of the frame will be a longer pole that hangs across the top of the wall. The frame will have to fill almost the entire entrance and be able to swing down from the top."

To build the gate frame, poles were tied together with wet leather straps that would later shrink, forming a tight bond. One end of the completed gate was swung from the poles at the top of the structure with the other end supported horizontally by a trip pole that could be dislodged by a rope, allowing the gate to swing down. The trip rope was then extended down and across the base of the trap.

With the work completed, Orin walked inside the trap to test the trip rope. He pressed his foot against the rope and was pleased to see the frame swing downward, banging heavily against the stop at the entrance.

"Now we have only to search for a newborn calf," Orin said. "We'll be ready, and I hope the spirits will be generous, also."

The two men, in addition to inspecting their snares, made daily trips along the meadow's edge, watching the cattle for clues of newborn calves.

The hunters returned to the task of securing food for the clan. In addition to themselves and the four women, they considered the wolves as part of their responsibility.

With the help of the wolves, the men were able to catch an occasional rabbit. Upon spotting the quarry, the chase would begin, and whenever the rabbit would change its course, one of the wolves would cut the corner to reduce the gap. Initially the young, inexperienced wolves had difficulty grasping the prey while running full speed, often stumbling over their quarry, but as they gained experience, they developed a technique of flipping the rump of the speeding rabbit with their muzzles before pouncing on the upset animal.

After one such successful chase, the dominant wolf refused to relinquish the prize to Dorik. He stood over the dying rabbit, baring his teeth at the clan leader while uttering a low guttural growl. Arriving at the scene, Orin swung his spear, delivering a painful blow to the rump of the startled challenger. The wolf momentarily turned to attack the young hunter, but reconsidered before skulking away.

"It seems those dumb critters never learn," Orin remarked to his father. "He thought he was the clan leader."

"They seem to have a lot in common with people," the older man agreed. "They want to be clan leaders. I believe they think they are people."

The men continued scouting the timbered edge of the broad meadow. The new growth of grass on the treeless meadow tempted a variety of grazers from the still dormant forest. Two startled yearling fawns were flushed from the tall brush bordering the meadow, but had little trouble outdistancing the pursuing wolf pack.

While the wolves were in futile pursuit, the hunters saw the clue for which they had waited several days. One of the cows nervously turned from where the other animals were grazing and trotted a short distance toward the wolf pack before stopping. Her attention momentarily shifted from the wolves to an area of heavy brush.

"I'll bet that's the one we're looking for," observed the older man. "She must have a calf somewhere over there."

"I'm sure you're right, but she'll never go to it if we have the wolves with us. Why don't you take them and the rabbit back to camp. I'll wait for the cow to go to the calf."

"That's a good plan," Dorik agreed. "There's no reason for us both to wait here. I'll see if I can find us something to eat and bring it back." The old leader whistled for the wolves to join him before departing for the shelter.

After locating a tree that offered a good view, Orin climbed onto a limb. His father and the wolf pack were hardly out of sight across the meadow before the cow left the company of the other cattle to enter the brush. Orin watched, and although he couldn't see the calf, he established its approximate location from the cow's behavior. Without waiting to nurse the calf, the cow, apparently reassured, returned to be with the other grazing cattle.

Orin had little trouble locating the newborn calf and rushed to it before it could get up. After tying the calf's feet, he hoisted the limp body to his back, and following the technique used the previous summer, tied the calf to a log he had earlier positioned on the meadow.

"After you left she went right to the calf," Orin explained when the older man returned. "I had no problem finding it. It was bedded down in the brush over there."

"Things are looking good," Dorik affirmed. "Now I just hope we can entice the cow into the trap. The pups didn't want to stay at camp. It took both women and the girls to hold them until I slipped away."

Shortly after the calf was tied to the log, the cow, followed by the other cattle, ran bellowing to its side. For a long period of time the cows lingered near the calf, sniffing curiously. After the cattle failed to observe any danger, and had returned to grazing, the men, following their earlier pattern, ran to the calf and log and moved them closer to the trap. The action of the herd was repeated until, after three or four such maneuvers, the men had positioned the calf inside the pole structure.

"I hope the cow can find the calf here inside the trap," Orin said.

"Don't worry," Dorik shouted, glancing back over his shoulder. "Here she comes now. Let's climb a tree."

"No, Dorik, we don't have time," Orin shouted as he began running. "Let's run inside the trap and trip it closed."

After running inside the pole structure, the men quickly tripped the door shut. The bellowing cow raced toward the cage, stopping only a few feet short. Snorting her anger, she circled the structure, attempting to reach her offspring. Several times the hunters tried to reach the nervous cow with their spears but were never granted an opportunity.

"If we wait, the cow should eventually go back with the other animals," Dorik suggested. "Then we can reset the trap door and hope the cow comes back to the calf."

The men continued to wait as the sun dropped below the western horizon. "We might have to spend the night here," was the wry remark of the younger man. "The women will be worried."

"I don't think so," countered the leader. "I think the cow is about to go back to the meadow."

As predicted, the cow finally moved away, periodically stopping to look back. When feeling safe, the two men tied the calf at the far inside end of the trap and reset the trap door. Before leaving, Orin carefully placed several small pine boughs across the trigger rope.

"There, now," he commented. "All the animal has to do is step on the pine boughs. I think we have a good chance of catching a cow tonight."

The men returned to the shelter to share a meager meal of roast rabbit. The wolves, after fighting for the scraps, then spent the balance of the evening futilely chasing squirrels. The women were told of the prospects with the trap and the clansmen went to bed that night hardly daring to hope that the next day would provide the abundance of meat that a fully grown cow would supply.

- 20 -

The first light of dawn offered minimum visibility for the two hunters and the young wolves as they anxiously proceeded toward the trap. Upon entering the shaded area of the woods, they searched the darkness, hoping to verify their success. The wolves, running far ahead of the men, could be heard snarling and growling. The men accelerated their pace, encouraged by the wolves' reaction. As they approached the cage, their first reaction was disappointment at not seeing the profile of the cow through the slits of the structure.

"I don't see anything in the trap," Orin said, "but something sure has the wolves excited."

The men's advance was brought to a sudden halt by a thunderous growl from inside the trap. Nervous and tense, they crept closer for a better look, but they had little doubt about the identity of the occupant. The tiger had consumed a large portion of the calf before the arrival of the men and wolf pack. Preoccupied with the wolves, the tiger appeared oblivious to the presence of the hunters. The annoyed beast repeatedly reached its paws between the poles to swipe at the growling and snarling wolves that raced back and forth beyond his reach. Dorik signaled Orin to follow as he circled the trap, approaching cautiously from behind the enraged tiger. The older hunter waited until he saw a vulnerable spot exposed on the enormous cat, and then, rushing forward, drove his spear hard into the beast's rib cage. The infuriated tiger whirled and lunged against the poles beyond which the two hunters waited.

"Watch out," Orin shouted. "He's breaking down the wall." Several poles splintered and the wall shifted, threatening to collapse. The shaft of the spear, after penetrating the side of the beast, had broken when the animal turned. The angry tiger again lunged against the crumbling pole frame, attempting to reach his attackers. Orin, gripping his spear with both hands, seized a momentary opportunity to plunge his spear forward, driving the point deep into the lower neck of the wounded beast. He quickly withdrew the spear and again plunged it near the earlier wound that was by then spurting surges of crimson blood onto the poles. Within moments the large cat's movements became slower as it turned its head back toward the wolves as if to signal a preference of adversaries. The tiger raised one paw and, as if in slow motion, made a feeble swipe toward the snarling wolf pack. The beast then stopped, ignoring the excitement around him, and allowed his head to drop lower and lower. The blood continued to pour in diminishing spurts from the two throat wounds, collecting in pools at his feet. The hunters watched with hypnotic fascination as the tiger, yielding to ebbing strength, allowed his body to slowly settle to the ground.

With the adrenaline in his body subsiding, Orin found himself weak and shaking from the excitement of the experience. He leaned against the trap poles to steady himself, allowing a broad smile to show on his face. The two men turned to each other with the sudden realization of their success and whooped a victory yell as they embraced in joy.

Dorik stepped back to view the dead animal and his grin gave testimony to his pride and pleasure. "I can't believe it," he said. "I simply can't believe it. To think that we could kill a fully grown tiger. No other clan would ever believe us."

Orin returned the smile. "We'll keep the head and skin as proof. What a trophy those teeth will make."

As they prepared to leave, the victorious hunters had difficulty convincing the wolves to leave the trap to accompany them back to the shelter.

"Amalee, Nomi," the leader yelled, as they approached the camp. "You won't believe what happened."

Amalee appeared at the entrance, holding the deerskin curtain aside.

"Hurry, woman," Dorik called. "Your son and I have just killed the tiger that's been worrying us for so long. You and Nomi bring your flints and come skin the carcass."

Amalee waited motionless until the hunters arrived at the shelter entrance. "I'm sorry, Dorik. If you want the tiger skinned, you'll have to do it yourself."

The clan leader remained speechless for a few moments. "What are you saying? You've never behaved like this before in all your life. Are you sick?"

"No, I'm not sick," she replied, "but Nomi is. The baby is on its way and she needs my help."

Orin rushed into the shelter and knelt beside the girl. Sweat beads covered the forehead of the young woman who lay prone on a bed of deerskin robes. Orin gently took her hand. "Are you all right? Am I about to have a son?"

Nomi forced a weak smile and closed her eyes, straining, as some unknown force dictated the actions of her body.

Amalee returned to Nomi's side to rest her hand on the forehead of the young woman. She looked up at Dorik to explain. "The labor pains have just started and it might be quite awhile. I better stay here with her."

Orin didn't wait for his father to respond. "Yes, mother, of course you should stay with her. I want my son to arrive, well and strong."

The two men took several of the women's skinning flints and reluctantly departed camp to return to the trap. The wolves ran ahead but soon became diverted in pursuit of a fox that had been attracted to the smell of the tiger blood.

The men had difficulty dragging the limp carcass of the enormous tiger from the confines of the trap. "We must be very careful to not puncture the skin," Orin reminded his father. "What a wonderful robe this will make."

Dorik looked up from where he knelt at his skinning task. "It'll be a fitting bed for you and Nomi to share with your new son."

"You are the clan leader," Orin replied. "It should be yours to keep."

Dorik raised one hand to silence his son. "The hide is yours. You made the kill. I'll hear no more about it."

The two men worked carefully, and after finally removing the skin, spread it on the ground to admire. The wolves were thrown scraps of the unfamiliar tiger flesh which they cautiously sniffed before carrying the pieces away to be eaten.

"I've never tasted tiger meat," Dorik commented. "I don't know whether it's good or not."

Orin flexed his biceps and grinned. "Perhaps it will give us the strength of the tiger. I could use the extra strength."

The tiger carcass was cut into smaller chunks which were temporarily stored above the trap to remove them from the teeth of the wolves. The hunters then rolled the skin onto a pole which they laboriously carried back to camp.

As the men approached the shelter, Carma and Retta ran to meet them. "Orin, Orin," Retta yelled. "The baby's been born."

"Is it a boy?" was Orin's excited inquiry.

Carma answered for her younger sister. "Yes, it's a boy. He was born just a little while ago. Mother says he looks healthy."

The men lowered the pole and tiger skin, allowing Orin to run into the shelter. Amalee held the infant nestled in a bundle of rabbit fur.

The young father's eyes sparkled as he gazed down at the child. "Let me hold him. I want to see my son."

"You'll do nothing of the kind," Amalee countered. "Not until you've washed that blood off your hands. My grandson deserves better care than that."

Nomi watched unobserved from her bed in the corner of the shelter and then slipped into a deep sleep of exhaustion.

The pieces of tiger meat were carried back to camp and hung in a nearby tree. The liver and heart were cooked, but they all agreed, as hungry as they were, the strange taste wasn't appealing. The wolves were rewarded with the discarded morsels. Although the remaining meat also had a strange and strong taste, it was welcomed by the hungry clansmen. The weather was cool enough to delay the stripping and drying process of the meat until the women were free to resume the tedious task.

Several days passed with Orin spending long portions of his time holding and talking to his newborn son. Amalee watched Orin's devotion to the baby and then finally explained the problem that had been worrying her.

"I'm becoming very concerned," she explained. "The baby is crying more and more and always seems hungry. I'm not sure Nomi has enough milk for the baby."

"What can we do about it?" Orin asked. "Why isn't there enough milk?"

"I don't know. If we were back with the clan, we could always find a nursing mother who would share her milk. There isn't anything that can be done here. If she doesn't start producing more milk, I'm afraid the baby will die."

Orin's face grew pale, and for a moment he was at a loss for words. "No," he finally shouted. "My baby will not die. Someday he's going to be a great hunter." He then turned and left the shelter, trying to hide his emotions.

With the passing days, Orin watched as Nomi repeatedly tried to satisfy the infant's craving for nourishment. Amalee also suffered, helplessly worrying about both the baby and her son.

"There must be something we can do," the desperate young man pleaded. "Can't you think of anything?"

The frustrated woman shook her head negatively. "If we could just find another nursing mother who could share her milk, but there's no chance of that."

"It isn't fair," Orin lashed out. "The new fawns in the forest and the new calves out there on the meadow have all the milk they can drink while my baby is starving to death. The spirits must be punishing me."

He lapsed into silence and slowly walked from the shelter to avoid displaying his grief. He walked aimlessly, finding himself near the stream that flowed the length of the meadow. As he gazed at the cattle and watched a calf nursing, his thoughts repeated his earlier statement. It isn't fair.

"It just isn't fair," he mumbled to himself. "Why can't my baby somehow have some of that milk from those cows."

The thought offered no solution. Even if I caught a cow with a newborn calf, he reasoned, how would the baby get the milk? Even if we tied the cow so it couldn't move, the baby could never nurse from a large beast like that.

Desperation drove the young hunter into a half-planned course of action. He didn't know how the baby was going to get at that milk, but he became determined to at least catch a cow. He suggested his plan to Dorik but was disappointed with his father's lack of enthusiasm.

"I'll help you try to catch a cow," his father agreed, "but only because, when you see the futility of your scheme, we can at least eat the cow."

* * *

The two hunters returned to the trap to repair the damage done by the lunging tiger. An attempt was made to scrape away much of the blood that had permeated the ground inside. An early spring shower assisted, but Dorik wondered whether the lingering smell might frighten the cattle away and render the entire effort useless.

The two men watched the cattle for a couple of days before the behavior of a cow allowed the men to repeat their earlier procedure. The calf was located, and following the earlier technique, was gradually moved to the trap and tied to the inner end of the structure. Even before the men could properly adjust the rope trigger, the long-horned cow ran bellowing from the meadow. She was followed by the bulls and other grieving cows. The smell of the earlier tiger kill, contrary to what the men expected, only increased the protective instinct of the cow for her calf.

"Here she comes," Dorik shouted. "Let's get out of here." The nervous hunters ran from the structure and frantically climbed the poles to a place of safety on top. The belligerent cow, upon seeing her calf inside, immediately entered the structure to sniff and identify her offspring. Orin quickly reached through the roof of the trap to disengage the supporting pole, allowing the heavy door to swing shut. After unsuccessfully attempting to back out of the structure, the cow returned to again smell the calf. The bulls and other cows congregated around the outer structure, sniffing the blood and bawling their call of distress. The hunters, happy with the success of the trap, had little choice but to wait on top of the structure.

The wolf pack, excited by the action, selected a young bull and began harassing the animal. The main animal herd, turning its attention to the attackers, temporarily abandoned the trapped cow in pursuit of the wolves. Although the inexperienced pups were incapable of disabling the bull, they were agile enough to avoid the long horns. As the attack continued, the cattle and wolves maneuvered the action well out onto the meadow.

The hunters descended to the outer edge of the cage as the cow repeatedly tangled her horns in the poles while attempting to gore the men. After repeated failures, the two men finally managed to slip a strong leather noose over the broad pair of horns. The end of the leather strap was looped once around a pole and then tightened with each opportunity of available slack. The men continued to tighten the bond until the head of the bewildered beast was drawn firmly against the wall of the trap.

"Now what will you do?" Dorik asked his son. "How do you plan to get the milk from the cow to the baby?"

"I don't know," Orin confessed, "but I know I have to try."

As Orin reached through the poles, attempting to reach the cows udder, the agitated cow resisted, kicking at the man's hand.

"We may have to tie her rear legs so she can't kick," Orin suggested. "If we tie this nearest leg to the pole, she won't be able to move around very much."

With the difficult task of securing the animal completed, Orin reached to the cows udder and shook one of the teats several times.

"I don't know how those dumb calves get the milk," he exclaimed "but I know there's milk in there."

Dorik offered an idea. "If we untie the calf and bring it back here, we can see how the calf does it."

They moved the small calf to the rear of the cow and placed it on its feet. Upon moving the calf's head toward the cow's udder, the young animal eagerly began searching for the teat. Within moments, the hungry calf began sucking, allowing milk to drip from the corners of its mouth.

"There it is," Orin excitedly said to his father. "The calf's getting the milk now."

Again Orin reached to the udder, pulling on one the cow's other teats in an awkward imitation of the calf's action. After several such attempts, a few drops of the white liquid was released. By attempting variations of the calf's method, he finally succeeded in forcing a small stream onto the ground.

"I've got it now," he explained. "If I squeeze the top of the teat tightly closed, and then squeeze the other fingers closed, one at a time, it forces the milk out the end."

"What are you going to put the milk in?" Dorik asked.

Orin stepped back from the cow. "You stay here and I'll run to the shelter to get one of Amalee's clay pots."

As he ran toward camp, he was followed by the wolves that had abandoned their attack on the young bull. Upon reaching the shelter, he quickly told of the success at catching the cow.

After ordering Carma to keep the wolves in camp, and after returning to the trap where Dorik waited by the cow, he repeatedly attempted to get milk into a clay pot.

"I was able to get it to flow before," he complained. "Do you suppose the cow is empty?"

"I doubt it," Dorik answered. "Maybe she only lets the milk flow for the calf."

After again moving the calf to the cow's udder, Orin discovered that when the calf was nursing, the milk flowed more freely. He continued the effort until the pot was partially filled. "Now let's untie the cow and take this milk back to my son."

The cow was released from her bonds, but remained a captive within the pen. The men carefully carried the clay pot across the meadow to where the small, frail baby was nestled in Nomi's arms.

Attempts were made to feed the infant by holding a smaller milk-filled pot to his mouth, but the child refused to cooperate. Although the baby would eagerly suck on the woman's small finger that had been dipped in the milk, it became obvious that the amount consumed would be insufficient. Amalee then thought of a solution. She sent Carma running to the lakeshore to bring back several hollow reeds. The older woman cut a short section and cleared the center by pushing a small twig through the reed. After sucking a small amount of the milk into her own mouth, she then placed the other end of the reed in the baby's mouth to allow a small flow to dribble through. With the first taste of the milk, the infant reacted with an instinctive nursing action. The young parents were overjoyed and choked with emotion.

Orin took the baby into his arms, looking down at the frail infant. "He's going to have all the milk he wants. My son is not going to starve."

Later, as he and Dorik left the shelter, they discussed the problem of sustaining the milk supply.

"We're going to have to get water and grass to that cow," Dorik suggested. "If she dies, there can be no more milk."

The two men immediately went about the task of gathering grass which they placed in the pen. They placed a large pottery container in the corner of the pen and instructed Carma to keep it filled with water.

Twice daily the cow was again tied and the calf released to nurse. With each success, Orin became more adept at milking and was soon carrying back a clay pot filled with milk. Although the cow continued to resist being milked, the calf soon accepted the men as a normal thing in its new life. The cow refused to eat or take water until the second day, and then only when left alone. Each time the men approached, she struggled, resisting any attempt to tie her, but the men noticed that each day the struggle diminished.

Nomi's baby thrived on the new source of milk and it soon became obvious that the child was gaining weight.

At an evening ceremony, the small clan gathered to have Dorik officiate in declaring a name for the new clansman. His voice was somber as he began. "I Dorik, leader of this clan, do hereby declare this child, sired by Orin, and carried by the woman Nomi, to be a member of the clan of Dorik, and to henceforth be known as Ojon. He shall bear this name with pride, that he may someday walk in the tracks of his father, and his father's father. And may the spirits favor him and guide his destiny."

The baby continued to grow stronger and, except for an occasional upset stomach, thrived. In time the baby was taught to drink from the special small clay cup that Amalee created especially for her grandchild.

The problems of maintaining the milk source increased. Carma and Retta were assigned the task of gathering grass and pushing it through the poles of the trap. The cow, when left alone, would eat a portion of the feed and drink some of the water, but her milk supply diminished. It became necessary to deprive the calf from fully nursing until Orin had milked an adequate supply for his son.

Orin considered releasing the cow to feed with the other cattle, hoping she would return to nurse her trapped calf, but

Dorik considered the risk too great. "I'm afraid she might abandon the calf to stay with the herd."

Dorik considered the problem before suggesting an alternate plan. "If we could build a wall of poles that covered a larger area just outside of the trap, we could perhaps then release the cow into that area to graze."

"How tall do you think the wall should be?" Orin asked.

"I believe, if we make it as high as a man's head, the cow wouldn't try to get over it."

The two men continued to hunt and set snares, but after each success they turned their efforts to the task of building a corral. By placing pole upon pole in a zigzag pattern, the fence was extended far enough onto the meadow to include a section of a small tributary stream of the larger creek. The task became greater than expected. As the project continued, they found it necessary to go deeper and deeper into the forest to secure the poles.

The work extended into midsummer. The project had earlier been a low-priority effort, but the cow was growing thinner and the milk supply diminishing. Orin's concern for his child pushed him to greater effort. When the corral was nearing completion, Orin offered an additional suggestion. "Some of those other cows that gave birth later in the season still have small calves. If we could entice another cow into our trap, we would have a more reliable source of milk."

"We could try," his father consented, "but the calves are getting larger, and they'll be much harder to catch."

Construction of the wall continued until only a narrow opening of about ten feet remained. The men placed poles on the ground near the opening that could quickly be placed across the narrow gap to close the corral.

The younger calves on the meadow had grown old enough to run and bed down with the herd, making the situation appear insurmountable.

Orin, though doubtful of its success, offered a plan. "Maybe if we wait until some of the cows and calves move over near that marshy area, we can use the wolf pups to panic the herd and drive some of them into that deep mud. With a little luck a calf might become separated and we might be able to catch it and tie it."

"I think you're wasting our time," Dorik countered, "but I can't suggest anything better. Lets give it a try."

The two men waited and watched until several of the cows with calves were grazing near the marsh. Taking the wolf pack with them, the two men approached the cattle. The animals grouped together with the bulls taking the customary defensive position between the hunters and the cows. With no anticipation of what to expect, Orin encouraged the wolves to attack. The bulls repeatedly charged toward the nimble canines before returning to the defense of the cows and calves. The two men waited and watched from a safe distance.

"All we're doing is irritating the cattle," Dorik cautioned. "If they become disturbed, they might leave the valley."

During the maneuvering of the cattle and wolves, the cattle herd drifted nearer the edge of the marshy area through which the stream flowed. The cattle had taken up a defensive position with their backs to the stream, limiting the maneuvering area of the wolves. As the cattle became weary of the attack, one cow plunged into the shallow water, wading through mud to the opposite bank. The action encouraged another cow to follow and soon the entire herd bolted toward the opposite stream bank in hopes of ending the attack. The retreat offered an unexpected opportunity.

"See that calf struggling in the mud?" Orin shouted. The men raced forward with Orin encouraging the wolves to continue the attack on the cattle. Orin dropped his spear as he rushed into the marsh to grab the floundering calf. The action of the wolves held the attention of the cattle sufficiently to allow the men to quickly drag the struggling calf back to the shore where Dorik rapidly bound its legs with a leather thong. As soon as the mother of the bawling calf noticed the absence of her offspring, she quickly recrossed the stream to defend it.

"Here comes the cow," Dorik warned. "Let's get out of here." The hunters ran a safe distance and watched the bellowing cow run to the side of her disabled calf.

After congratulating each other on their success, the two men coaxed and scolded the wolves into following them back to camp. With the wolves gone, the remaining cattle recrossed the creek to be near the side of the tethered calf.

As they had done before, the men, with each opportunity, moved the calf until reaching the newly finished corral. With the calf well inside, the men could hardly believe their luck as they watched the entire cattle herd follow the mother cow into the corral. Quickly stacking the poles across the gate opening, the two men retreated to wait for the reaction. The animals appeared no more than curious, occasionally sniffing at the fence poles, but made no effort to breach the wall.

"I think we now have too much success," Dorik commented. "I never expected this to happen. There's enough meat in there to feed a large clan for several years, and yet they might as well be out on the meadow. Now that we have them in the big pen, I don't know how to handle them."

"I don't know, either," Orin said. "We can't go inside the pen with the cattle. Maybe if we opened the gate and let them all out, the cow will stay with the calf."

"No, I don't think so," Dorik responded. "I think that when the others rush to leave, she would follow them. If we had a safe means of separating the calves from the cows, we'd have all the meat we could use and perhaps still get the milk the baby needs."

Orin scratched his beard, weighing the problem before offering his suggestion. "I have an idea. If we remove only the upper poles from the gate, perhaps the larger cattle will jump over the remaining poles, but the calves can't. What do you think?"

Dorik studied the fence and gate before answering. "It's worth a try, but we should tie the lower poles securely to the fence so they won't get knocked down."

The two men cautiously approached the gate beyond which the cows and calves waited. The bulls defiantly faced the men. After Dorik and Orin finished tying and securing the lower gate poles, they removed the higher ones. The dominant bull occasionally charged toward the two men but, on each occasion, stopped short of the remaining poles.

"We better be prepared to find a safe place to go before we topple any more of the poles," Dorik suggested.

"Maybe we can climb over the fence as the cattle leave," Orin suggested.

"And maybe we'll have cattle on both sides of the fence. Then what could we do?"

The thought reduced the enthusiasm of the younger man for a few moments before he responded. "If we bring the wolf pack out to the meadow, perhaps the cattle will turn their attention to them as they leave the pen."

They adopted the plan with Dorik holding the wolves under control while Orin cautiously returned to the gate. The younger hunter shoved the remaining higher poles from the rack and quickly retreated, prepared to run for the safety of the trees nearby. The animals cautiously moved to the corral entrance to investigate before one of the younger bulls decided to escape. After easily jumping over the barricade, the bull continued trotting out onto the meadow. Immediately a cow followed and soon several others were attempting to leave at the same time.

Orin's attention was drawn to the splintering sound of breaking timber as one of the cows entangled her legs in the remaining poles. "They're getting away," he called to Dorik. "We'll never get them back inside the pen again." He envisioned the loss of the entire herd, including the calves.

The sound of splintering timber unnerved the remaining animals, momentarily turning them back from the gate. Orin, grasping the opportunity, ran to the corral opening. Several calves as well as two cows and a yearling bull had retreated to the far side of the corral, giving Orin the opportunity of quickly stacking the toppled gate poles back on the rack. Glancing behind him, he was reassured to see the escaped animals preoccupied with the wolf pack. The young man could hardly believe his luck. He waved to his father, signaling his success. The older man called off the attack and took the wolves back to the camp.

By the time Dorik rejoined his son at the corral, several cows from the meadow had missed their calves and had returned with the entire herd to the corral fence. There was a sustained bawling by cows and calves as they faced each other across the pole structure. The bulls, bellowing and snorting, pawed the dirt, undecided as to where to vent their anger. The men safely watched the commotion from the far side of the pen.

"The main herd should give up soon and go back to grazing," Dorik reasoned. "I'd sure like to get that yearling bull, but we could never get close enough to kill him without getting inside the pen with him, and I'm not that anxious to move into the spirit world."

"I've been thinking about that problem," Orin responded. "If we rearrange the poles and add two walls feeding into the pen, we could build a second gate a few feet from the first and possibly isolate an animal as it tries to enter or leave the larger pen."

"I think I know what you have in mind," Dorik agreed. "Let's get started. I can't wait to sink my teeth into some roast meat from that young bull."

Orin placed higher priority on getting milk for his child. They released the cow that had been captive since spring, freeing her to join the other cows in the corral, but retained her calf in the trap as a means of enticing her back. Orin reset the trap door, extending a long rope from the door release latch to a nearby bush. "I can always trip the door shut from here if necessary," he explained.

With the trap reset, the men began the task of rebuilding the corral entrance while also watching the penned cattle. With the hope that one of the other calves would find its way into the trap, Orin was even more fortunate. When the tethered calf in the trap began bawling for its mother, one of the other cows moved in to investigate and sniff of the calf. The natural curiosity and motherly instinct of the cow had become too great. Orin quickly released the trap door.

Reminiscent of their earlier efforts, the two men securely tied the struggling cow after which Orin lifted the trap door open enough to allow the cow's calf to enter. With the advantage of previous experience, Orin was able to once again fill a pottery urn with milk.

The following morning the two men checked the penned animals. The previously released cattle grazed nearby with the mothers of the penned calves periodically returning to check on their bawling offspring. The two men began rebuilding the entrance of the corral, reducing it to a passage width of about four feet. They set the parallel fence poles in such a manner as to allow a second set of poles to be inserted across the gate opening, thereby controlling the movement of an animal in or out of the corral.

The sun had descended to near the horizon when they were finally ready to test the new structure. As a final preparation, they secured the outermost gate and then lowered the poles from the inner corral gate.

While impatiently waiting, they watched the sun sink below the mountain ridge. The animals inside the pen avoided the new structure.

"Any more good ideas?" chided the older man to his son. "I thought we were supposed to have fresh roast meat on the fire stones by now."

"I can't help it if the dumb things won't enter the chute," Orin grumbled.

Upon returning to camp, the two men explained the details of the project to the women who offered their hopes for greater success the following day.

"Perhaps the great Spirit of the Hunt is angry," Amalee suggested, "but at least you have some of the cattle in the corral and we have fresh milk for baby Ojon."

Nomi went to the rear of the shelter, returning with the partially filled urn. "Something strange has happened to the milk," she explained. "It has become thick on the top and I don't know whether it's safe for the baby."

Amalee took the urn to study the contents. She dipped her finger into the thick surface layer and touched it to her tongue. After licking her lips to better analyze the taste, she again tested a sample. "It tastes different," she said, "but I'm sure it's all right. In fact, I think it tastes sweeter. I wonder what made the milk separate like that?"

Following Amalee's remarks, each of the clansmen sampled the rich cream that had risen to the surface.

"I'll get some fresh milk in the morning for the baby," Orin offered, and then, as an afterthought, added, "but don't throw that out. Do you think it would hurt an adult to drink some of it? If cow's milk is good for a baby, it should also be good for adults. Perhaps if Nomi drank some of the milk, she would produce more herself."

Nomi, reluctantly at first, and then eagerly, consumed the remaining milk from the urn.

"Well?" Orin inquired.

"Well what?" she countered.

"Does it taste all right?"

"It tastes delicious," she answered, smiling. "In fact, it tastes about as good as anything I've ever tasted."

"If we could get enough," Orin added, "I'd like to try some myself."

The next morning, as the two men walked toward the corral, Orin commented, "I stayed awake a long time last night, thinking. I believe I know a better way to control the cattle. It should not only give us all the meat we want, but could probably give us all the milk we could ever use. I believe the only reason the remaining cattle haven't left the valley is because they won't abandon the ones we have in the corral. If we had a second large corral right next to the one we've already built, and if we could entice a few of the other cows into that corral, we could then release one group at a time to graze. I believe the released group would always return to the other corral to be near their calves. By alternately retaining one group while we release the others, the cattle would have a chance to graze. Cows are so dumb, I don't think they'd ever catch on. We could keep the calves in a special pen to entice the cows back and could then catch and tie the cows to get the milk."

"Your ideas wear me out," Dorik said, laughing and shaking his head. "You've been right so much in the past, though, I guess I'll have to go along with you. With the prospect of all this meat, at least we don't have to worry about hunting right now."

After Orin explained his plan, the two workers began the task of building a second corral which shared a common wall with the existing corral. Each of the corrals was connected by gates to a small pen, with other gates opening to the meadow. To expedite the project, the women also supplied their labor. The effort was occasionally interrupted when the cows with captive calves attempted to reach their offspring. After the cows entered the unused corral to be near their calves, the gate would be closed. The gate to the calf pen would then be opened, allowing the cows access to their calves. The men occasionally found themselves frantically climbing the fence to avoid the long horns of the agitated bulls. Upon completion of the task, the men were delighted at how well the plan was working.

Later when the cattle from the first corral were released to graze, the young bull was detained and isolated in the small, double gate entrance.

Dorik said to Orin. "At last we're going to enjoy some delicious meat. I feel almost guilty killing a helpless bull."

"He wouldn't hesitate in killing you," Orin answered. "Juicy strips of rib meat, sizzling on a cooking rock, should soothe your guilt feelings."

Using their spears, they slaughtered the animal after which the women were put to work skinning and cutting the flesh into long thin strips suitable for drying. The hunters urged the women to work faster for they were all aware that, in warm weather, some of the meat would spoil before it could be dried. The men volunteered to help carry a few of the larger sections of the carcass back to the camp where it was hung from the limbs of nearby trees. The wolves were allowed to feast on the bones and waste scraps.

When darkness prevented the women from pursuing their work, the clan members congregated around the cooking fire, gorging themselves on cuts of meat being roasted on the large, flat rocks embedded in hot coals.

Carma, who was in charge of caring for the baby, offered him small pieces of juicy meat to suck on.

"I've been thinking about our valley here," Dorik remarked. "Orin's plans for the corrals seem to have solved most of our problems. If we always keep the young calves penned, and if we never release all the cows at the same time, I think we can expect the grazing animals to always come back to the corrals. I'm very grateful to Orin for planning it all so well. We could probably live comfortably here forever."

The younger man was slightly embarrassed by the praise. "Dorik is the one we should be grateful to. If he hadn't left Agar's clan to join us, we probably could never have survived."

"So long as we're all expressing our gratitude," Amalee added, "I'm also grateful, for if it hadn't been for all of you, I would have died back there on the trail."

A moment of silence passed before Carma spoke. "What's going to happen to us. Are we going to spend the rest of our lives here? Aren't we going to ever see any other people? I miss all my friends in the clan."

The adults all glanced at each other, waiting for someone to answer the child. The situation posed by Carma had at some time been considered by each of the clan members, but further thought had always been postponed by the problems or pleasures of the moment. Amalee looked at Dorik, searching for an answer.

"I don't know, Carma," Dorik responded. "Life is so good here that I hate the thought of ever leaving. I suppose that someday, when you girls are older, we'll have to find mates for both of you. And when baby Ojon grows up he'll want to take a mate, otherwise our clan will die off. I suppose someday we'll have to locate and join another clan."

Summer passed into fall and the clan pursued its preparations for the coming winter. The shelter was repaired and fresh pine boughs were stacked on the sloped roof to shed the rain. Nuts were gathered and stored in leather pouches to be hung from the ceiling of the shelter. Small tart apples and other fruits were picked and dried. A large supply of dried meat hung on strings from the ridge pole of the shelter. Their experience with the captive cattle gave a feeling of security to all the adults.

Orin and Dorik continuously tested various arrangements of chutes through which the cows would have to pass to reach their calves, and in which they could easily be restrained while being milked.

The men observed that the calves, as they grew larger, accepted the men and could more easily be moved and controlled without the struggle that was characteristic of the older animals. As the two men watched the calves nursing, Orin offered his thoughts to Dorik. "I'll bet that by the time these calves grow up into cows, they'll be accustomed to us and will be more gentle."

With Orin getting milk from two of the cows, Amalee informed the others that, after the baby and Nomi had consumed all they wanted, there was usually a surplus.

The milk supply of Nomi also increased, as did the baby's appetite. Baby Ojon was growing rapidly, his color and robust appearance giving evidence to the older clansmen that the milk was a healthy food. Amalee and Nomi molded and baked new pots to accommodate the changing life-style of the clan.

With an apparent guaranteed supply of meat and milk, the clansmen turned their increased attention to improving the comfort of their existence. Animal skins were cured and tanned for use as bed robes as well as new and better clothes for all the clansmen. Deerskin, soft and pliable with the hair intact, was the preferred available garment material.

Though meat was not critical, the hunters returned to the forest to set their snares. They enjoyed the excitement of the hunt which also gave them an opportunity to be away from camp when the women were engaged in heavy tasks.

The behavior of the five wolves began to change. The animals developed a pattern of leaving camp together, often remaining away for two or three days. Upon returning they were usually hungry and invariably fought over any bones or meat scraps that were discarded by the clansmen.

The first time the young wolves failed to return for several days, Dorik became concerned. "I'm afraid they might not return some day," he remarked to Orin. "We'd sure miss them."

Both men appreciated the value of the wolves for hunting purposes but felt helpless to keep them from periodically leaving.

With the arrival of colder weather, the willows and trees along the stream displayed various shades of red and gold. The sun travelled a more southerly arc across the sky and the animals grew heavier coats of fur or hair in preparation for the coming winter. The adult clansmen felt comfortable with the supply of dried fruits and nuts stored in the shelter but agreed that, with the uncertainty of winter, they should have extra dried meat for emergencies. Another yearling bull was killed for that purpose. After being soaked in salt brine, strips of meat were hung near the fire to dry.

As the calves grew larger, the men began experiencing greater difficulty in separating the cows and calves. The two men spent less time hunting, devoting their energies to repairing or improving the corral. Although the system of enticing alternate groups of cattle back into the pens was working, questions were raised in the minds of the men.

Orin shared his thoughts with Dorik. "I wonder if the grazing cattle will quit coming back to the corral to be near the penned ones after the snow falls? When grazing becomes difficult, will one group abandon the other group?"

"I don't know," Dorik responded. "I certainly hope not."

During a cold and rainy milking session, Orin began considering alternatives. "I'm cold," he complained to Dorik, "and the icy water runs down my back. I wish I could do the milking in the comfort of a shelter."

"Then why don't we build one over the milking chute?" Dorik responded. "It shouldn't be that difficult."

The two men began gathering more poles and making more rope. Within a few days they had a pine bough cover over the chute, and although initially the cows were reluctant to enter, after a little prodding, the animals accepted the new structure.

The clan members all developed a taste and craving for milk. Without exception, they were each gaining weight, and conversation often centered on the merits of its use. Baby Ojon was growing and began crawling, eager to explore his surroundings. Retta willingly spent a great deal of her time guarding the child from the hazards of the campfire.

Amalee created new pottery containers for the increased milk supply and continued to be fascinated by the fact that cream would rise to the top after a period of storage. She and Nomi experimented with new recipes for cooking roots or seeds in the rich cream. The comfortable life-style was a constant reminder to the men of their need to reinforce their control over the cattle.

The milk was usually consumed before it could sour, but on one occasion Amalee went to the crock to get cream that had been skimmed from an earlier milk supply. "That's strange," she said to Nomi. "The cream tastes bad. I think it's spoiled."

Nomi tasted the liquid and agreed. "Maybe it was too warm. Meat spoils faster when it's warm so perhaps milk does too."

"I'll leave it in the crock and give it to the wolves later. Maybe they won't mind the taste."

The women became preoccupied with skinning and stripping meat from the young bull the men had slaughtered, forgetting to empty the crock at the back of the shelter. As Amalee moved the pot outside the shelter in preparation of discarding the contents, she again decided to taste it.

"It has an odd taste," she said, "and it's curdled, but if I add a little salt, it might still be good for cooking."

After separating the whey from the remaining curd, she again tasted the soft white cheese. "It's different," she commented, "but it's not bad. I'll have to try different ways of making and using it."

At night, Orin and Nomi, while embraced in the comfort of their bed robes, often discussed the blessings of the spirits that had guided them to such a paradise.

"I constantly think of baby Ojon and I'm grateful for the milk that saved his life," she confided. "If he had died, you would have been justified in sending me away from the camp."

"Foolish girl," he responded, kissing her gently on the neck. "I love you and would never send you away." He smiled, and in a joking tone, added, "Besides there's no one to replace you in bed."

Teasing, she pushed a finger into his ribs. "Is that why you keep me around? You just want me to prepare the food and be in bed when you want me. I don't think you really love me."

"I do," he countered, "but if you were a good mate, you'd give me another son."

"But that proves I'm a good mate," she countered.

A few moments passed before he realized the significance of the word. He raised up in the bed and grasped her shoulder. Her face was faintly illuminated by the fire near the shelter entrance. "What are you saying? Are we going to have another baby?"

"I think so," she replied. "I wanted to wait until I was sure, but now I'm almost certain."

He drew her near, gently kissing her. Turning his head, he called, "Dorik! Amalee! We're going to have another baby! Ojon is going to have a brother."

"If you ever awaken me like that again," Dorik responded gruffly, "the new baby might end up without a father. Now get back to sleep and consider the possibility that the baby might be a girl."

The first snow of approaching winter fell gently and quickly melted, but as winter progressed, the fury of the previous year was repeated. The snow continued to accumulate, and before each snowfall could melt, another storm arrived to add to the ever increasing snow cover.

The greatest fears of the two men became a reality. The cattle were not getting enough feed, and the animals that were free to graze in the meadow became increasingly reluctant to reenter the corral. It became apparent that the system that had served so well during the summer wouldn't work during the difficult winter. With the arrival of the deep snow, the cattle required every moment of daylight time to forage for enough dormant grass to survive.

"We'll have to turn them all loose," Orin suggested to his father. "The cows are growing thinner and are barely giving enough milk to keep the calves alive."

"Before we let them go, let's separate two or three of those yearling bulls and hold them in the corral. We can then slaughter them and hang the meat where it will freeze. At least we'll have enough meat for most of the winter."

The men isolated two young bulls before reluctantly releasing the cows and calves. The bulls were slaughtered and the carcass quarters were hung from high limbs in the shady pine grove near the shelter. The wolves, although unable to reach the meat, served to discourage other carnivores from attempting the same.

When the winter snow became deep, the men returned to the technique of hunting with their snow walkers. On each of the hunting forays, the wolves eagerly followed but were becoming noticeably more irritable and uncontrollable.

* * *

The sun had settled below the hills to the southwest, replaced by a three-quarter moon adding a luminescent glow to the surface of the deep snow. The clansmen snuggled warmly between their heavy bed robes, stirring occasionally to toss pieces of wood on the low fire that burned near the shelter entrance.

The adults were suddenly awakened by the rush of the pet wolves from the back of the shelter. The animals leaped over the bedrolls, racing out of the shelter into the deep snow. Orin's ears caught the sound of the long, mournful call of a wolf from a great distance away, and shivers ran through his body as the tame wolves responded with the same eerie call. Orin and Dorik quickly went to the shelter entrance to push back the leather flap. The pale moonlight revealed a wolf pack far out on the frozen lake bed and the men watched as the tame animals ran to meet their wild relatives. The domestic wolves, conditioned to subservience to the clansmen, approached the hunting pack with tails drawn low and heads lowered. In response to a challenge by the pack leader, the tame wolves cowered by rolling onto their backs, exposing their throats to the mercy of the leader. From the security of the shelter, the men only partially saw or understood the drama that was unfolding on the lake. After completing the ritual, the wild wolves moved off toward the forest beyond the lake, accompanied by the five tame animals.

"I had hoped our wolves would protect the cattle from any wild pack," Dorik grumbled, "but it looks like they're joining them. I'm afraid a pack that size could easily kill some of our weaker cows."

The following morning Retta and Carma were terribly disappointed to learn of the disappearance of their canine friends. Dorik and Orin said little, but were equally disappointed to lose their hunting companions.

"I assumed they would leave sooner or later," the clan leader remarked. "We'll miss them terribly. We'll have to go back to our old way of hunting."

Through the following days the men occasionally donned their snow walkers to spend the afternoons setting and checking snares in the nearby woods. The frozen quarters of beef supplied their daily needs and were only slowly being depleted. The men hunted, not only for the joy and anticipation, but to escape the close confines of the shelter.

"Next summer, I think we ought to build a larger structure for our home," Orin suggested.

Dorik concurred. "I've been thinking the same thing. I'd like to build one much larger and leave an opening in the top so we could keep our winter fire in the center of the dwelling."

Orin's mind began working on the possibilities. He gathered dried willows, experimenting with various designs. The sisters became fascinated, watching him construct a miniature dwelling with his bundle of willow sticks.

"It's easy to build the walls by laying the poles across each other," he explained to Dorik, "but it's difficult to leave an opening to get in and out." He finally settled on a design, feeling he had resolved the problem. "If we build a double wall of poles on one end," he explained to his father, "and support the ends of those walls short of each other with enough room to get in and out, we can then hang robes over the opening and have the shelter well protected against the wind. We can lay poles across the top of the structure and cover them with pine boughs like we've done here. We can use mud to plug the openings between the poles."

- 21 -

The days of late winter grew longer, and the snow was slowly being consumed by the increased sunlight. The creek became a roaring muddy river, overflowing its banks and flooding portions of the great meadow. Spring rains stole an additional share of the diminishing snow cover, turning the trails into muddy, slippery paths. The supply of dried meats, nuts and roots lasted far longer than the previous difficult winter, and the frozen meat lasted until it would have otherwise spoiled. The hunters, using snares, were occasionally successful in supplementing their diminishing food supply.

Orin and Dorik maintained a close surveillance of the cattle herd.

"I don't see the old cow with the crooked horn," Orin commented, "but as near as I can count, she's the only one missing."

The thought produced a worried look on Dorik's face. "If the wolf pack had returned, I'm sure we'd have seen them. I sure hope we don't have another tiger in the area."

The two men searched the edge of the meadow for tracks and other signs of large carnivores but found only signs of deer, rabbits and the footprints of one of the smaller members of the cat family. After crossing the far end of the meadow and starting back toward the lake, Dorik saw a mud print that caught his attention.

"This looks like a bear track," Dorik informed his son, "but I can't believe a bear would kill a full grown cow."

The two men followed the tracks well out onto the meadow until, upon approaching the stream, they saw the remains of the missing cow.

"She's been dead quite awhile," Orin observed. "I think the bear has been feasting on the carcass, but I don't believe it killed her."

Dorik examined what was left of the animal. "I think you're right," he said, while examining the bones. "The cow's leg is broken. She must have broken it here on these rocks and couldn't get up. She probably starved to death right here before the bear discovered her."

The two men returned to camp, reassured there was no great threat to the cattle herd. They each harbored plans for the coming summer on the assumption they could entice the herd back into the corrals with the newborn calves.

The men spent the early spring days setting and checking snares, producing an occasional success. Fresh deer meat, though not plentiful, became the main staple of their diet.

Considerable thought was given to the possible location of the new dwelling.

Amalee meekly offered an opinion. "I think it would be nice to build it near the spring, close to the watercress bed. Then we could always have clean, fresh water without carrying it so far."

The men, having no other site in mind, felt there was some merit to the woman's suggestion. If the women didn't have to carry water so far, it would allow them more time for other chores.

The clansmen began collecting and stockpiling the long, straight poles that would be suitable for the new dwelling, and the women were put to work burning the poles off at the places designated by Orin.

The weather improved and became warmer, allowing the construction of their new dwelling to begin. Orin positioned the entrance facing south with only a short walking distance to the small stream that flowed from the spring. While Nomi struggled to fulfill her duties at the camp and new construction, she was hampered by her growing pregnancy. The birth of her second child was growing near.

During the night, Dorik was awakened by a movement across his bed robe. The action sent a surge of adrenaline into his veins, bringing him to a full alert condition. He reached for his hand axe, and was about to swing at the unknown intruder when a whining sound disclosed the identity of the beast. In the light of the dim fire he saw one of the domesticated wolves in the corner of the shelter. After alerting the other clan members, he stoked the fire to better illuminate the animal.

"Fluffy has come home," Retta excitedly exclaimed. "She loves us and left those wild wolves to come home to us."

"I think she came home to have puppies," Amalee suggested. "She looks that way to me."

Retta ran to hug the older woman. "Oh Mama, can I have one of the new puppies when they come?"

"Dorik will make that decision," she answered. "She'll probably leave again before the pups are born. I'm surprised that she came back at all."

"Perhaps her mate was killed," Orin suggested. "If that is what happened, she might stay here."

After feeding the wolf, Retta coaxed her to cuddle near her bed robe, and was reassured by Dorik that she could have her choice of the litter.

* * *

The men maintained a close surveillance of the cattle, searching for signs of a new spring calf. The vigil was finally rewarded and the men repeated the old familiar technique of moving the calf to the corral. The cow was allowed to come and go freely except when she would enter the chute to nurse her calf. Orin and Dorik resumed the milking procedure, supplying Nomi with the important nourishment.

"If you drink milk before the baby is born," Orin insisted, "perhaps your own milk supply for the baby will improve."

Nomi shared the supply with her son, but felt guilty not sharing with the girls or other adults. Within a few days, a second calf was caught, resulting in additional milk for the entire clan.

Work continued on the new dwelling, but Nomi was excused from the heavier work, allowing her time to perform her regular chores. Amalee informed the men that the child could be born any day.

- 22 -

From his position on the wall of the new structure, Orin nervously called to his father. "I see two men a long way out on the meadow," he shouted, pointing toward a pair of small silhouettes in the distance.

Dorik lifted his hand to shade his eyes. He waited a moment, studying the figures. "Yes," he confirmed, "there are two of them all right, but I can't tell whether they're men from our old clan. I think we ought to go out to meet them. In case of trouble, I'd rather confront them out there."

After Dorik explained the situation to Amalee, advising her to take the girls to the shelter, the two worried hunters picked up their spears and moved out across the meadow.

A multitude of questions and fears haunted the mind of the younger man. Could one of the men be Agar, or be from Agar's clan? Even if they're from another clan, will Dorik want his clan to join up with them and move on? Although he hoped they were strangers, his greatest concern was Agar. His instinct was to run to Nomi's side and escape with her into the hills. Even if such an act was possible, it was impractical. Nomi was expecting a baby at any time and was in no condition to travel. If Agar was one of the men, Orin knew that he'd either have to fight him or run, and if he was to run, it would have to be without Nomi.

Dorik and Orin walked in silence, each one occupied with his own thoughts. The distant figures remained motionless, waiting for the distance to narrow. Upon reaching a point where recognition might be possible, Orin and Dorik paused, watching the two strangers, one of whom was pointing. Suddenly the hunter who was pointing commenced running and quickly disappeared into the nearby woods.

Orin then recognized the remaining traveler. "It looks like Vodim," he announced to his father. "That means the clan is nearby. That also means that Agar is near." The thought produced a sickening feeling in his stomach.

"Let's go talk to him before we form any conclusions," Dorik suggested. "Vodim is a good man and will give us the answer."

As Orin and Dorik moved forward, Vodim stood motionless, waiting. No one spoke until they stood facing each other.

"Hello, Vodim," Dorik said, speaking in a soft and friendly tone. "How are you?"

"I'm fine, Dorik, and how are you?" Without waiting for an answer, he turned to Orin. "You look well, Orin. Are Carma and Retta all right? And the girl, Nomi, is she with you? Is she all right?"

"Yes, Vodim, they're all well. We also brought mother with us, and she is also well."

Vodim's eyes widened. "She survived back at the camp where we left her?" He appeared surprised and pleased.

"Yes, Vodim," the young man affirmed. "She was awfully weak when I found her, but she's recovered and is completely well now."

Vodim looked in the direction of the lake. "Where are they now?"

Dorik answered. "They're all back at our camp. Who was your partner who just departed, and where is the clan?"

"That was Armid," Vodim answered. "He's on his way back to the clan which will be camped just the other side of this ridge. We're on our way north to the hunting grounds and Armid and I have been scouting this side of the trail searching for game."

"Tell us what happened after we left camp," Dorik asked. "Is Agar still clan leader?"

Vodim answered affirmatively, adding, "I'm afraid he's become a very bitter man. He's vowed to kill either of you if he ever finds you. He feels that Orin deserves death for taking some members of the clan away, and he feels you betrayed him by deserting the clan. Under the circumstances, I would have done the same as you, but that doesn't change the irrational attitude of Agar."

"What will you do now?" Dorik asked. "What are your plans?"

"I still have some of my family with the clan, so I have no choice but to stay with them, but if you don't mind, I'll wait here and let the other hunters come to me. I'm sure that when Armid reveals your whereabouts, Agar will bring them over here."

Again, Orin was gripped by a feeling of panic, nervously glancing in the direction of Armid's departure.

"We might as well wait back at our camp," Dorik suggested, nodding his head toward the lake.

As the three men began walking, Vodim told of the travels and experiences of the clan following Dorik's departure.

"Agar was as mean as a bear after you all left the clan," Vodim explained. "He forced us to travel at a tedious pace until we finally located the bison herds. We were able to get all the calves we wanted, and an occasional cow, but after a few days, Agar suddenly decided to move the clan on farther north to hunt reindeer. We lost one of the smaller clan children when we crossed the river. When we finally located the reindeer herds, hunting was good and we killed all the calves we wanted, but Agar kept moving us from one area to another, always searching for other hunting groups. I think he was hoping to find all of you with one of the other clans."

Vodim stopped walking, interrupting his story to view the valley and surrounding hills. "You certainly found a beautiful place here by the lake. Have you been here long?"

Dorik briefly summarized the activities of his small group. He captured Vodim's full interest when he described the methods and success of corralling the cattle. "In all my years of hunting," Dorik added, "I would never have believed that meat could be so dependable. We kill only what we need and it's great to have the animals here in the valley when we need them."

As they approached the shelter, Dorik called to the girls. Upon recognition of their father, Carma and Retta ran to Vodim's side, hugging and kissing the man.

Amalee also emerged from the shelter and walked several paces to meet the men.

After Vodim lowered Retta from his arms, he took the woman's hands. "Amalee, you look marvelous," he said. "You look younger than you have for years. You don't know how happy I am to see you and to know you're well."

"You look well also, Vodim," Amalee replied, still holding his hands. She waited a moment before continuing. "Vodim, you were a good mate to me and a good father to the girls. I'll always remember and be grateful for that. When Agar took me away from Dorik, assigning me first to his own hearth and later to you, I was resentful and bitter. I'm sure you knew that, but you accepted me and treated me well. I grew to respect you and was proud to bear you two fine daughters. When the clan left me on the trail, I knew you were very disturbed, but I also knew that you had no choice."

Vodim released her hands but offered no comment.

Amalee continued. "When Dorik left the clan to join Orin and the rest of us, he generously took me back as his mate. Dorik is now the leader of our small clan. He knows of my deep love for him. My future rests with his decision."

Vodim started to speak but found himself at a loss for words. To terminate the awkward situation, he turned to his daughters. "My, how you've grown, Carma. You're almost a woman. And Retta, how beautiful you are, just like your mother."

Amalee attempted to further ease any tension. "You must be hungry, Vodim. We have some roast meat that you might enjoy."

As the group moved to the fire, Amalee handed Vodim a strip of meat left from their earlier meal.

"When do you think the hunters will arrive?" Dorik asked, looking at Vodim. His concern was clearly evident.

"Not before tomorrow," Vodim answered, "and probably not before midday. The camp is a half day's travel from here." He studied Orin and then Dorik for a moment before adding, "Why don't all of you take a few supplies and move south for awhile. Agar won't want to retrace our travels, and I doubt if he would wait around here very long. You could then return in a few days."

Dorik shook his head. "I'll not run from that man. I'll meet him right here." He then turned to his son. "I'm speaking for myself, Orin. You and Nomi are free to do whatever you want. I would respect any decision you make."

Orin studied the face of his father before responding. "I'd rather die than run away from that horrible beast. I'm determined to face him, regardless of the outcome."

"You'll have to wait until after I've had my chance," Dorik said. "I intend to do better than I did last time."

Vodim interrupted with a warning. "Agar will probably use his hand axe. Are you sure you want to stand up to him?"

"I'll face him with my fists, if necessary," Dorik angrily answered. "I should have challenged him long ago."

From his waist strap, Orin drew the hand axe that Dorik had awarded him much earlier in the ceremony. He displayed the weapon to Vodim, offering an explanation. "This is the only hand axe we have in camp. We haven't found any flint to make another."

Vodim turned back to Dorik, drawing his own hand axe from his waist strap. "Dorik," he said, extending the weapon. "I want you to take my hand axe as a gift. I have another one at the camp."

"I do thank you, Vodim," Dorik replied, "but if Agar recognizes your axe, he'll take his vengeance out on you."

"No, I don't think so," Vodim countered. "He knows that he's lost a lot of the support of his hunters and won't risk losing any more. He only wants to get back at you. He's trying to save face from his earlier mistakes."

When the female wolf, returning from her usual afternoon search for rabbits or squirrels, approached camp, she saw Vodim. She bared her fangs, snarling a defiant challenge. The hunter reacted by quickly raising his spear in a defensive posture.

Orin stepped toward the wolf, issuing a crisp command. "Stop it! Quiet there!" He grasped the wolf by the nape of her neck, subduing her.

Vodim's mouth was agape at seeing the wolf obey. His surprise turned to alarm when Orin then ordered Retta to take the animal inside the shelter. Orin then explained the presence of the wolf and told the story of the pack.

"The beast gave me a worry," Vodim responded. "I'm amazed that a wolf would let a child handle it."

Nomi, her stomach enlarged, awkwardly assisted Amalee in preparing an evening meal. The men remained near the shelter, recounting their experiences of the past two years.

Vodim expressed awe and admiration for what the small group had accomplished. "Seeing what you've done here makes me envious. I wish the clan could find a place like this so we wouldn't have to be on the trail so much." He paused, weighing the advantages before adding, "But of course Agar would never accept any ideas that came from either of you. He's a very stubborn man." The conversation continued until long after the sinking sun had withdrawn its light from the valley.

Although Vodim was invited to share the sleeping robes inside the shelter, he preferred to bed down outside near the fire. "I prefer sleeping out here, away from that beast," he explained. "I'm just not used to sleeping with a wolf, and I don't think the wolf is ready to accept me." He went to sleep concerned about the safety of his daughters who could love and pet such a ferocious animal.

While cuddling Nomi in their sleeping robe, Orin felt the baby's movements inside her body. He allowed his mind to wonder whether he would ever see the child. Nomi offered no conversation. Her silent anguish allowed Orin the privacy of his own thoughts.

Sleep was reluctantly bestowed on the expectant mother, but was withheld much longer from the frightened and bewildered father. Orin lay wide awake well into the night worrying, more for the future of Nomi and his son, Ojon, than for himself. He worried about the coming fight, feeling guilty that his father should insist on being first to confront Agar, when it was clearly his own fight. The familiar sickening feeling again returned to his stomach.

His tormented mind probed for answers. Why did Vodim and Armid have to stumble into this valley and destroy all my hopes and plans? If it wasn't for my actions, he reasoned, the others would still be members of Agar's clan. If I just hadn't lost my temper at the hot pool. Maybe I should never have left the clan. But if I hadn't, I would never have found Amalee still alive. I don't know what to think. It's all so confusing.

His main concern was for Nomi and his son, Ojon. If Agar has his way, he speculated, will he take Nomi as his mate and keep my babies as a reminder of his authority? What will happen to Amalee? Will she be given back to Vodim or will Agar also take out his vengeance on her?

Sleep eluded the tormented young man. He was still waiting for the first light of dawn when his exhausted mind finally surrendered to fitful sleep.

When he awakened, the camp was bathed in sunlight. Nomi had departed the bed and the only inhabitants of the shelter were the two sisters and himself.

"Where are Dorik and Vodim?" Orin inquired of his mother who sat peeling roots near the fire.

"They left early to look at your cow trap and the corrals," she explained. "They had a bite to eat before they left. You better have something also before you join them."

Orin, in a dazed condition, picked up and began chewing on a strip of cooked meat as he wandered aimlessly toward the corrals. He saw the other two men at a distance, but had no enthusiasm for joining them. He started toward the new construction, intending to continue his work, but his sickening feeling returned. As he sat on one of the poles with his head in his hands, he mumbled, "Why, oh why, does this have to happen? Why can't the spirits prevent all of this?" After a short time he rose to his feet and aimlessly began moving poles in a nervous effort at cabin construction. He became oblivious to the passage of time until, glancing at the sun, he realized that it was near midday. Looking around for Dorik and Vodim, he assumed they had returned to the shelter. He walked to the spring and drank heavily from the cool water to moisten his dry mouth. He then began walking slowly back toward the camp.

Lifting his head from a slumped position, Orin's eyes caught a movement in the distance and his heart began pounding. Approaching along the edge of the meadow were several men. Orin attempted to count, but concluded only that there were about ten or twelve. In a daze, he continued walking toward the shelter. Nearing camp, he saw Dorik and Vodim watching the same approaching hunting group.

As he joined the two older men, Orin saw his mother and Nomi emerge from the shelter. Dorik turned and pointed at the women with a stern command. "I want you both back inside the shelter and stay out of sight. You are not to come out until ordered."

Orin saw tears on the face of Nomi as the two women reluctantly retreated. There was no conversation from the three men as they waited for the arrival of the hunting group.

Agar, advancing forward of the other men, approached the shelter and stopped. His eyes scanned the area before settling on Vodim. "It looks like reunion time for you, Vodim," he chortled. "Are you waiting for me to get your daughters back for you?" His sarcasm emphasized his anger and nervous tension.

"If you have anything to say, then save it for me," Dorik said, stepping forward to face his old adversary. "I'm the only one you're concerned with now."

Agar glanced contemptuously at Dorik. "I'll take care of you later," he said. He then turned to face Orin who was standing a few feet away. "But first I'm going to tear the guts out of this disloyal, worthless worm."

Dorik quickly stepped forward, taking a position between Agar and Orin. "No, you won't," he shouted. "Your gripe is with me. You'll have to settle with me first."

Agar waited a few moments, studying the scene. He then turned to his hunters with a sharp command. "I want you men to hold this old traitor in check while I take care of his miserable son. I'll take care of him later."

As Dorik raised his arms and began moving toward his antagonist, Agar retreated a few paces, again shouting to his hunters. "Didn't you hear me? I told you to hold that man. If you don't obey, you'll have me to contend with later."

The hunters reluctantly advanced toward Dorik, where, after a short struggle, they held his arms tightly behind his back. Agar, who had been facing Orin, then momentarily turned his attention back to Dorik who was still struggling to free himself from the hunters.

"I want you to watch this," he emphasized while drawing his hand axe from his waist band. "I want you to watch me cut that boy of yours into pieces. I want you to see a sample of what you're in for as soon as I finish with him."

Orin, in a partial daze, had been watching without being fully aware of the implications. He suddenly realized that the moment of action had arrived. Fear pumped adrenaline into his bloodstream and he felt a tightening of his muscles. He drew his own hand axe before turning to face the threat.

As Agar advanced to within a few feet of Orin, he suddenly lunged forward toward the startled youth, simultaneously swinging his hand axe in a downward arc. Orin, seeing the descending weapon, raised his left arm to deflect the blow. The shaft of the axe was diverted by the younger man's arm, but the inertia of the swing and the weight of the man behind it were too great. Orin lost his balance, falling backward to the ground. Agar's momentum carried him beyond the fallen youth before he quickly turned and lunged back, again swinging the axe downward toward his prone victim. Orin saw the descending weapon and the enraged fury of Agar charging downward toward him. Bracing his legs, and with a desperate effort, he twisted and rolled his body enough to avoid the pending blow.

As the weight of the older man crashed down on his victim, Agar's free hand groped for the younger man's throat. Orin released his axe, and summoning all his remaining strength, pushed the determined leader from him. Orin then struggled to his feet barely in time to face a new charge from Agar whose hand axe was again raised for attack.

Vodim shouted from the circle of men who surrounded the two adversaries. "Hold it, Agar. Stop it. Orin doesn't have his weapon."

Without removing his eyes from the youth, Agar shouted his response. "Good! That's his tough luck. Then he won't have it with him in the spirit world, either, will he?"

"Come on, Agar," Vodim again pleaded. "It isn't a fair fight. At least let the boy have his weapon."

A few of the hunters mumbled agreement but refrained from identifying themselves.

Agar ignored the comments. As the enraged clan leader advanced toward Orin, brandishing his hand axe in his raised hand, Orin slowly backed away, leaving an ever greater distance between himself and his own axe that lay useless on the ground. The panicked youth, his eyes focused on Agar's threatening weapon, raised his arm, hoping to again deflect the blow. As the axe began its downward swing, Orin stepped backward, catching his heel in the hole of some long departed burrowing rodent. Upon losing his balance, the youth fell backward, thrusting his arms behind him to break his fall. As Orin waited in a semi-prone position, Agar moved forward, and as though waiting to gain the maximum attention, held his weapon poised until assured his men would all witness the kill. As Agar lifted his axe slightly higher to begin the downward blow, he became distracted, first by a commotion and then by a growl from behind him. Agar turned his head just in time to see the wolf, with fangs bared, leap toward him in a powerful lunge. The surprised hunter turned with his arms raised to defend himself. Using his elbow, he managed to deflect the body of the attacking animal. As the wolf whirled to again attack, one of the hunters ran forward to drive his spear point into the shoulder of the animal. The wolf fell to the ground with a pained and useless front leg. As the hunter withdrew the spear and was again about to plunge it into the animal, Retta screamed. All eyes turned to the young child who ran to her pet, throwing her body as a protective shield over the injured animal.

"Get that girl away and I'll kill the beast," shouted the hunter who stood over the child and wounded animal.

"We'll take care of the wolf later," Agar shouted. He quickly turned his attention back to Orin who was stooping low to retrieve his weapon. Agar again lunged toward the youth in an effort to regain the advantage he had earlier enjoyed. Orin had still not recovered his full upright stance when Agar's arm and axe again began a downward swing toward his head. From his crouched position, Orin's braced legs allowed him to rapidly propel his body to one side to avoid the arc of the rapidly descending weapon. The momentum of the axe carried the downward action well beyond the range of the intended victim. As Orin whirled, his eyes caught the opportunity offered by Agar's lowered weapon. His own arm and axe were in motion from the frantic twisting action of his body and his right foot was dug into the ground to regain his balance. Summoning all the strength of his powerful muscles, Orin increased the momentum of his hand axe. Swinging with a tremendous force from above and across the lowered arm of Agar, Orin drove the sharp flint edge deep into his enemy's temple. Agar dropped motionless to the ground. He was instantly dead.

- 23 -

Everyone stood motionless. Not a word was said, nor was any movement made for a long time. At last, as the significance of the event was recognized by the hunters, they released the arms of Dorik. Orin still stood panting, staring down at the body of his vanquished enemy. Suddenly he felt weak. He could no longer stand. He looked around for something on which to sit, but found nothing. His knees buckled as he lowered himself to the ground. With his head at the lower level, the blood flow slowly returned to normal, clearing his mind. He felt foolish for showing a weakness that he didn't understand, but when the full awareness of his victory revealed itself, a feeling of joy and excitement surged through him and he barely refrained from shouting with joy.

Vodim walked to where Retta was shielding the wolf. He took the weeping child in his arms, carrying her back to the shelter. Dorik picked up the wounded animal and carefully carried it to a nest of pine needles near the fire.

As Nomi emerged from the shelter from where she had witnessed her mate's victory, tears of joy slid down her cheeks. She ran to Orin, and in an emotional display that normally would have been frowned on, threw herself into his arms, burying her tear-strewn face in his chest.

Dorik returned from where he had left the wolf and placed a hand on his son's shoulder. He started to speak, but choked and remained silent. From the edge of the group, Amalee watched and waited, emotionally drained.

There was a loud murmur of whispering from the group of hunters who had retreated a short distance. Finally Gors, spokesman of the group, advanced to where Orin stood.

"What are your orders?" he asked of the young victor.

"What do you mean?" countered the youth.

"You defeated Agar. You are now the clan leader." Gors placed a hand on the youth's shoulder, but then feeling he may have over-extended his prerogatives, withdrew his arm.

"No," Orin said, looking at his father. "Dorik is our clan leader. He is the one to give orders."

Dorik quickly evaluated the mood of the assembled men before responding to his son. "You are the one who defeated Agar. By tradition, you are the one to become clan leader."

"But I don't want to leave the valley. I don't want to spend half of my life, and the lives of my children and friends, traveling the trail, always searching for game."

"Then that is your privilege," Dorik emphasized. "You may keep any or all of the clan here in the valley. You may also order them to leave and never come back. It is your decision."

The weight of the authority and responsibility was almost too staggering for Orin's mind to comprehend. There was a long silence before he at last turned to Vodim with his first directive. "I want you to take the men back to your camp and bring the rest of the clan back to this valley. In the meantime, I have a lot of thinking to do before I make any decisions."

214

* * *

The hunters took the dead leader to the marsh near the end of the lake, where, after tying a heavy stone to the body, they allowed it to sink slowly into the mud.

Vodim led the men back across the ridge to inform a surprised and perplexed clan of the day's events.

Amalee and Nomi busied themselves preparing a feast and celebration. With the confrontation over, Orin felt a joyous relief, but when he allowed his mind to comprehend his responsibility and obligations, he couldn't help but withdraw into serious thought. He at last succumbed to the enthusiasm of the small clan, joining in the feast and singing that lasted until long after the sun had set.

The following morning he awoke at first light. He reached out to draw Nomi a little closer and forced his thoughts to focus on the matters to be decided. His happiness with life in the valley, and the progress with the cattle, weighed heavily on his judgment. He considered the options. Can I simply send the clan on its way and allow them to pick a new leader? If I do that, would Carma want to go with the clan? Then there is Retta and my own son, Ojon, and even the unborn baby. Is it fair to isolate these children in this valley and run the risk of never finding mates for them? Can I order the clan to pass through the valley each journey on their way to and from the hunting grounds? That would solve the problem of finding mates. His logic refuted such a consideration. Once I release the clan to choose their own leader, he reasoned, I forfeit my authority, and the new leader may then choose to never return. The problem haunted and tormented Orin until he decided to postpone any decision. He could easily afford to let the clan spend a few days near the lake before assuming such responsibility.

The new young leader watched his mother and Carma bathing the wounds of the female wolf that had probably saved his life. I owe everything to that wonderful animal, he reasoned. She came to my defense without any thought of her own safety. There is a loyalty in that animal far greater than anyone can imagine. I know I'll always have a fondness for that wonderful creature.

Orin again became absorbed in thought regarding his new responsibilities. He repeatedly summarized the possibilities while later discussing them with his father.

"Don't look to me for answers," Dorik said to his son. "I know what you're thinking and I know your problems with those thoughts. You're the new leader of the clan and I have faith that the spirits will guide you in your decisions."

"Thanks a lot," was Orin's joking comment. "It looks like you're the real winner. All I wanted to do is build better ways to capture and handle the cattle."

"Then why don't you use the clan to do just that?"

Dorik's comment brought a silence to the conversation. Orin allowed his thoughts to dwell on Dorik's last statement. If he used the entire clan, could he expand the cattle catching and milking operation? Are there enough animals to supply meat and milk for the entire group?

I doubt it, he reasoned. Of course, I could certainly use some help in building larger corrals. In fact, I would love to eventually build a pole wall around the entire meadow to ensure that the cattle would never leave the area. But I can't keep the clan here just to help me control the cattle. That would mean more mouths to feed. I doubt if the size of this herd could continuously feed our entire clan. Maybe we could continue to supplement the meat of the long horned cattle with some other source of game. We could always trap a few deer, but I know from clan experience that when the clan stays in one place too long, the number of deer diminish."

He was still laboring with those thoughts when Carma ran to his side. "Look, Orin," she announced excitedly. "I see all the other people coming down the meadow and all my friends will be there. I can't wait to tell them about our wolves, and all about the other exciting things we've done."

Orin saw the enthusiasm in the eyes of his sister. "Why don't you run out and meet them?" he suggested. "I'm sure your friends have a lot to tell you, also."

The young girl raced across the meadow with her long hair trailing in the light midday breeze.

When the clan at last arrived at the lakeshore, Tomar approached Orin. "I've heard the story of the fight and your victory. In fact I've heard it several times. You are to be congratulated. May the spirits reward you with health and a long life."

"Thank you, Tomar," Orin responded. "I'm not sure that I deserve the leadership, nor am I sure that I want it. There are many men stronger and more deserving than myself."

"You're too modest. I'm sure that everyone in the clan is willing and anxious for you to assume the leadership. I'm also sure your authority will be tested soon enough. How you carry it will determine how long you carry it."

Tomar's message only increased the weight imposed on Orin's already burdened shoulders. He also felt a need for Tomar's advice to reinforce the thoughts and plans that were beginning to form in his troubled mind. After seating the old spiritual leader on a log, Orin related the experiences in the valley. As he portrayed the problems and benefits of spending a winter in the snow country, the old sage listened, wide-eyed with amazement. When Orin described the trap and the capture of the tiger, Tomar shook his head in disbelief. When he saw the tiger robe, he again shook his head, but only to emphasize the incredibility of the feat. When Orin finally told him of catching and milking the wild, long-horned cows, the old man refused to believe that such a thing could be possible.

Orin and Dorik took the hunters down to the corrals to see the captive cattle. As they approached the fence, the corralled bulls bellowed and charged toward the frightened clansmen who scattered in wild retreat. From the safety of distance, the hunters watched with amazement to see Orin and Dorik stand their ground across the fence from the huge beasts. The bulls repeatedly charged toward the men, always stopping short of the pole enclosure where they then vented their anger by bellowing and pawing the earth.

Gors shook his head in amazement as he remarked to Vodim, "I sure thought they were on their way to the spirit world."

After the hunters cautiously rejoined Orin and Dorik, they were told of the operation.

"We keep the herd divided," Orin explained. "We also keep the calves in the inner pen and when the grazing cows return from the open pasture to nurse the calves, we close that corral gate and release the animals we've been holding in the other corral. In that way the cattle all have a chance to graze out on the meadow during part of the day but later always return to be with the other animals. Cows aren't as smart as wolves or foxes."

Orin and Dorik were then surprised to see that one of the cows, upon being deprived the opportunity of delivering her calf in the security of the brush, had given birth in the corral.

One of the hunters asked Dorik why he didn't try to kill the newborn calf before the cow was capable of defending it.

"We save the calves as a means of enticing the cows back into the corral," Dorik explained. "We also believe that the cattle will remain in the valley if we kill only as many as we need. By doing that, there will always be some cattle left for the future."

The men listened with rapt attention.

"See those cows in the other corral," Dorik continued. "The gate is open and they are free to come and go as they want. The animals always try to stay close together as a single herd, so every day, after the free animals have grazed their fill, they return to be near the captive ones. Orin and I will now close the gate to that corral and release the cows from this one so these animals can graze."

Orin, who had been listening to Dorik's explanation, added a suggestion. "I think we should have a feast today and allow the entire clan to celebrate. We'll slaughter one of the bulls. If we save the cows, there'll be more calves to sustain the herd."

The hunters watched as Orin and Dorik closed one gate and opened the other, and then saw the animals file out on their way to the meadow.

Vodim appeared puzzled as he asked Orin, "Surely those bulls are strong enough to break down that pole wall?"

Dorik answered for his son. "Yes, they are. You and I know it, but the bulls don't seem to know it. They're not the most intelligent animals in the land."

After the cattle left the corral, the new calf and mother cow were moved to the calf pen. The animals that were retained attempted to follow the released cows, but when one of the less dominant bulls entered the chute, Dorik pushed the poles across the entrance to prevent his escape.

"Now, when we're ready," Orin explained, "we'll have all the meat we need for our feast."

The animal was slaughtered and the clansmen, initiating the festivities, built fires along the lakeshore. The clan women were put to work skinning and butchering the carcass. Orin lingered with the members of the old clan to enjoy the songs and laughter that echoed across the valley.

He was deep in conversation with several of the hunters, explaining his plans, when Retta ran to his side. "Mama wants you to come to the shelter," she announced urgently.

"What does she want?" Orin asked, his eyes searching Retta's face for an explanation.

"I don't know, Orin. Mama is with Nomi in the shelter, and I heard Nomi moaning. I don't know what's wrong."

Orin ran to the shelter. As he entered the structure and faced his mother, she looked up from her kneeling position.

"Well, you got here just in time," she said. "Your mate has just given you another fine baby boy."

Orin let out a whoop of joy, and without pausing to check on the condition of Nomi, ran toward the celebrating clansmen to announce the arrival of his second son. "We'll name him Orik," he announced. "He'll grow up to be a fine hunter, just like his brother, Ojon."

The celebration lasted far into the night. The hunters, one after another, approached Orin to congratulate him on his victory and his new son, and to proclaim loyalty to the leadership that he wasn't sure he wanted.

The following morning Orin called Dorik and Tomar to join him in formulating plans. "I'd like to keep the clan right here in the valley," he announced, "but I don't believe there is enough game in the hills, or that the cattle herd is large enough to sustain the entire clan. Perhaps if the hunters occasionally scout the neighboring valleys, we could provide for everyone."

Orin then turned to Tomar. "I seek the wisdom of your many years to help me make a decision about the future of the clan."

"I'm impressed and amazed at what you've done here in this mountain valley," the old man said. "I have a strong opinion, but you may find it prejudiced. The benevolent spirits have granted me forty and seven years of life with this clan, for which I am grateful. Each time I travel the trail of our hunting journeys, I find it more difficult, and each time I wonder how many moons of life I have left."

Dorik placed his hand on the shoulder of the old man. "Tomar," he said, "you shouldn't think like that. Our clan needs you. There is no one with your wisdom or power to invoke the favor of the spirits. We'll always need you."

"Always is a long time," Tomar responded. "For myself, I would welcome a permanent home such as those enjoyed by the sea clans. It would also be good for the women of the clan to be relieved of the burden of the trail. Since our arrival here in this valley, I've pondered the benefits and problems of adopting this new way of life. If the clan could be sustained here, I see many benefits to be gained. I'm sure there will be problems beyond our imagination, but if the spirits have guided your actions so far, we can assume they will continue to do so."

The other two men waited for Tomar to continue, but when the old man remained silent, Orin said, "I've decided, for now, to keep the clan here in the valley. The final decision can always be made as fall weather approaches.

Orin assigned Dorik the task of teaching the hunters the technique of shelter construction. He saw the benefits of using his own structure for training the clan members, and soon had the women hauling mud and pine boughs for the roof. The gaps between the poles were filled with a mixture of mud and straw that earlier experience told him would reduce the cold winter drafts.

The clansmen exhibited awe and admiration for the strange new pole home and, with Dorik's advice, were soon working at collecting poles for their own cabins. Dorik considered the first year as crucial, suggesting that two families share in the construction and use of each shelter.

Orin recommended that the families make their own selections for sharing. Old animosities surfaced when a few families had difficulty finding others to share in the construction task. After the voluntary pairing effort failed, Orin was confronted with the first arbitration duty of his new leadership.

"But my mate can't get along with those other women," one of the hunters complained. "If we could share with Umik and his family, the women would get along better."

"But Umik has already made his arrangements with another hunter," Orin explained. "I can't split them up just to satisfy your mate. Why don't you share with Armid? He has only his one mate, Lana, and he hasn't yet found anyone to share a cabin with. Why don't you combine hearths with him?"

"None of the women get along with Lana," complained the hunter. "I never hear anything but complaints about her."

Armid, who had overheard the conversation, became angry. "It's because of women like your mate that I've decided to build my own shelter. I think all the women of the clan are jealous of Lana's beauty, and your mate is the worst. She's a pig."

Orin stepped between the two antagonists. "If you can't peaceably find a family with whom to share a cabin, then I'll have to assign one."

His uneasy feeling was heightened when he considered what he would do if his orders were challenged. To his great relief, the two men mumbled indiscernible oaths at each other, departing in opposite directions. The situation presented a problem that he had not foreseen. He began to realize that in assigning hunting or work teams, he would always have to consider the personalities and antagonisms of the clansmen. He wasn't sure he wanted that responsibility.

He was again faced with a similar problem when he called his hunters together to dispatch teams to scout the nearby hills and valleys for game.

With the new cabin complete, Dorik moved his family to the new quarters. Nomi had recovered her strength, and the new baby was thriving on an adequate supply of mother's milk. Carma and Retta continued to nurse the wound of the injured wolf which managed to limp along with them as they carried the variety of clay pots and robes to their new dwelling. Orin invited Tomar to share the hearth of the new cabin, knowing the old man would be valuable in maintaining the fire. Homan was assigned to the hearth of another family.

Carma and Retta were gathering cattail roots near the lake when they were startled by a duck frantically fluttering into the air. Carma searched the reeds, hoping to find a nest of eggs. A faint peeping sound summoned her attention under a covering of marsh grass. "Over here, Retta," she called. "Come see what I've found. A baby duck is just breaking out of the shell."

The two girls knelt, watching the infant bird struggle to free itself.

"May I hold it?" Retta pleaded. "Isn't it cute?"

Carma consented. "Be careful you don't hurt it. Oh, look, I think another one is breaking the shell."

The two girls lingered at the nest until three more had hatched. They carefully carried the young ducklings and the remaining eggs back to the cabin.

"Please, Mama, may I keep them?" Retta begged.

Amalee consented, suggesting that the small birds were too small to be eaten. She added, "You might as well throw those other eggs away. They wouldn't be any good to eat either."

The girls took the small ducks and remaining eggs out to the ground near the cabin and were thrilled when the small ducklings attempted to follow them where ever they went. They were enjoying their new playthings when, to their continued delight, they watched each of the remaining eggs erupt with a new chick. By the time darkness forced the youngsters into the cabin, they were being trailed by eleven small waddling baby ducklings. The girls placed their playthings in a nest of rabbit fur and listened to the chirping as they drifted into a dreamy sleep.

The following day Amalee reminded the children to not be disappointed when the small ducklings perished. "Without the mother duck to watch over them, I don't see how they could possibly survive."

"But Mother," Carma pointed out, "they are already pecking at the ground. Maybe they'll find enough to eat. I just love the way they follow us around."

Amalee shrugged her shoulders. "I don't know. Just don't be disappointed."

* * *

Dorik maintained a watchful eye on the construction of the other cabins being assembled near Orin's and his. The hunters divided their attention between building and hunting with only moderate success at the latter. It became necessary to supplement the rewards of the hunt with an occasional animal from the corral. The women were sent on periodic missions to harvest the thin crystals of white salt that seemed to grow from the face of the outcropping at the salt lick.

The female wolf, Fluffy, recovered from her wound. Her swelling milk bag indicated the imminent birth of pups. After the wolf was absent from the camp area for several days, Orin and the sisters expressed deep concern that she might not return. When she did reappear, it was obvious she had delivered her pups.

Orin watched patiently and then followed her on her return to the forest and new offspring. Upon locating her shallow den, and after considerable coaxing, the mother wolf allowed him to carry the seven small pups back to the cabin. Dorik cautioned the girls to not handle the small furry creatures if the mother displayed the slightest belligerence. The mother wolf showed only a gentle nature and watched with alert attention when Carma held and petted one of the pups. The wolf had to be occasionally scolded for showing too much interest in the small ducks that also shared the living quarters.

The clansmen worked from dawn to dusk assembling the crude shelters. There was considerable grumbling by some of the members who doubted the wisdom of spending the winter in such a far north land. There were occasional whispers of organizing a group to abandon the valley and return to the cave. Any thought of challenging Orin for clan leadership was subdued with the knowledge that Dorik, a still powerful man, would exercise full support for his son. Tomar firmly endorsed the new young leader and few clansmen were willing to forgo the favors of the spirits with whom the old man was so influential.

* * *

As the summer season faded, Orin was faced with a difficult decision. The construction of the cabins had progressed to a stage that offered assurance of shelter for everyone. The women of the clan had not dried enough meat for the winter, but with the cattle available for emergencies, Orin felt confident. He would have to decide on how many animals to kill to supplement the other food that had been accumulated.

If only I could be certain that the cattle will never leave the valley, he said to himself. The very thought was enough to cause doubt about his earlier decision to keep the clan in the valley. He realized that, with the arrival of snow, he would have to release all the cattle from the corrals. Once the cattle were all together, would they leave the area in search of new feeding grounds?

He expressed his worries to Dorik. "If we slaughter too many of the bulls, the cattle herd might become wary and leave the valley when we release them for winter. If such a thing happens, all my plans for us here will vanish."

"I've had the same thoughts," his father admitted. "I would sure hate to lose all that meat."

Orin considered the problem for a few moments before commenting. "If we could build a pole fence around just part of the meadow, perhaps we could keep that dominant bull and some of the cows inside that area all winter. The others might then stay around. We can later change those inside with the others on the outside. Do you think the idea practical?"

"That would be a tremendous undertaking," Dorik answered. "The people are exhausted from building their shelters. There's already a lot of grumbling in some families, but I agree that it might be a safeguard against the loss of the cattle."

Orin made his decision. He called his hunters together for a conference. "You men have worked very hard these past moons and your mates and children have accomplished the tremendous tasks of building your cabins. You can be proud. I want you to know that I've conferred with Tomar and Dorik and we feel that, with your cabins now complete, the clan can comfortably spend the winter in this valley."

To soften the impact of the news of the next project, he then made a commitment about which he had serious reservations. "I assure you that, before the snow arrives, we'll slaughter enough cattle to sustain the clan until spring." When the whispers of satisfaction subsided, Orin continued. "Tomar, Dorik and I feel that the clan should construct a new fence similar to the corral, but extend it to enclose part of the meadow. We'll keep a few of the animals inside the fenced area which should ensure us that the other cattle will remain in the valley."

There was considerable whispering and mumbling. Before he could hear any complaints, he added. "Give it some thought. We can discuss it more tomorrow."

Work commenced on the zigzag pole fence with Dorik supervising the project. To accelerate the progress, he had the clansmen utilize many of the pine trees that had already fallen throughout the forest slopes near the valley. The fence spread out from either end of the existing corral, extending to form a large rectangle on the meadow. Orin sacrificed hunting time to keep the men working on the project until, after a moon's time, the two pole walls merged from opposite sides of the meadow. As the gap diminished, Dorik became worried, not only for the safety of clan workers, but concerning the possible reaction of the grazing cattle. Would the animals hesitate to pass through the gate of the outer fence? He quickly realized that his concern was unfounded. By the time the gap narrowed to a few feet, the animals had worn a well defined path through the meadow grass. Dorik established the fence top at the level of a man's chest with the knowledge that the workers could always add more poles to increase its height.

After the project was complete, the gate poles were placed across the narrow opening. Orin and Dorik watched as the animals being held in the inner corral were released. The cattle proceeded across the fenced meadow area to the gate through which they usually passed. The older dominant cow, that normally ruled the grazing animals, paused short of the poles before advancing slowly to sniff the new barrier. The other animals waited nearby until they lost interest and moved back into the fenced meadow to feed. The gate was then opened. Orin was satisfied and reassured that by retaining only a few of the dominant cows and bulls throughout the winter, the rest of the animals would stay nearby.

The project was completed just in time. The first indications of approaching winter were becoming evident. The days were growing shorter and early mornings often found crystals of ice on the grass. Increased plumes of smoke curled skyward from the roof openings in the new cabins. The baby ducks had diminished in numbers, but had grown in size, spending an increased portion of their time swimming and feeding near the marshes of the lake. One of Fluffy's pups died from an inadequate milk supply but the other six thrived and romped with the girls. Children of the other families shared the joy of playing with the young wolves.

On a crisp sunny morning, Vodim called on Orin and Dorik. He carried a large, loosely woven basket that puzzled the two observers.

"What do you have there?" Dorik asked.

"One time when we were trading with the sea clans, I saw several devices that looked like this. They told me only that they were fish traps and I thought no more about them. I've been watching the fish that swim near the inlet of the lake. I got to thinking that maybe Olvi could weave one of these traps and I showed her how I thought they were made."

"But there's a hole in one end." Dorik pointed out. "If a fish can swim in, can't he also swim out?"

"I'm not sure it'll work, but as you can see, the end here is tapered in toward the opening in the center of the basket. I suspect that when the fish swim into the basket, they're too dumb to find the opening to swim back out. Anyway, I had Olvi weave the thing for me and I'm anxious to try it out."

The two curious observers accompanied Vodim out to where the stream emptied into the lake. After Vodim tied a rope to the basket, he lowered the device into the water.

"It's too light," Orin suggested. "It'll float. Maybe if you put a few small rocks inside, it will be heavy enough to sink."

The men experimented and soon had the trap resting on the bottom. They peered into the water hoping to see a fish enter the device.

"Perhaps the fish can see us and won't go in while we're here," Dorik commented. "Let's move back and wait."

The men moved a few feet back from the water and sat discussing the problems and prospects of the clan. Periodically Vodim got up to peer over the tall marsh grass near the stream's edge.

"Hey, we've got one," he called to the other two men who rushed forward to watch Vodim pull the basket from the stream. A two-foot-long fish thrashed about inside the woven frame.

After Vodim reset the trap, the three men carried the still struggling fish back to the cabins to display their catch. The women of the clan were soon put to work weaving similar devices.

Amalee and Nomi continued to experiment with the surplus milk. The other clan members were offered samples of the cream and cheese that had become a favorite food in the clan leader's cabin.

Dorik began teaching some of the other men how to tie and milk the cows, allowing them to keep part of the product. As more clansmen became aware of the pleasures of drinking milk, the operation was expanded. With the advice of other men, the milking chutes were redesigned and expanded, allowing the cows to more easily nurse their calves and be milked at the same time.

Within a short time the men concluded that the menial task of milking cows was more closely related to women's work than to the dignified status of hunting. The men continued the exciting job of catching and tying the cows, but allowed the women the pleasure of doing the milking.

- 24 -

The sun had risen well above the horizon when Orin entered the cabin of Armid. "Is Armid around?" he inquired.

Lana arose from the bed of fur robes where she had been resting. "Oh, is that you, Orin? I haven't seen you lately."

Orin waited for his eyes to adjust to the darker interior. "Yes, I came to talk to Armid, but I can see him later when he returns."

Lana moved closer to Orin before speaking. "You don't have to leave. You can wait for him here, if you'd like." She was clad only in a brief, lower deerskin garment that was her normal night attire. Orin felt suddenly awkward in the presence of the woman who was two years older than himself. His eyes lowered to survey the body that had changed little from her early teen years. His eyes paused on her full breasts and then reluctantly returned to her face. He began to leave, but yielding to the attraction, decided to stay for a short while.

He searched for words to justify his presence. "It's been three years since Agar assigned you to Armid, hasn't it? His eyes again slowly examined her body before he added, "You've never had a child, have you?"

"Perhaps the spirit can't enter my body to start a new baby." She smiled and lowered her eyes before continuing. "Perhaps Armid was not the right man for me."

The bold talk unnerved the young leader somewhat, but her manner and words sent invisible arms reaching out to draw him closer. He was not conscious of his next action, but her upturned face demanded attention. He lowered his mouth to her warm lips, and as the kiss intensified, his arms drew her body to him, pressing her firm breasts to his chest in a lingering embrace. She drew back a step, flipping her head to throw her long strands of hair behind her back. She took Orin's hand and moved toward the robes that covered a corner floor of the room.

Orin suddenly became aware of voices outside the cabin. As his head cleared, he realized that Armid and a fellow hunter were approaching. "I'll see you later," he whispered, and after squeezing her hand, moved out to meet and discuss with the hunters the problems that had originally brought him to the cabin.

The clan women and children worked diligently at harvesting and drying the tart apples that grew in abundance along the stream below the lake. They searched the valley for nut trees, competing with the squirrels in gathering the rich yield. Early storms left short-lived, shallow blankets of snow across the meadow and on the limbs of pine trees. Many of the hunters harbored feelings of doubt and concern about the coming winter, but they also knew they were committed and resolved to make the best of whatever came. Orin demonstrated his snow shoes to the clansmen, strongly suggesting they duplicate the devices.

Heavy snow was late in arriving and the clan benefited from a prolonged milking season. Orin enjoyed the arrangement with the other milkers who dutifully gave a portion of their milk supply to the family of the leader.

"It isn't right," Dorik advised his son. "The cattle and the valley belong to everyone. You should be out there working along with the other clansmen."

"I have other responsibilities that keep me busy," Orin said in defense. "We developed the system with the cattle and corrals, and I feel we deserve that much. I don't want to talk about it any more."

Dorik shook his head and walked from the cabin. The boy must not be feeling well lately, he reasoned.

When the first heavy snow of winter arrived, the milk supply diminished and Dorik, with Orin's consent, released the calves and cows from the inner pens. They retained several cows with calves, along with the dominant bull and five young bulls, in the newly enclosed pasture. The other animals were released to forage on the broad open expanse of the unfenced meadow.

Whenever snow restricted the normal duties of the women, a few would often congregate at one of the shelters to share fascinating bits of gossip about their absent neighbors.

When the heavy snow arrived, the well stocked winter food supply afforded the clansmen the leisure time to explore their lower-priority endeavors.

The hunters began experimenting with the snow shoes that their women had labored to weave. They were enthralled with the clever devices.

The young boys of the clan assembled under the tutelage of Vodim to learn the skill of making rope and tying knots.

The girls generally acquired their skills, including curing and tanning leather, by participating in the chores with their mothers.

Orin remained wide awake in bed, separated from Nomi by his younger son whose occasional crying had become annoying. He allowed his thoughts to revive the memory of his interrupted encounter with Lana. The young clan leader envisioned himself beneath the bison robe, enfolding her body in his arms. His imagination kindled an excitement, stirring a deep response in his body. He reached across the sleeping child to place a hand on the body of his sleeping mate. "Nomi, are you awake?" he whispered.

The woman failed to stir.

"Nomi," he repeated, "are you awake?

A light murmur preceded her response. "What? What is it? What do you want?"

"I didn't know you were asleep. Do we have to have the baby between us? Can't he be in a separate robe with Ojon?"

"He's too young," Nomi mumbled. "I have to keep him here to nurse him during the night. What was it you wanted?"

Orin waited before answering. "Oh, nothing. Forget it."

"Why did you wake me, then?" She turned to face Orin and the child.

Orin, feeling isolated by the baby, answered, "I just wanted to talk."

"What about?"

"Oh, just about the clan.

"What about the clan?"

"I've been thinking about Armid. He seems strange to me. He and Lana live all alone in that little cabin they built and they don't even have any children."

"If you ask me, she doesn't want any children," Nomi mumbled. Her voice faded toward resumption of sleep. "I think all she wants to do is lay in bed and think of other men. She's just lazy."

"That's unfair." Orin protested. "After all, she helped build their cabin."

"The other men helped. Everyone likes Armid. I don't think Armid and Lana could even have finished it by themselves. Why don't we go back to sleep?"

Orin didn't answer, but remained awake for a long time envisioning the enticing bosom and slender body of the woman that Nomi so obviously disliked.

The days became shorter and the winter deepened with few hardships for the clansmen in their comfortable cabins. Although the food supply diminished, the reserve cattle still foraged inside the fenced pasture. The remaining animals foraged in the outer meadow, often returning to the pasture fence to be near the other cattle within the pole barrier.

Orin called his hunters to a conference. "I want a few of you men to cross the hill and try to kill some of those wild pigs you told me about."

"That's a half day's walk even when the ground is dry," Umik complained. "We couldn't possibly get there and back in one day."

"I realize that," Orin confirmed. "I know it'll be a difficult task, but I feel we need to kill more game and I don't want to deplete the cattle."

"We can't even be sure of killing any," Umik continued. "I don't know what the situation will be like in this deep snow." There were whispered voices of agreement.

"Do you feel that you're not up to it?" Orin countered. "Do you think it's too big a job?" Orin waited for a response from the silent group before continuing. "I only want three men for the task."

A few men shrugged their shoulders, accepting the odds of not being among the ones chosen.

"All right, then," he said. "I assume you're agreeable. If you're successful at killing any pigs, bring only what you can comfortably carry on your backs. Hang the rest high on a tree limb and we'll send another team out later to bring it back."

The hunters all nursed serious doubts regarding the wisdom of the venture, but with the prospect of being exempt, no one raised an objection.

"Then we're all agreed," Orin continued. "I've decided on Umik, Armid and Gors to make the trip. You'll earn the gratitude of the entire clan. The women and children will truly appreciate your efforts."

A voice was heard to grumble an indecipherable oath.

"What was that?" the young leader asked.

In silence, the men all turned and waded through the snow back to their cabins.

The following morning the three hunters, loaded with extra robes, and an adequate supply of dried meat, strapped their snow shoes to their cowhide foot bindings and grasped their spears to begin their unenthusiastic trek across the pass of the eastern mountain ridge.

- 25 -

A slender moon cast a dim light on the cabins from which thin wisps of smoke curled. Orin opened the flap of his own cabin entrance and stepped out into the crisp night air. He looked at the surrounding cabins before returning to the fire that burned at the center of his shelter.

The sound of snoring gave evidence of deep sleep from the bed robes of Dorik and Amalee. He glanced at his older son who lay curled in the comfort of an ibex robe. Nomi stirred in response to the whimpering of the baby and then drew him to her breast to nurse. Her closed eyes suggested her desire for sleep.

"Nomi," Orin whispered, "are you awake?"

"No," she mumbled, "not really. What is it?"

"I'm going out to check the cattle. I might be gone awhile so don't worry."

Receiving no response, Orin pushed aside the flap opening and moved out into the shadow of the trees. He walked quietly to the cabin that had occupied his dreams for the past several nights. Pausing at the cabin entrance, he slowly lifted the deerskin flap.

"Lana," he whispered, "it's me, Orin. Are you there?"

In the dim light of the low embers, he saw the woman rise from her bed and move to his side.

She took his hand and led him to the far corner of the shelter. "I knew you'd come. I've been waiting for you."

He started to speak but was silenced by her fingers gently touching his mouth. She drew his head lower and the fingers that silenced him were replaced by her warm and inviting lips.

"Shhh," she whispered. "Don't talk. Just hold me close." She pulled the slip knot of his waist band and slid his body robe from his shoulders.

Yielding to an excitement deep within him, he drew her body closer and felt the warmth of her breasts against his chest. His mouth again located the welcome lips that eagerly responded to his passionate kisses.

Her hips pressed tightly to his and she felt the urgency of his mounting passion. "Ooooh," she moaned, and before easing her slender body lower to the bed, reached for his hand to draw him to her side. "I love you, Orin," she whispered. "I've watched you and craved for you. Please don't say anything. Just come to me."

He quickly shed his remaining garments and lowered himself beneath the cover that was held open to welcome him. As his mouth again engaged her lips and lingered in a long embrace, his hand searched to explore her firm breasts. His fingers felt the flatness of her stomach and explored her yielding thighs as she moaned a soft acknowledgment of her pleasure.

"I do love you, Orin," she whispered. "I've longed for this moment and hope I can satisfy your desires."

She withdrew her arm from around his neck and moved her hand along his body. Her fingers lightly touched his heaving chest. She turned her head, allowing her lips to nibble lightly on his neck. Her hand moved lower along his waist and felt the firmness of his muscled stomach. Her teasing fingers explored his hips and thighs before locating the object of her desires. As her fingers nimbly explored, she sensed the demanding urge that was taking possession of his body and mind.

Her fingers gently teased until she sensed her lover could stand no more. "Now, Orin," she whispered, "I want you. I need you."

Lana drew him to her to satisfy the ever growing urge that begged for fulfillment.

With the release of his bursting passion, he drew her ever nearer and sensed the emotion of her own fulfillment.

The ecstasy lasted for a long period until, as their passion slowly ebbed, he gently released her. Totally exhausted, he rolled onto the robe beside the equally drained woman.

Lana drew his face to hers and gently touched her lips to his chin and then to his mouth. He slid lower to cradle his head against her warm breast, allowing his mind to drift into a dreamy sleep. Lana stroked her hand across his beard, whispering softly, "You're mine, Orin. You're all mine."

Orin returned to the bed where Nomi still slept. He lay awake for a long time reviewing and reliving his experience from earlier that night.

Why are Nomi and the other women so critical of such a beautiful woman? he pondered. Is it jealousy? It must be.

He envisioned Lana as his second mate, allowing his mind to contemplate the pleasures of having the woman at his side where he could constantly see and touch her beautiful body. His mind easily justified his desires. Why do I care what Nomi or the other women think? After all, I'm clan leader, and if I decide to take her as my second mate, that is my privilege.

He awoke from his sleep to realize that the day was well along. He looked from his bed and saw only Nomi and Amalee sitting by the fire threading leather thongs into his boots to repair a small tear. He watched the quietly working women for a few moments before asking, "Where are the babies and the girls?"

Nomi rose to her feet and moved to Orin's side. "Oh, you're awake? You really slept late this morning. We took the children over to Olvi's so they wouldn't disturb you. Did you have any problem with the cattle last night?"

Orin didn't answer, but rose from his bed and tied his fur garments to his body. Nomi handed him his boots and helped bind them to his legs. As he stepped out into the crisp air, he picked up a strip of meat that rested on a rock near the fire. He wandered aimlessly down to the corrals and the milking pens that had been empty for such a long time. After walking to the fenced pasture, he counted the few animals that pawed the snow searching for grass. The number was insignificant to his line of thought and immediately forgotten. His eyes moved back toward the dwellings, selecting the cabin that relentlessly dominated his mind.

Why am I so hesitant to tell Nomi of my desires? Am I not her master? Am I not the clan leader? Why do I act this way? If I am the leader, I should have the backbone to act like one.

With firm determination, he started back toward his cabin. His decision was made. He would tell Nomi that he was taking a second mate. He would deal with the problem of Armid later. He could always assign Agar's widows and children to the hunter. That was his privilege as clan leader.

Upon arriving at the cabin, he pulled back the flap and stepped inside.

"Oh, there you are," Amalee said. "Nomi is out looking for you."

Orin sensed a problem. "What's wrong?"

"Gors returned from the pig hunt a short time ago. I guess Armid was badly injured, and poor Gors walked all night getting here. Umik is staying with Armid, waiting for help. Dorik is out organizing the other men for the rescue effort."

Orin turned and ran to the cabin of Gors. He stepped inside and saw the exhausted man lying on a robe near the fire.

"What happened?" Orin asked.

"I'll tell you what happened," replied the hunter, emphasizing his disgust. "We located the pig wallow and began setting up an ambush. The pigs were downwind from us and apparently smelled us. The boars charged at us and we all ran for a tree. Armid slipped on the ice and a big tusker ripped his leg and hip badly. Umik and I were finally able to wound the boar enough to pull Armid to safety, but he's lost a lot of blood. We were able to bind the wound and stop the bleeding, but he's very weak and can't stand on his injured leg. I don't know whether he'll live or not."

A sick feeling of guilt and self-recrimination prevented Orin from looking directly into the face of Gors. He at last glanced up and asked, "Have you seen Dorik?"

"He was here a little while ago. I think he's trying to organize some help."

As Orin left the cabin, he saw his father approaching, accompanied by several other hunters. "I heard about the accident," Orin said as the men drew near. "Are you going out to help him?"

Dorik stopped to stare at his son before replying. "Yes, Orin, we're going out to help him, and that includes you." The tone of his voice left no doubt as to who was in command. He then turned to the other men, adding, "Go get your food and equipment and we'll leave just as soon as everyone is ready."

Amalee, anticipating their needs, had packed two pouches of dried beef and shelled nuts. She handed one to each of the men of her family and also gave Dorik a roll of soft, tanned deerskin with an explanation, "This might be useful in binding his wounds."

Seven men moved out across the packed snow of the small village. In addition to their weapons, they each carried snow walkers and a three-day supply of food. They easily followed the earlier tracks of Gors, where, upon reaching deeper snow, they paused to strap the crude snow walkers to their feet.

A high, thin film of clouds partially obscured the blue sky, displaying a bright ring around the image of the sun. The men walked in silence, each taking turns leading the column. Dorik periodically glanced skyward, wondering if the high clouds were portent of a coming storm. As the day continued, the men nervously watched the sun move closer to the horizon on its low path across the southern sky.

The small group crossed the mountain pass and then followed the tracks that descended along a small stream. Cascading water could be heard gurgling beneath the ice, occasionally appearing through openings in the snow-covered crust. As the men descended into a small clearing, they startled several deer that had been feeding on the tender willow shoots. The surprised animals struggled through the deep snow at a speed that could easily have been exceeded by the snowshoe clad hunters. The men looked to Dorik for a clue but turned their attention back to the trail when the grim man appeared oblivious to the animals. He continued plunging straight ahead without speaking a word.

* * *

When the earlier tracks of Gors finally led them to a grove of poplars by the stream's edge, the men responded to a shout from Umik who had been waiting with the injured hunter.

"Over here," he yelled as they approached, and then added in a lowered voice, "I hope you're not too late."

In addition to his own robe and the one of Armid, Umik had bundled the injured man in the extra sleeping robe of Gors which had been left behind for that purpose. Dorik lifted the layers of deer and bison robes from the inert body of the wounded man. The blood had crusted and covered the greater portion of the man's leg. When the crude bindings were removed, the wound again began to drip blood from the open wound. Dorik wrapped Amalee's soft deerskin bandage around the major cut, binding it snugly.

Dorik then replaced the robes around the semiconscious hunter after which he turned to the other men. "It looks like the tendon may have been severed. If he survives I doubt that he'll ever walk again." The crisis had established Dorik as the temporary leader with his fellow hunters looking to him for orders.

After Dorik finished binding the leg, Vodim asked, "Do you want me to find poles for a carrier?"

"Thank you, Vodim," Dorik answered. "We'll use the largest robe available and bind it to the poles. Let's get started. We have no time to lose."

The men searched for suitable poles of about ten-foot length, testing them for strength. After Dorik selected two of the better ones, the men pursued the task of cutting small slits in the robe through which leather straps were laced and tied to the poles.

Dorik glanced at the horizon, noting the darkening clouds that totally obscured the sun. The decreasing light suggested night was imminent. "Let's eat a bite and get started," he ordered. "We might as well take advantage of what little light remains."

After loading the bundled, inert figure of Armid onto the carrier, four men reached for the pole ends.

"Orin, you take one of the front positions," Dorik

237

ordered. His demanding voice called for no reply.

The progress was slow and awkward. The extra hunters walked beside the litter, ready to relieve the burdened men if they tired, or if a snowshoe needed adjustment. After a short period of struggling through deep snow, the relief men reached for the poles to assume the burden.

As Vodim reached to relieve Orin, the young man shook his head. "No, I'm not tired. I can continue."

"But I haven't had a turn," Vodim stated. "I want to do my share."

"Then go relieve someone else." The tone of Orin's voice dismissed any further conversation.

The difficult travel continued until darkness forced them to halt. The total blackness prevented further progress. After lowering the carrier to the snow, the men wrapped their remaining robes around their chilled bodies and stomped their feet to maintain the necessary blood circulation to avoid frostbite.

"The moon should be up before too long," Dorik announced, "but with this heavy cloud cover, I doubt that it will do any good. All we can do is to wait and see."

Time passed slowly with Dorik periodically touching the face of his patient to confirm that Armid was still alive. Eyes searched the starless sky looking for some hint of light. One of the men stopped moving his feet and was reminded that his toes could freeze.

"We have one disabled man," Dorik reminded him. "We can't carry anyone else."

The moonlight failed to penetrate the thick overcast. An attempt was made to travel in the darkness with the extra hunters groping ahead and calling back to signal the route. Dorik finally cancelled the effort, considering it too hazardous.

The night seemed to last an eternity and became a torture to the shivering men. A cold wind stung their faces and hands. When the first light of dawn finally penetrated the thick overcast, the chilled, uncomfortable men resumed their efforts. The cold wind, that had earlier stung their faces and hands, pummeled their faces with granules of sleet. The drifting snow obscured their earlier tracks, forcing them to occasionally pause for reorientation. Visibility deteriorated, often forcing the group to retreat in search of a better route. As the men plodded on, numbed by the cold, they finally crossed the pass that offered a gradual descent toward the valley floor. Upon entering the pine forest on the western slope of the ridge, the wind intensity diminished, but fallen and rotting logs posed an even greater problem. It was awkward and difficult enough for the men to cross the obstacles while wearing the crude snow walkers, but even more so when supporting the burden of the wounded man. Exhaustion finally brought the valiant hunters to a halt. They huddled together, drawing their feet up under their robes. Some of the men surrendered to short periods of sleep, dreaming of hot baths at the thermal springs on the old migration route.

"Get on your feet!" Dorik shouted, jolting some of the men from the deep lethargy of drowsiness and fatigue. Two men had to be shaken to force them to grasp the reality of the moment.

The group continued the struggle, moving tediously down the slope. The deep snow precluded recognition of any landmarks that might confirm their whereabouts. Dorik withheld his thoughts from the men but allowed himself to speculate on their chance of survival if darkness again caught them in the blizzard. Those thoughts prompted him to push the men a little harder, with an occasional reminder that a warm fire awaited them.

The forest growth at last became less dense with dormant willow bushes on the gentle grade giving hope that they were about to reach the meadow. The blowing snow continued to obscure their visibility, but a contagious enthusiasm drove them at a faster pace.

"Umik, you go on ahead," Dorik ordered. "Send back every suitable man you can find."

Exhausted and numb from the cold, Umik pushed ahead of the others until he finally arrived to within shouting distance of the cabins. After the camp was alerted, fires were quickly stoked in preparation for the return of the remaining hunters. The few men who had remained in camp retraced Umik's partially obscured snow tracks to meet and help the weary rescue group. When the exhausted men were relieved of their stretcher duties by the relief men, the pace increased.

Women waited in the snow outside the cabins, searching the waning light for the heroic rescue party. When the carrier was finally lowered to the floor of Armid's cabin, a tremendous feeling of relief was expressed by the women. With heavy darkness settling over the remote valley, the men returned to their own cabins where they collapsed near fires that were stoked by their women and children.

The women assumed the chore of nursing the wounded man. Lana waited in the corner of the room, responding only when given direct instructions.

"Get us some hot water," Olvi ordered, "and go to my cabin and bring me my pouch of medicine herbs. Uval will know where it is."

Lana moved to comply, but wished she could be elsewhere. Olvi and Amalee washed the wound and attempted to bind the torn flesh back together. Willow bark was soaked and layered over the swollen leg. Armid occasionally opened his eyes and moaned, receiving sympathy from the two older women and a vacant stare from his own mate.

When nothing more could be done, the two older women made the hunter as comfortable as possible. They then returned to their own cabins to care for their exhausted mates.

Amalee found Nomi seated, supporting Orin's head in her lap. The two men of the family had eaten a few bites of warm, roasted meat before collapsing into a heavy sleep. Amalee stoked the fire before stooping to pick up baby Orik, who had stirred and was whimpering.

Orin occasionally moaned as Nomi gently stroked his forehead. "He must be dreaming," she explained. "He keeps mumbling something about Armid. I couldn't make out all that he said, but I could understand a little. He kept saying, 'I'm sorry Armid, I'm really sorry.' I don't know what he means."

The returned hunters slept well into the following day. When they at last stirred, the women served them hot stew that simmered in clay pots beside the fire.

* * *

It was late afternoon, and the storm had receded when Tomar returned to the cabin. "I finally heard most of the story of the injury and the rescue," the old man stated. "It was a truly heroic effort. The clan storytellers will be repeating the details for generations to come." He waited for a comment before continuing. "Orin, I've come to believe that you are a very intelligent leader. You have accomplished things beyond imagination. However I'm puzzled by one thing. What made you decide to send those men on such a difficult and hazardous mission?"

Dorik interrupted before Orin could speak. "Let's say it was just a case of temporary poor judgment. I'm sure it will never happen again. There is nothing more to say."

- 26 -

With the passing days, Orin showed little interest in making decisions. Dorik remained silent, observing the actions of his son. No important orders were necessary. The hunters paired off, setting snare lines or organizing their own hunting forays. The men preferred being away from the cabins if weather permitted.

When hunting failed to produce enough to sustain the clan, Vodim took it upon himself to corral and slaughter one of the bulls from the fenced pasture. No objection was expected.

Armid ran a fever for several days before he slowly began improving. Olvi and Vodim periodically stopped in with food, trying to raise his morale.

"You'll be fine in no time," Vodim offered as encouragement. "That leg will heal and you'll be as good as ever."

Armid attempted a weak smile, but remained mute.

The days slowly grew longer, and the snow, that had partially melted and compacted, crusted solid in the early morning cold. Carma and Retta joined the other clan children in play, climbing the gentle slopes before sliding down the slippery surfaces. The partially grown pups chased the playful children, loving the attention they received. The ducks took up residence at the spring, feasting on the tender watercress shoots. They occasionally waddled to the lake, amusing the children by slipping and falling on the icy surface.

While working at their chores of scraping and softening a cow-hide, Nomi confided her concern to Amalee. "I'm worried about Orin. He's so moody. He doesn't joke and tease like he used to. I'm afraid he may be getting sick."

"I've noticed that, too," Amalee agreed. "Maybe it's just the long winter. It will soon be spring and I'm sure he'll be all right then."

Amalee expressed the same worry to Dorik, offering an opinion that she had withheld from Nomi. "I'm afraid he's despondent about sending those men to the pig wallow. Goodness, he had no way of knowing there would be an accident."

"I'm afraid his problem is deeper than that," Dorik responded. "It's something he's going to have to work out for himself." Dorik seemed reticent about continuing the conversation so Amalee dropped the subject.

Tomar spent most of his days visiting the other cabins, often engaging the women in long conversations. Although the local gossip often included Orin's poor decision in organizing the pig hunt, the old man defended the youth's leadership, reminding them all of the benefits they enjoyed from the cattle herd.

"He's still very young," the old spiritual leader explained. "He's entitled to make a few errors. I'm sure he's learned from that mistake and will eventually become a great leader."

Dorik was grateful for Tomar's support. The old man could only guess at the full cause of Orin's despondency, but felt that time and opportunity would resolve the problem. Tomar suspected that if it wasn't for the stature of Dorik, one of the hunters might be tempted to challenge Orin for leadership of the clan.

Spring arrived with many familiar problems. Sloppy mud became deeper near the cabin entrances. With the melting snow, and occasional heavy rains, water flowed under the logs onto the dwelling floors. It became increasingly difficult to find suitable firewood, and there were complaints of fever and diarrhea which seemed to spread from family to family.

Two happy thoughts countered the gloomy mood. The weather was certain to get better, and the clan would not have to make the long spring migration for which they would normally be making preparations at that time of year.

Several sunny days produced a marked change. Buds appeared on many of the trees with flowers showing among the meadow grasses.

Tomar sat complacently on a log that had been placed at the sunny end of the cabin. He often rested or dozed in the sun, enjoying the warmth. Orin accepted an invitation from the old man to seat himself.

"Well, it looks like I survived another winter," Tomar joked. "Each year my bones ache a little more and my joints become a little stiffer. I expect each year to be my last, and with these aches and pains, I find the prospect appealing."

"You're not the only one with problems," countered the serious young leader. "Everyone is troubled by something."

"You're right. Enough of this complaining. Let's talk about more pleasant things."

"Go ahead," Orin suggested.

"Well," the old man began, "I'd sure like to be around to see this valley in another ten years. I've been giving much thought to what you've done. I watch the cattle and see a difference in the cows that have matured from captive calves. I've watched those wolf pups and can hardly believe they are descendants of the ferocious packs that roam the plains, killing the bison and reindeer calves. But more amazing than anything else is the way those baby ducks have accepted domestic life." He paused to emphasize the point before continuing. "I've come to a conclusion. I firmly believe that almost any animal can be tamed if captured young enough. Maybe I'm saying that wrong. I believe that almost any animal will remain tame if captured young enough and continues to live with people. I believe that is the explanation for the sheep that the woman interpreter told us about back at the hot springs, and it explains why they would return to their master's huts each night."

Orin showed a sudden spark of the old enthusiasm that had eluded him for so long. "Do you believe that the goats, living high on those mountain cliffs, could be tamed?"

"I certainly do. I believe that a reindeer or a red deer can be tamed. I even believe those vicious pigs, if born in captivity or captured soon enough after birth, can be tamed."

This last thought sent a small shiver along the spine of the young man. He didn't answer, but settled into deep thought.

As Amalee had predicted, the arrival of spring lifted the mantle of despondency from the shoulders of the young man who had willingly worn it since the accident. The previous sunny days had helped Orin make a difficult decision. He was determined to at least attempt a partial reconciliation with the guilt that haunted him. He walked briskly among the cabins, greeting his fellow hunters. Upon approaching the cabin of Armid, he saw the crippled hunter sitting on a log near the flap entrance. He approached and seated himself on the log beside the disabled man. Armid made an attempt to get up, but failing, turned his back toward his visitor.

"How are you feeling, Armid?" Orin asked. "Does your leg still pain you a lot?"

"I'll live with it," the embittered man mumbled.

A short silence prevailed as Orin moved around to look directly into the face of the disgruntled man. "Armid," he said, "I want you to know how sorry I am."

The wounded man again struggled to rise.

"Please hear me out," Orin insisted. "I am truly sorry. I accept full blame for sending you men out on a hazardous and unnecessary mission. There is no excuse for my actions. Please forgive me."

Silence prevailed for a short time before Orin finally continued. "I have given much thought to my mistake and have made a decision. If the men of the clan want me to resign my leadership, I will not contest it. I will accept their judgment. I will request Vodim to speak to all the men, and if the opinion is against me, I will relinquish my position as leader."

For a long time Armid stared up into the face of the tormented young man before he at last spoke. "I believe you really are sorry. I believe you truly regret what happened. I confess I hated you. I considered you arrogant and irresponsible. The spirits know that I have reason to dislike you, but if you are man enough to face me and say the things you've just said, then I'm going to be man enough to forgive you."

Orin sat beside the offended man and grasped his hand in a firm and friendly grip. With a loss for further words, he then rose to his feet.

As Orin turned to leave, Armid called him back. "I want you to know that I'm going to ask Vodim to send each hunter to me before making his decision."

Orin again turned to go.

"Wait just one more moment," Armid added, "I want Lana to know."

Orin felt awkward and would rather not face the woman in front of Armid, but he also felt committed to his course of action.

Armid called to his mate, and after what seemed a long time to Orin, the attractive woman appeared at the entrance of the cabin.

Her hair hung in long curls around her neck, but her beauty was marred by reddened eyes that avoided the face of the leader. Her voice was barely audible as she said, "I know. I heard everything that was said."

Two days elapsed before Vodim appeared at the door of the leader's cabin.

Orin invited him in and faced the man whose hearth had provided his food through many of his younger years. "You've come with the decision of the hunters?" Orin asked.

"I have," Vodim replied.

Orin felt a slow sinking feeling in the pit of his stomach. He had no right to expect a favorable decision. "I don't mind losing the leadership of the clan. What I do mind is losing the respect of the men. But I'm afraid I'm too late for that."

"You have a powerful friend in Armid," Vodim stated. "The men all feel that, if he can forgive you, they certainly can also. You have the support of the hunters of the Clan."

* * *

Spring weather brought new life to the meadow. New calves were born and transferred to the calf pen. One of the cows, that as a calf had spent her first summer in the calf pen, delivered her own calf, offering little resistance at the milking chute. Orin allowed the clansmen to take a fair share of the available milk and found pleasure himself again preparing the cows for milking.

Orin engaged his time in building a small pen near the mud of the lakeshore. His project drew the interest of the curious clansmen.

"You'll just have to wait and see," he responded to the many questions. He then organized and led a group of four hunters across the ridge to the vicinity of the pig wallow that produced so many haunting memories.

"Now we're not going to take any chances," Orin cautioned. "We first want to locate the pig herd and then locate the trail they use between the oak grove and wallow."

When the trail was located, he produced a net he had constructed by tying ropes in a crossed-pattern spacing of half a foot. The overall net was about ten feet long by three feet high.

The pigs were located rooting beneath the oaks at the far side of the grove. Orin, with the help of the other men, quietly strung the net across the trail, tying the upper ends to trees that grew on opposite sides. The ropes from the lower ends of the net hung limp, extending into the branches where two well-briefed men waited. Orin and the other hunter then circled, approaching the pigs from the far side. As he advanced, the old dominant tusker conformed to expectations. The huge boar snorted a challenge before rushing a few paces toward the two men who waited near a convenient tree limb. The technique followed the pattern used by hunters many times in the past, altered only by the addition of the net across the path. After the old boar was provoked into charging, the hunters scrambled into the tree. Spears were used to effective advantage and soon the old tusker crumbled to his knees from loss of blood. The lesser boars snorted, making abortive charges from a distance, but loss of their leader confused and demoralized them. Upon seeing the old boar roll onto his side, the remaining pigs panicked, retreating at full speed along the trail. The other hunters, waiting in the trees, remained tense and alert. As three young pigs, leading the retreat, raced headlong into the net, the hunters above pulled with maximum strength to lift the lower span, catching and holding the tangled victims. Orin and his partner ran along the trail, chasing the retreating, frightened, younger pigs. They arrived in time to grasp the rear legs of the struggling animals, restraining them long enough for the men above to descend and assist. After a considerable struggle, the men were able to tie the legs of their victims with stout leather thongs.

After checking the sexes of the captured pigs, Orin was pleased to note they had captured two sows and a boar. The animals would be the beginning of his domestic pig enterprise.

The difficulties of moving the pigs back to camp became greater than Orin had contemplated. The animals were larger than anticipated. "I had hoped to catch smaller pigs that we could carry on our shoulders," he explained to his men.

At one man's suggestion they adopted a technique similar to the one used to rescue Armid a few moons earlier. Orin didn't enjoy being reminded. The men, as before, located a strong, slender pole threading it through the outer edges of the net. They placed the trussed animals in the hanging net, and with a man shouldering each end of the pole, began the trek back to the valley.

Orin allowed himself the grim reminder of the earlier winter trip, noting the comparison, but on this occasion he considered the burden a pleasure.

As they approached the village, they were met by a throng of shouting and curious children. The returning hunters were deluged with questions.

"What are you going to do with them?"

"Are you going to kill them?"

"Are we going to eat them?"

Retta answered the questions for the leader. "Orin's going to put them in that new pen that he built."

The children raced ahead to acquire favorable positions at the railing of the new structure. When the animals were released inside the well-constructed pen, they ran, frantically testing each foot of the enclosure. The children squealed, jumping back each time the pigs attempted to push their way through the poles near them.

The food scraps and roots that were placed in the pen were ignored for a few days until hunger forced the animals to reluctantly accept their captivity and the food.

The wound on the leg of Armid healed, leaving a long, jagged scar. The severed tendon allowed him to support only limited weight on his heel, depriving him of the full use of his foot.

Orin called a conference of his hunters and grimaced when the crippled clansman, supporting himself on an improvised crutch, joined the circle.

"I'd like to make a suggestion," Orin commenced. "We have been so successful at domesticating wild animals that I would like to make an effort at capturing some baby goats. Tomar believes that it has been done before by other clans, and thinks the animals would be an easy and useful source of food. What do you think?"

There was enthusiastic approval.

"Very good, then," Orin offered. "I'll take some volunteers with me and we'll begin our search. It may take a long while."

Vodim stepped forward with a suggestion. "I think you should stay with the clan. I know a mountain area where there are many goats. This time, if you'll permit, I'd like to lead the effort."

Orin's deep respect for Vodim made consent easy. The following day, six men departed on the unusual mission.

- 27 -

The strawberries that dotted the meadow were ripening and the women and children carried baskets to gather the small sweet fruit. More berries entered the mouths of the children than accumulated in their containers.

Dorik again cautioned the clansmen to avoid the part of the meadow where the cattle grazed. The animals would normally avoid the clansmen, but as they became increasingly familiar with humans, the cattle would often exhibit a curiosity by approaching anyone who ventured near them. Orin reissued the warning that the cattle could be unpredictable and the bulls might pose a real danger.

The sun had passed its zenith and was descending when Umik's mate summoned Orin from his cabin.

"You look worried," Orin said. "What is it?"

"The children have been picking strawberries out on the meadow and when they returned, my boy Kim wasn't with them. Some of the boys were playing tag, but when they came back, Kim wasn't there. I haven't been able to find him and I'm worried."

Orin accompanied the woman to her cabin. He loudly called the child's name, later asking other children if they knew where the boy was.

"I'm certain he's all right," Orin assured the worried mother. He probably wandered off somewhere. Is he the only child missing?"

"I'm not sure. There could have been others with him. His friends didn't mention any other child."

Orin called all the children together and identified them. Five-year-old Kim was the only child unaccounted for. He felt an increasing concern. "Let's get every man, woman and child over eight years of age and we'll start a search."

The designated clan members gathered near the fence of the outer pasture. When they were finally assembled, Orin issued instructions. "You are to pair up and search along the stream and in the brush at the edge of the meadow. Everyone is to report back to me before dark. Be careful. We don't want any injuries."

The worried young leader then departed at a jog to explore the stream that wound its way the full length of the valley. He searched the brush on either bank and repeatedly shouted the boy's name. After passing the herd of grazing cattle, he continued the search farther south along the stream. After travelling a distance that he felt was beyond the range of the small child, he crossed an expanse of waving grass to search the brush bordering the lush meadow. He worked his way back north, shouting the child's name while searching every small ravine. He had travelled well back toward the corrals when, from a distance, he heard a child scream. He stopped, searching for the source, and then saw a young girl pointing toward a few people out on the meadow some distance away. Orin turned his attention to where the girl was pointing and saw the source of her fright. A woman and two children were running from the area. Armid, hobbling awkwardly with the aid of a forked stick, followed. Beyond the crippled hunter stood the old dominant bull, pawing the ground and bellowing his rage as a preface of attack.

Orin broke into a run, racing frantically toward the crippled man. The distance narrowed, but as his legs propelled him nearer, he saw the bull lower his head and begin charging toward the helpless man. Orin attempted to shout but his strained breath muted the sound. He watched in terror as the distance between the bull and Armid diminished. Orin's muscles strained, driving him at a speed that matched the closure rate of the bull. As he drew closer, it appeared to Orin that he would soon collide with a horn of the bull's lowered head. Summoning his final effort, Orin plunged toward Armid who had turned and waited, paralyzed with fear. Orin's shoulder, hitting the chest of Armid with the full impact of his lunge, sent both men sprawling onto the grass. The young clan leader felt the long horns brush his leg as his lunge carried him on toward the ground. After regaining his feet, Orin quickly turned to face the bull. The speed of the enraged animal had carried the beast a considerable distance beyond the two men. Waving his arms, Orin moved several steps away from Armid, attempting to draw the bull away from the fallen man.

With the bull's attention diverted, the mind of the desperate youth frantically searched for answers. Now what can I do? Could I outrun him? Doubt cancelled any such hope. His eyes glanced around in search of an alternate means of escape. The meadow offered nothing closer than the corral fence which appeared too far away. He again frantically considered trying to outrun the bull. Could I make it to the fence before he caught me? I doubt it.

Orin cautiously moved laterally to place himself between the bull and the fence. If I run, I'll have my back to him, he reasoned. I have to keep my eyes on him.

Again the animal pawed the ground, lowering his head to attack. As the bull began to charge, fear pumped additional adrenalin into the young man's body. His first thought was to jump high over the horns, attempting to absorb the blow on the shoulders of the beast. The alternate thought left no time for further consideration. He flexed his knee, bracing his foot in the damp soil. His desperate plan was to wait until the last possible moment before plunging to one side.

I must wait until he's almost on me, Orin reasoned. Too early a plunge would allow him time to veer toward me. He waited, watching the wide-spread horns bearing down on him. When the animal reached to within a few feet, Orin lunged. He narrowly cleared the horns, landing prone on the ground before again scrambling to his feet. As before, the bull's momentum carried him well beyond his target. The enraged animal turned and again studied the tiring youth. Orin stepped slowly backward toward the fence.

The bull, appearing confused by his failure to contact the man, turned his head momentarily before returning his attention to Orin. The bull's deep, red eyes glistened as he lowered his head in preparation for his next assault. The animal's momentary indecision allowed Orin to move a few more steps closer to safety.

The threatened young clan leader heard voices shouting, and from the corner of his eye, saw Umik waving his arms while moving out from the corral fence toward the bull. Umik stayed within a safe distance of the fence but continued to wave his arms and shout, attempting to distract the enraged animal. The bull momentarily turned his head in the direction of the noise, allowing Orin additional time to retreat. The increased pace of Orin's backward movement recaptured the attention of the bull. After snorting, and again lowering his head, the bull began accelerating toward his intended victim. Orin quickly judged the distance to the fence and elected to run. He turned, and sprinting at maximum speed, raced toward the pole barrier. The pounding hoof beats behind him were growing louder and, as he neared the fence, he heard the heavy breathing of the beast. With a final effort, Orin jumped, grasping the top railing to catapult himself over the barrier. As his body hit the ground, he heard the crashing sound of breaking timber. With the wall partially collapsed from the impact, the animal disengaged his legs from the poles and turned to resume his attack. Orin quickly regained his footing and began moving parallel along and behind the fence. The bull followed, facing him from the opposite side while snorting his threat. Upon reaching the open gate of the control pen, the bull entered, attempting to reach the hunter. With the safety of the pole barrier between them, Orin continued to draw the attention of the still dangerous animal while Umik and Dorik quickly slipped poles across the pen opening. With the gate secured, and the bull safely enclosed, the hunters emitted loud sighs of relief and immediately gathered to discuss the situation.

Several women ran onto the pasture to help Armid back to safety. The crippled man hobbled toward Orin who began walking out to meet him.

"I'm sorry about the problem I caused," Armid said, apologizing. "I shouldn't have gone out onto the meadow. It's just that I refuse to sit and feel sorry for myself. I wanted to get out and help look for the child."

Orin placed an arm around the shoulder of the hunter, attempting to ease his mind with a touch of humor. "Don't apologize. Without your help, we could never have managed to get that old bull inside the pen."

Lana, who had observed the drama from the safety of the corral, approached the group of men. She remained silent as she took her mate's arm to assist him back to the cabin. Her eyes avoided Orin as she departed.

The search for the child continued. Within a short while word was relayed that Kim had been found. The women located the child asleep beneath a willow bush and carried him safely back to his happy mother.

Orin, Dorik and a few of the men lingered at the corral. Orin studied the still enraged animal in the pen. "We have to figure out a safe way to take the meanness out of those old bulls. There must be some way. I wonder if we'll ever be able to tame them?"

Dorik expressed his doubts. "We'll just have to always maintain strong fences and keep everyone away from them."

"There are younger bulls to help maintain the herd," Orin suggested. "I think we should kill this old monster and have a special clan celebration."

With the old bull locked in the chute to be slaughtered, the celebration was soon underway. A communal fire roasted large chunks of meat skewered on green poles. The festivities lasted until long after dark with many of the men lingering near the fire long after the women had taken their sleepy children to their beds.

After Orin and Nomi were settled comfortably in their bed, Nomi announced to her mate that another child was on its way. "This time," she suggested, "I'd like a daughter."

Orin laughed and drew her into his arms, adding his reassurance. "If you want a girl, then that's what it will be."

Vodim and his team were gone for several days before returning from their search for goats. To the delight of the children who ran to meet them, the men brought back five yearlings. Pens were constructed by the hunters who were assured by Tomar, that even if these animals never became tame, the following generation of offspring would.

Life in the clan still had many hardships, but the women were all in agreement that the spirits had been generous in providing them with the means of living in a permanent settlement.

At an evening meal near the fire outside the cabin, Retta played with the pups that romped and teased her for attention.

Tomar, watching the young wolves, offered a prediction. "I'm convinced the day will come when almost every family will keep a beautiful pup like those, not only for protection, but for the sheer joy of companionship."

Dorik sat on the ground at the side of Amalee. He looked around at the many cabins and out across the meadow before commenting to no one in particular. "I wonder what the future holds. I wonder what Ojon's and Orik's children and grandchildren will see. I wonder what later generations, far off in the future, will someday be doing in this very valley. I wish I could come back sometime and see."

Orin lifted himself to his feet, his eyes taking on a dreamy stare. A sudden chill sent a strange feeling tingling along his spine. He waited a long time before he spoke. "I have a strange feeling that we have just begun to see the changes that future generations will experience."

- The End -